Tempting Tatum

KAYLEE RYAN

Cover Design: Sommer Stein Perfect Pear Creative Covers
Cover Photography: Toski Covey Photography Custom Design
Editing: Hot Tree Editing
Formatting: Integrity Formatting

DEDICATION

To my family.

Your continued love and support throughout this journey is empowering.

CHAPTER 1

I'm sitting against the wall with my knees pulled to my chest, my face buried, rocking back and forth. I keep hearing the doctor's words run through my mind. *"I'm sorry; there was nothing I could do. They're gone. Your parents didn't survive. I'm so sorry. Is there anyone we can call?"* My parents, they're gone. The accident that came across the airways earlier today, that was them. The thought never crossed my mind when I heard about the accident. They were not supposed to be there. They were supposed to be in Kentucky for a few more days, settling Nana's estate. Why were they there on that road at that exact time? Why them? Pain slices through me. Hot tears roll down my cheeks, causing my eyes to burn. I struggle to pull air into my lungs. Feeling a faint touch on my arm, my head jerks up to find the doctor who just sent my entire world spinning out of control. I know he's talking, but my ears are ringing. His voice and his previous words are on constant replay.

Panic is starting to set in and I need to get away. Josh…I need Josh. Just the thought of him wrapping me in his arms has me springing into action. I jump to my feet and run. I hear the doctor yell my name. I don't care. I have to get to Josh.

I need him.

I bust through the emergency room's doors and I'm assaulted by bright sunlight. It's a clear, beautiful sunny day, even though there's a dark cloud hanging over me. A cloud of death. My parents, they're gone. I run straight to the parking lot without even looking; the honking of horns just causes me to run faster. I spot my Ford Fusion, finally on my way to Josh. I fumble with the keys, my hands shaking. I manage to get the door unlocked and climb behind the wheel. Gripping the wheel tight, I rest my forehead against it, closing my eyes

1

trying to gain control of my tears. Taking a deep breath, I start the car and slowly pull out of the lot. I point my car in the direction of the only person who can soothe me, Josh.

Josh and I have been dating for the last year. We met the summer before our senior year at Ohio State University. Josh is an architecture major while mine is marketing and public relations. We both graduate next month. I place my hand to my chest to dull the ache. My parents won't be there to see me graduate.

Somehow, I'm able to make it to his condo. I don't remember the drive. Pulling into the lot, my foggy brain suddenly remembers that he is in class for at least another two hours. I contemplate calling him, but decide that I'll just use the key that he gave me a few weeks ago, when he begged me to move in. Being surrounded by his things will help until I can be with him. He's all I have now.

Decision made, I make my way into the building and hit the button for the elevator. Once inside, I release the breath I was holding as more tears flood my cheeks. My heart is pounding as I struggle to pull breath into my lungs. His apartment is on the third floor. Almost there. I slouch against the wall and pray that I can make it there without any stops. I'm not exactly up for chitchat. I just need Josh. I need for him to wrap his arms around me and make the pain go away. The elevator dings and the doors slide open. I turn right and make it to Josh's door. I reach for the handle and turn, not thinking that I need my keys and, well in this case, I didn't. The door is unlocked. Through the tears and heartache that has taken over me the last few hours, I don't think anything of it. That is until I look up and see Josh, my boyfriend, with some blonde chick slouched over the arm of the couch. He has a tight grip on her hair as he plunges himself inside of her, over and over again. I stand there frozen, shock preventing me from moving. I hear what I can only describe as a strangling noise, and Josh whips his head toward me. Shit, apparently that noise is me. Josh pulls himself from the blonde.

"Tatum, what are you doing here?" he asks me. He reaches for his pants and hastily throws them on. He pulls a throw off the back of the couch and tosses it over the blonde. The same throw that he and I have snuggled under, made love on.

I don't answer; I can't. I can't pull my eyes from the train wreck in front of me. I want to scream. I want to tell him what a piece of shit he is. I want him to know he let me down, but I can't speak. My words are stuck. Just two short hours ago, I was notified that I lost both of my parents in a fatal car crash, and the one person who I needed, the one person who I thought could bring me comfort, was just buried five inches, sad but true, into some blonde bimbo. What do you say to that?

"Tatum, are you okay? What happened?" he asks, like he's concerned. Blondie is just standing there with her lady bits on display looking confused.

Really? "Are you fucking kidding me? Am I all right? You just had your dick in her." I wave in the direction of the bimbo who is currently holding *the* throw around her naked body. "What part of this is okay?" I yell.

He moves toward me. "Honey, it's not what it looks like."

For every step he takes, I retreat the same. "Stop!" I scream at him. He stops. "How could you? How long, Josh? How long have you been screwing around on me?"

He reaches for me. I smack his hand away.

"You know what? Fuck it! We are through. I don't care if this was the first time or the tenth; I'm done." I back up further until I can feel that I'm standing in the doorway. "I needed you." I say as tears run unchecked down my face. His betrayal slicing me to my core. I am broken, broken and alone.

"Tatum…" Josh says as he follows me to the hallway, reaching for me.

"Don't touch me! You lost the right to touch me!" I scream.

Josh raises his hands in the air, but he doesn't back up. His eyes are boring into mine. His are dark and angry. "Tatum, just stop and listen to me!" he yells.

His neighbor, whose name I can't remember, steps out of his apartment. "Is everything all right here?"

"Mind your own damn business." Josh growls in reply.

"No, it's not all right. I'm trying to leave and he won't let me."

The neighbor, who has a good two inches and at least thirty pounds on Josh, steps out into the hall and in front of me. "Leave, he won't follow you." He tells me. His eyes never leaving Josh.

"T—thank you." I manage to croak out as I turn and flee from the building. I take the stairs, not willing to wait on the elevator. I stumble a few times through my tears, eventually making it back to my car. I start the engine and pull out of the lot, heading toward home. My parents' home, where I continued to live all through college. We live right outside of the city limits and my commute to school every day is only thirty minutes. My parents and I were always close, and living at home saves us both money. I'm an only child and they have always treated me as an adult.

I make it home, again, I'm not sure how. I turn off the ignition and sit. My eyes are swollen and painful, my vision blurred. My gaze is locked on the front door. I don't want to get out of my car and walk through that door. When I do, and they aren't there, that means this entire day is real. Not just a horrid nightmare that I can wake up from.

The shrill ringing of my cell phone causes me to jump. I glance down at the cup holder to see my best friend Leah's name flash across the screen. *She knows.* I stare at my phone. The hum of the vibration, as well as the ringtone, fills the car. As soon as she gets my voicemail, she calls right back and the vibrating ring starts all over again. She's relentless, my best friend. I know she's already on her way to find me. I need to answer so she knows I'm oaky, well physically okay. I'm not sure about my emotional state, not sure I will ever be the same.

Again, the ringing stops and immediately starts. Taking a deep breath, I grab the phone and swipe across the screen, placing it to my ear. I don't say anything, and I don't have to.

"Tatum, oh God. I just heard. Where are you?" she asks, anguish in her voice. Leah and I have been best friends since kindergarten. She knows my parents well. Knew my parents well. *Shit!* They're gone. I feel panic set in as I struggle to drag air into my lungs. "Is Josh with you?" she asks.

"No," is all I can say at the moment, and that is a valiant effort. I feel like an elephant is sitting on my chest.

"Tell me where you are." Her voice is now pleading.

"Home," I croak out.

"Stay there, I'm on my way. I'll call Josh."

"No! Please don't," I beg her. I don't want to be anywhere near him.

"Okay, just stay there. I'm about five minutes away," she tells me.

I nod my head, even though she can't see me, unable to form words. I hit end on my cell and drop it back into the cup holder. I try to focus on taking slow, deep, even breaths. I need to get myself under control.

My cell rings again. I peer down at the screen and see that it's Josh. My chest aches from his betrayal. Josh cheated on my. My parents are gone. My entire life is crashing and burning. A sob escapes my lips as the doctors words continue to play through my mind. *"They're gone. Your parents didn't survive. I'm so sorry."*

I jump at a gentle knock on my window, the sound a welcome one due to its creator. Leah. She is peering through the window watching me, tears rolling across her cheeks. I fumble with the door handle, trying to get out of the car. A task that minutes earlier seemed too daunting. Leah is here; I'm no longer alone. Seeing me struggle, she pulls open the door. I step out and she immediately engulfs me in a hug. I sag against her, letting go of the pain, as I sob into her shoulder.

Leah hugs me tighter. "I am so sorry, Tate," she whispers through her own tears.

I'm not sure how long we stand there, but my best friend never wavers. She holds on tight and allows me to grieve the loss of my family, and the future I thought I was planning with Josh.

I pull away from her embrace, and without saying a word, she grabs my hand and slowly leads me to the front of the house. Instead of going to the door, she makes her way to the porch swing that is slighting swaying with the warm breeze. She takes a seat, and reluctantly, I sit beside her. *My parents loved this swing.*

As if she can read my thoughts, she says, "They would sit out here for hours. I remember in high school on warm summer nights, they would be here when we would get home at night. You always said it

5

was to make sure we made curfew, but they just loved each other that much. They enjoyed being with each other." She pauses to collect her thoughts. I don't say anything, because she's right. My parents were high school sweethearts; the love they shared was once in a lifetime. *Will I ever have that?* My mind flashes back to Josh and the blonde bimbo. I open my mouth to spill the horrid details, but Leah speaks first.

"It seems fitting that they were together. They were never far apart, and I'm not sure how one would have gone on without the other," she says softly.

I let her words sink in. She's right. My parents shared a bond, a love so deep that either one would have been devastated without the other. I know they loved me. I'm an only child as my mother had complications during my delivery and was unable to have more children. However, what they shared, it was if one was not complete without the other.

"I think you may be right," I tell her.

She squeezes my hand in recognition. What would I do without her? Then it hits me that she's moving. Leah and her fiancé Brent are moving to Murfreesboro, TN. Brent is a pediatrician. He just finished his residency at Nationwide Children's Hospital here in Columbus. He accepted a private practice position in Tennessee. Leah is a registered nurse; she will be able to find work once they get there.

Sure they will only be seven hours away, but right now, they're all that I have.

"I know what you're thinking," she tells me. "I'm only a phone call away. You can drive to me in a day, and a flight will get you there in a couple of hours. I will always be here for you," she says, giving my hand another squeeze.

"The hospital called and said that I needed to come right away." my voice is trembling. Taking a deep breath, I try to get myself under control before I continue. "I had no idea why, and they wouldn't tell me on the phone. When I got there and asked for the nurse who called me, I was led into a private room. Once I heard the news, it was like I was living outside my body. I know the doctor was talking, but I couldn't hear a word he was saying. Josh popped into my head, and all

I wanted to do was go to him. I wanted to feel his arms around me, and hear him tell me everything was going to be okay."

I stop to take a breath. Leah offers me a small smile of encouragement. She has no idea the bomb I'm about to drop on her. "I knew he had class, but I just wanted to feel close to him. I decided to use the key he gave me a few weeks ago and let myself into his apartment. I'm not sure how I got there; the drive is a blur. I made it to his apartment and turned the handle; it was unlocked. Looking back now, that should have been the first clue, but my head was so jumbled that it just now dawned on me."

I shake my head to clear the thought. "Anyway, I opened the door and found Josh with some blonde bimbo bent over the couch. I'll spare you the remaining visual. Needless to say, I told him we were through. He tried to stop me, but his neighbor heard the yelling and stepped in. He blocked Josh while I got away." I wipe my hands across my cheeks to remove the tears. It's a wasted effort because they continue to flow. "I didn't even get the chance to tell him about Mom and Dad."

"Fuck him!" Leah spits venomously. "I never liked that jackass anyway. You wait until I see him again," she seethes.

I smile through the tears, because this girl has had my back for years, and I hers. I love her; she is my sister of hearts. "I'm going to miss you," I say.

"You can always come with us. The condo has three bedrooms and we would love to have you," she replies. "Let's get you through the next couple of days, and then we can talk more. You ready?" she asks, gesturing toward the door.

"Not really, but I can't live on the front porch." I stand up, as does Leah. I hug her tight. "Thank you for being here." I release her and pull my keys out of my pocket. Time to face reality.

CHAPTER 2

BLAISE

The blaring vocals of George Strait's "Fireman" jolt me out of bed. I look at the clock on the night stand and it's ten fifty-nine. *Shit*. I reach for my phone and swipe at the screen. "Hello," I mumble.

"Blaise, you up?" I hear my brother chuckle on the other end of the line. He knows that I'm not, or that I wasn't rather.

"Seriously, why are you calling?" I ask him, frustrated. I was out until three this morning at an auto accident. I was on call he knows this.

"Just making sure you're up. Mom will so not be impressed if you miss Sunday dinner," he replies.

Well, shit.

"Thanks, I'm up. Noon as usual?" I ask, even though I already know the answer.

"Yep, don't be late," he says with a chuckle as he hangs up. Asher is my twin brother. My baby brother as I like to call him. I did arrive ten minutes earlier than he did. Our father is the fire chief. Asher and I have followed in his footsteps to some degree. We both volunteer for the department, but our first love is our tattoo shop. We rotate hours at the shop to blend with our volunteer hours with the department. It works for us.

I throw my phone on the bed, grab some clothes, and head to the shower. Sunday dinner at my parents has become a tradition. Asher and I moved out when we were twenty-one, and recently our little sister Ember, well she's twenty-two, but still little to me, has moved out as well. I worry about her living on her own. Living alone doesn't seem to faze her, except she complains of boredom. Ember is a social butterfly; that's what my mom calls her. Asher and I were four when she was born, and we have always gone out of our way to protect her. Hell, Dad beat that into our heads from the time she was born. Not just for Ember, for women in general. Always treat them with respect and never lay a mean hand on them. That philosophy was born and bred into us.

My mom is the administrative assistant to the mayor of Murfreesboro. She and my father have been married for twenty-eight years. She, and I quote, "Just wants her babies to be as happy as she is." In Mom terms, that means get hitched and have me some grandbabies. Of course, Asher and I are first on the hit list, with Ember just graduating from college. She graduates in a few weeks with her degree in elementary education. She wants to teach kindergarten. Ember has always loved kids.

At one time, I thought I would be the first to make my parents grandparents. My ex, Beth, and I dated for two years. I was ready to ask her to marry me. The day I had planned to ask her, she showed up on my doorstep. She had news for me. Apparently, she had been sleeping around behind my back. She was six weeks pregnant and the baby wasn't mine. It had been longer than that since we had slept together. The department was short-staffed due to an injured man. With the hours I picked up there as well as my time at the shop, there was not much time for anything else. I was trying to make the shop a success so I could buy a house. Asher and I were living in an apartment at the time. It didn't seem to bother Beth; I guess that should have tipped me off. I was blinded by…well, a lot of things. I was preoccupied with the shop, picking up at the department whenever I could, and things between us were…fine. I assumed that proposing was the next step. She talked about it often and I was willing to give that to her. That day on my doorstep, she came clean. She had been seeing this guy for over a year behind my back. That was three years ago, and I haven't been in a relationship since. Sure, I date, hook up here and there. I'm selective though. I don't like the thought of using women for sex and, well, Beth pretty much ruined me ever being in another relationship. Why chance the heartache? I put all of my focus into the shop and volunteering for the department.

As I pull up to my parents' house, I spot Asher and his girlfriend Grace. He informed me earlier in the week that he was going to propose, and that if things went well, he and Grace would be finding a place of their own. I'm happy for them. Maybe someday, I might have a change of heart and be where he is. I wanted that life with Beth: marriage, kids, all of it. Hell, if I'm honest, I want it now. I just haven't found anyone who I'm willing to risk my heart for.

I climb the steps to the front porch and reach for Grace. I throw my arm over her shoulder and kiss her cheek. "Hey, beautiful, thanks for meeting me here," I say with a wink.

Grace giggles.

Asher growls, "Hands off my woman!"

I throw my head back in laughter. Fucking with him never gets old. Grace is the one and only girl I've seen him this way with. He loves her; even a blind man can see it. I give Grace another squeeze and then release her. Asher pulls her into his chest and kisses her temple.

As soon as I'm through the door, I smell Mom's cooking and my stomach growls. I can hear Mom and Ember talking as they finish lunch. Asher and Grace are still out on the front porch and Dad is sitting in his recliner watching ESPN. I hand out my fist for him to bump and he shakes his head with a smile as we bump fists. "Smells good," I say.

"Yep, your mother is one of the best cooks around. One of the reasons I married her," he chuckles.

I laugh. My parents are so in love with each other, my mom could burn every meal and Dad would still look at her like she hung the fucking moon. She looks at him the same way. I look up to see Asher and Grace walk into the room; they both have that look.

"Come and get it!" Ember yells from the kitchen. Dad and I usher in like a herd of cattle while Asher and Grace follow behind. Lunch is amazing. Mom made fried chicken, mashed potatoes and gravy, and macaroni and cheese, with apple pie for desert. Yum!

"So how was last night?" my dad asks. Being fire chief, he already knows, but he likes to get our side every time. This leads Dad, Asher, and I into talks of the department and staffing issues. Mom and the girls are planning a trip to go shopping to get some items for Ember's new condo.

"You sure you are okay there all by yourself?" Asher asks her.

"Yeah, you know you can always stay in our spare room," I chime in.

Ember rolls her eyes. "Guys, come on. I lived at home all through college. It's time for me to spread my wings. Speaking of which, I really want my tattoo. When can you work me in?" she asks.

Ember doesn't have any ink. She is going to be a kindergarten teacher so she has to remain professional. However, she is the first out of our family to go to college and finish, even out of all of our cousins. This is a huge accomplishment. She wants Asher and I to both give her a tattoo. She says she would never be able to choose either one of us. So we agreed that once she graduated we would do it.

I glance over at Asher; he shrugs his shoulders. "We'll have to find a time when we can both be in the shop. We'll work it out for after graduation." I'm so fucking proud of her. I would hate the tat to jinx her before she holds that piece of paper in her hands.

Ember smiles so big I'm afraid her face might crack. "You guys are the best brothers ever!"

"Oh, go on," Asher and I say at the same time. This causes the entire table to bust out in laughter. We do that a lot; it's a freaky twin thing.

I take in my family and Grace, well she'll be family soon enough. Asher already said when she says yes, that he's going to push for a short engagement. He's confident, and by the looks of them together, he has a right to be. It's a great feeling to know that you have so many people in your corner. As involved as our family is with the department, we know all too well that life is short and you have to live each day to its fullest. However, even for us, we sometimes take our family, each other, for granted.

CHAPTER 3

I watch as Leah shows the last guest to the door. Once I hear the sound of the lock click into place, I drop down on the couch and curl up in the corner. I feel empty, a hollow version of myself. Within the blink of an eye, my life was in flames. How do I come back from this? How do I move on without them?

Josh continued to call my cell relentlessly. Brent called and had my number changed. He stopped by a few times, but Brent and Leah threatened to call the cops. I'm done with him. I can't deal with his shit. I don't want to. He no longer exists in my world. I needed him; he was fucking someone else. That is the end of our story.

Leah has been staying with me. I can't stay here alone, without them. I hear her on her cell talking to Brent. He's been great through all of this. Sacrificing time with his fiancée so that she can be here with me. Leah and Brent, they're all I have left. Bringing my knees to my chest, I rest my head, letting my mind wonder.

The day after the accident, I had to go to the police station to hear the results of the investigation. Leah had to work, so I went alone. My mind developed a constant string of images from the details the investigator shared with me. I keep seeing their accident play out, and it's tearing me up inside. Officer Morgan assured me that they didn't suffer, and died on impact. How in the fuck is that supposed to make me feel better? Leah has tried to get me to talk to her, but I can't. It's bad enough that I see the accident play out in my mind and in my sleep. Every time I close my eyes, the details are on instant replay. Every loud noise causes me to cringe. It consumes me. I can't talk about it. I refuse to talk about it. She hasn't pushed me, just hugs me and tells me that she is here for me. I have heard that so many times in the last five days, but Leah is the only one I believe.

Josh showed up that first night, banging on the door, causing all kinds of commotion. Luckily, Brent was here. I'm not sure exactly what he told him. I know he told him about my parents, but I have a feeling he also threated some type of bodily harm. Brent is a big guy, tall about 6'2 and broad shoulders. At first sight, you wouldn't think of him as a pediatrician. The man is great with kids, and he loves my best friend fiercely. When I asked Leah about his interaction with Josh, she said I need not worry about it. Brent loves her and she loves me, therefore, Brent would never let anything happen to me. I'm not sure what I did to have these two amazing people in my life, but I am, and will be, eternally grateful.

The couch dips; I raise my head to see Leah sitting beside me. She places her hand on my knee. "Can I get you anything?"

"No, thanks." I haven't had much of an appetite. "How's Brent?"

She smiles. "Good. He wanted me to apologize again for rushing out after the service. When you're a resident, you don't have much to say about your schedule. Especially since the loss was not immediate family," she says softly.

"I understand. I don't know that I would have done this past week without the two of you," I tell her.

"Well, you don't ever have to find out," she says as my cell rings.

I reach for it and look at the screen. "It's Josh." This is the first time he has called since the night Brent warned him away. Leah said she saw him in the back of the church during the funeral. I didn't see him. I didn't see a lot of people. My mom was an only child and my dad had an older brother who passed away from a heart attack a few years ago. My gran, who just passed a few months earlier, Dad's mom, was my only living grandparent. I have two cousins and my aunt Brenda who is now re-married. Our family was small, but loving. I grew up always feeling loved and wanted. Now…well, now all I feel is pain in my chest.

"Hey, why don't you go pack a bag and we'll head over to my place? We can curl up on the couch and watch movies. Girls night," she says hopefully.

She seems to always know how I'm feeling. She's moving away in less than a month. What will I do without her? I need to soak up as much girl time as I can, as it will be a rarity once she moves to Tennessee.

"That actually sounds great. I need to get out of here for a while. Give me five to pack a bag and change."

"Yay! Okay, I will go finish cleaning up the kitchen and we'll be all set. I'm thinking take out, pizza maybe?" she asks.

Again, she knows me so well. The kitchen is filled with casseroles, meat trays, vegetable trays, and I don't even know what else. The thought of consuming any of it makes me ill.

I quickly change and pack a bag. "I'm ready," I yell to Leah as I make my way down the hall, back to the living room.

"Great, I called and ordered us a pizza, pepperoni and banana pepper. They said forty minutes so we should be there in plenty of time."

Leah and Brent live in a condo. It's close to the hospital and only fifteen minutes from my parents' house. Shit. My house. I fight against the tears that threaten to fall. I turn to gaze out the window, trying to get my emotions in check. Without saying a word, Leah reaches over and grabs my hand. She squeezes tight and continues to drive. She doesn't make me talk. I love my best friend

We arrive at the condo just in time. The pizza delivery guy pulls in right behind us. I insist on paying for the pizza, so Leah heads inside to get drinks.

"Marco," I yell as I enter the condo.

I hear Leah laughing. "Polo," she yells back through her laughter. When we were kids, we spent hours in the pool at both her house and mine playing that game.

"It's good to see you smile," Leah says as I place the pizza box on the coffee table.

"We wore that game out," I reply. I avoid the fact that my smile has been missing. I don't want to think about it, and I don't want to talk about it. Not right now, anyway.

"Well, guess what's on?" she asks cheerily.

"What?"

"Jeff Dunham." She laughs just talking about it.

"Sounds good." It actually sounds damn good. I don't want a romance, not with my break up with Josh still lingering. I was honestly stressing over what movie we would watch and what emotions it might bring out in me. Kicking back with the comedy channel is just what the doctor ordered.

Leah smiles as she shakes her head and laughs, mimicking the character Peanut. He's our favorite.

We both have our fill of pizza, which for me was one slice. Leah doesn't push, but I can tell by the look on her face that she's concerned. We settle in on the couch, both of us curled up in a throw. I feel myself begin to grow tired as the stress of the last five days catches up with me. It's not long before sleep claims me.

I wake up with a jolt. I sit up on the couch and survey my surroundings. It takes me a minute to realize I'm on Leah and Brent's couch. I place my hand over my racing heart, another nightmare.

"Hey, you, you okay?" I hear Leah's voice. I turn and see that she and Brent are sitting together on the love seat. He's eating leftover pizza.

"I'm so sorry; I dozed off. What time is it?" I ask.

Leah smiles softly. "Tate, it's eleven thirty. You slept for four hours."

"Wow," is all I can say. Four hours seems like an eternity compared to what I have slept at one time in the last week.

"Tate, I'm glad you're awake. We were actually just talking about you," Brent says with a wink. Leah is damn lucky to have found such an amazing guy.

I scoot back on the couch and cross my legs. "Really, do tell," I retort.

"Well, you see, my new job is going to require me to work a lot of hours. The practice that I'm joining takes on call shifts at the hospital as well as regular office hours." He reaches for Leah's hand and laces their fingers together. "My beautiful fiancée will not have to be in a rush to find work. I want her to focus on planning our wedding. She's not going to know anyone, and I'm afraid she's going to miss you terribly."

Leah smiles at me and shakes her head yes. "So much, you don't even know," she pleads with a smile.

"So, I was wondering if you would please consider coming with us. We have the space, and I would feel better knowing Leah won't be spending too much time alone. Besides, she needs her maid-of-honor to get these wedding plans rolling. I plan to make an honest woman out of her sooner than later," Brent tries to convince me.

I watch him closely for any signs that Leah might have put him up to this. He seems sincere. I don't say anything so he continues.

"You're like a sister…to both of us. We want you to come with us. Please say you will."

I can feel the tears that are wetting my cheeks. "I—I don't know what to say."

"Say that you'll come. We can all use a fresh start. I even kinda sorta may have a job for you, or at least a lead," he tells me, batting his eyelashes.

"What?" Leah turns to face him. "What about me? I need a job," she huffs.

"You, my future wife, have a wedding to plan; then work, unless I can convince you to start having my babies," he says as he wags his eyebrows at her.

Leah's smile lights up her face. Instead of the anger she was trying to portray just seconds ago, she's now putty in his hands. She leans in and kisses him on the cheek.

"What kind of job?" I ask, trying to let the idea really sink in.

"Well, I may have mentioned to my new office manager that my fiancée and her best friend would be coming with me." He winks at me. I just shake my head and smile.

"She asked what each of you did, and she said she may have a job lead for you. Her sister works for the city of Murfreesboro, not sure in what capacity, but she said they are looking for a public relations person. Someone who can help represent all areas of the city such as police, fire, and even the hospital in some cases."

"Wow, that actually sounds kind of perfect," I say.

"Well, then say you'll come with us, please, Tatum," Leah pleads. "I need you with me to plan this wedding." She lightly elbows Brent. "It also sounds like I may need a sitter in the very near future," she says, laughing.

"Yeah, Leah, please…wait…what? D—did you just…?" Brent stutters unable to form a sentence.

Leah smiles and shakes her head. "Hell yeah!" Brent rejoices as he devours her in an all-consuming kiss.

I can feel the grin spread across my face. I'm so happy for both of them. They are starting their lives together.

We can all use a fresh start. I think about going back to that house and being here all alone. I think about Josh and running into him. The life Brent has painted has much more appeal. I think a fresh start is what I need. Am I making a rash decision based on emotion? Maybe, but I will have my two best friends with me. How many people get the chance to start over and have people they know and love come along for the ride?

The lovebirds finally come up for air and smile at me. Neither one the least bit embarrassed of that fact I witnessed such a personal life changing decision between them. "When do we leave?" I ask.

"Really?" Leah jumps off the love seat and tackles me. "Holy shit, this is great. Thank you so much. I can't believe you said yes."

Brent joins us and wraps his arms around both of us. "To new beginnings," he cheers and we all laugh.

18

CHAPTER 4

BLAISE

I pull into the lot of Self Expressions; I see that Asher and Ember are already here. Today is the day that we give our baby sister her first tattoo. Ember has been bugging the hell out of us since she turned eighteen to ink her. We told her as soon as she found something she was sure she wanted on her body for the rest of her life that we would be more than happy to do the work. Asher and I have seen so many people come through our doors with spur of the moment tattoos. We spend just as much time doing cover-ups as we do first timers.

Asher and I opened Self Expressions about six years ago. As soon as we graduated high school, we trained at the academy to become volunteers on the department. We worked our asses off and saved every damn penny to see our dream take shape. Here we are six years later with a thriving business.

As soon as I walk in the shop, I see Ember bouncing on a stool at the reception desk. Today is Sunday and we're closed, so it'll just be the three of us.

"About damn time you got here; let's do this," Ember singsongs.

I smile at her; I can't help it. Her enthusiasm is infectious. She has been waiting for this for the last four years. "All right, sis, what are we doing?" I ask her.

"Here," she hands Asher and I both a piece of paper, "I want one from each of you." She smiles sweetly.

I open the folded piece of paper and read, "Every journey begins with a single step." I look up at Ember; she's biting down on her smile. "I want that one on the outside of my right foot," she tells me.

We both turn to face Asher; he opens his folded piece of paper and reads aloud, "The future belongs to those who believe in the beauty of their dreams." He looks up at Ember.

Eyes sparkling, she says, "I want that one here, on my left side." She points to the middle of her torso, right over her rib cage.

"You sure about this, Ember?" Asher questions. "This is permanent," he reminds her.

"Ugh! Yes! I. Am. Sure. I've had four long years to decide what I want. I want this, no regrets," she says, bouncing on the balls of her feet.

"Well, all right then. Let's do the foot first. Hop up in the chair," I tell her, trying like hell not to laugh at how excited she is. It's the little things.

"EEEKK!" she says as she skips to the chair and wiggles out of her flip-flops.

I sit down on my stool and sheath my hands in my gloves before preparing my gun and ink. "Ready?" I ask her.

"Yepper," she replies.

I shake my head and smile. "So, how's the apartment?" I ask her as my needle touches her skin. She winces, but stays still

"It's amazing. I still get lonely at times, but I love being on my own. No worries, big brother," she tells me her voice quivering.

I pull back my gun and watch her as she bites her lip. Asher and I tried to warn her. Instead of I told you so I say "Good. You know if you need anything, you can come to us, right?" I know I don't need to remind her, but really I want to. It's for my peace of mind as much as it is hers.

"Yes, Blaise. I'm fine, really," she says.

"So when are you able to get into your classroom?" I ask as I place the needle back against her skin.

"Mrs. Smith asked if I would come and help her clean out. Since she is retiring, she is leaving most of her materials for me," she replies, excitement in her voice.

"Don't move, silly girl," I laugh.

"Oops, sorry. I'm just excited I'm finally starting my career, living on my own, and getting my ink. Life is good." She says through clenched teeth.

"Well, if you keep wiggling around, your ink is going to look like one of your students did it," Asher chuckles from across the room.

"I know, sorry. I'm just so excited and it's a little uncomfortable," she mumbles.

"All right, you're all set. Asher has his station set up for your other one," I tell her as I hold a mirror out beside her foot so she can get a good look at it.

"Blaise, I love it. Thank you!" she says, wrapping me in a bear hug. I hug her back just as fiercely, and then help her off the table.

Ember hobbles over to Asher's station and takes off her tank top. Underneath she is wearing a bikini, and I bite my tongue. She's not a little girl anymore, but the thought of some asshole taking advantage of her still gets me riled up. I can tell by the look in Asher's eyes that he's thinking the same thing.

Ember notices as well. "Oh, hush you two. I'm twenty-two years old and I can wear a damn bikini if I want. This is actually the most modest one I have," she tells us.

"Em, spare us the details, please," Asher begs her. She flashes us both a cheesy grin and settles in on the table.

"Are you both going to make it to dinner tonight at Mom and Dad's?" Ember asks.

"Never miss," I say as I clean up my station. I watch as she closes her eyes and fights back the tears. The ribs are touchy even for someone who has had ink. She's taking it like a champ.

"What about you, Ash? You and Grace coming?" she asks him taking deep even breaths.

"Yes, little sister, we'll be there. We would be crazy to miss one of Mamma's meals," he says.

"Aunt Ruth and Uncle Tom are going to be there as well," she informs us.

"How are they?" Asher asks.

Ember shrugs her shoulders. "Don't move," Asher tells her.

"Sorry, Mom says that Uncle Tom is getting around pretty well after the fall, but I haven't seen them for a couple weeks, ahhh" she says wincing in pain.

Uncle Tom fell a few months ago on the ice. Broke his ankle in three separate places. He had to have reconstructive surgery and has been laid up.

"It'll be good to see them," I say.

"Okay, you're all set," Asher tells her. She immediately releases the breath she was holding. Asher offers his hand and helps her sit up and get off the table. She hobbles over to the wall that encases a floor to ceiling mirror to view our handiwork. She stares at her left side; then turns to check out her foot. She does this a couple of times, before she lifts her head to face us. When she does, there are tears in her eyes.

"Happy tears, I hope?" I ask, worried that we just inked our little sister and she hates it.

Ember nods her head. "Hell yes, these are happy tears. I love you both so much!" she says. She limps over and kisses each of us on the cheek. We both have to bend down from the height difference.

"Well, I'm off to pick up Grace. Meet you guys at the house?" Asher asks.

"Sure. Ember, you want to ride with me?" I ask her.

"Yes, hopefully the tingling in my foot will be gone by the time we're done so I can drive." She smiles.

I toss my keys at her. "Here, I'm just going to make sure everything is locked up. I'll meet you in the car."

I do a walk-through of the building, making sure the front door is pulled tight, and meet Ember in the car.

"All set?" she asks.

"Yep, just wanted to make sure everything was turned off." Being a volunteer firefighter and the son of a fire chief makes you cautious. Never can be too careful.

"I just talked to Mom; she's made a ham and all the trimmings. My mouth is watering just thinking about it."

I rub my stomach; I skipped breakfast this morning. "I plan on tearing it up myself. Nothing beats Mom's cooking."

"One day, when some lucky girl steals your heart, one that deserves your heart, you might think differently. Asher used to say the same thing, now all he can do is brag about Grace's cooking," she laughs.

"Yeah, you might be right, but it's going to have to be someone special. I'm not exactly thrilled at the prospect of getting my heart trampled again anytime soon. So this girl you speak of, she needs to be one in a million," I tell her.

"I agree, big brother. I agree."

As soon as we enter the house, the smell of home cooking invades us. I glance over at Ember, and she's licking her lips. I wink at her as I dash off to the kitchen. "Hey, no fair. I'm not operating at 100%," she whines as she trails behind me. I hear my dad and Uncle Tom laughing at us.

I burst through the kitchen door and see Mom and Aunt Ruth sitting at the island, drinking tea. "Hello, ladies," I say as I bend down and kiss each of them on the cheek. I sneak my arm around Mom and grab a roll. She slaps my hand. "What? I'm starving," I tell her.

"Well, a few more minutes won't kill you. As soon as Asher and Grace arrive, we can eat," Mom says.

Ember sticks her tongue out at me as she limps through the door. Mom scoots off her stool and tells Ember to sit. She reaches for a roll and Mom slaps her hand also. "You two," she says with a smile as she shakes her head. She looks at Aunt Ruth and shrugs her shoulders like *what do you do?*

"Well, let's see it," Mom tells Ember.

Ember hold up her right leg so Mom and Ruth can see her tat. The only problem is it's still covered. "Blaise says I have to leave it covered for at least two hours. I'll show them to you before we leave?" She looks at me for confirmation.

I shake my head yes. My mouth is full of my second roll, which I snatched while Ember had them distracted.

"Finally!" Ember says looking at the door. I turn to see Asher and Grace are finally here. My dad and Uncle Tom are right behind them. Seems like we all brought our appetites today.

There is limited conversation at the table; we're all too busy shoveling it in. Asher and I clean up while everyone else heads out to the back deck. We make quick work of clean up as we have done this since we were little tykes. Joining everyone on the deck, I take a seat beside Aunt Ruth.

"Oh, Nancy, are you all still looking for a new public relations person?" Aunt Ruth asks.

"Ugh. Yes, the hunt is really at a standstill. Most of the new graduates already have job placements, so we are just waiting to see who else might pop up."

"Well, I may have a candidate for you. The new doctor we hired, Brent Wethington, he and his fiancée are moving here and her best friend is coming with them. Seems she has had a rough way to go the last few months and wants a new start. Dr. Wethington says she has a degree in Marketing and Public Relations. He is supposed to bring me a copy of her resume tomorrow; it's his first day," she tells my mom.

"Really? Thank you so much. The sooner we get someone hired, the sooner I can go back to my normal routine. Not that I mind picking up hours, but I'm worn out."

"Mom, can I do anything to help?" Ember asks.

"Thanks, sweetie. I might have to take you up on that if we don't find someone soon," she says.

"Well, hopefully this girl will work out. Dr. Wethington didn't tell me her name, just that he would stand behind the decision to hire her. I'll fax her resume to you tomorrow."

"Thank you. Fingers crossed," Mom says, crossing her fingers.

CHAPTER 5

After making the decision to pack up and move my life to Tennessee, my world has become a flurry of activity. I had three weeks to prepare to move, get the house settled and, not to mention, graduate from college. I thought about joining Leah and Brent at a later date, but Leah begged me to drive with them. I think she's afraid I'll back out. Really, I don't think I would. The more time the idea has a chance to take root, the more excited I am about it. At first, I was going to put the house on the market, but Leah and Brent talked me into closing it up and waiting to see how I feel about it in a few months. They are afraid I'll make a rash decision based on emotions. I'm sure they're right. So, I hired the people next door to look after it, really their fourteen-year-old son. He's going to keep the lawn mowed and the weeds from taking over. At this point, I don't think I can live here ever again, but time will tell

I finish packing the last box and survey my room. Twenty-two years broke down into boxes. I'm taking my bedroom furniture, but leaving the rest. Leah and Brent have furniture from their current apartment. I offered them anything in the house they might want or need. Leah says she just needs me.

"Tate, you ready to go?" I hear Brent yell down the hall. A few seconds later, he appears in my doorway. "I loaded all the boxes by the door. Is this the rest of it?" he asks gently.

I offer him a smile. Brent and Leah have been so good to me. I honestly don't believe I could have made it through these last few weeks without them. They're starting their life together and invited me to tag along. I haven't told them yet, but as soon as I land a job and get my bearings about me, I'm going to find a place of my own.

Hopefully, close to them. They need their space. Hell, they decided they are going to start a family right away; they don't need me underfoot for that. Besides, I don't want to listen to their sexcapades as they practice.

"Yep, that's the last of it. I just need to walk the spare set of keys next door, and I'm good to go," I tell him. "I'll meet you guys at the truck." Brent rented a U-Haul for the trip. He refused to let me help pay, saying I was lucky he happened to be going my way. Leah is a lucky girl.

I take one last look at my room, turn and walk away. As I walk through the house, I am flooded with memories of my parents. I look to the backyard at the pool. My dad had it installed when I was thirteen. He always said that he wanted our house to be the "hang out" so that he always knew I was safe. As I pass through the kitchen, images of my mother making dinners and birthday cakes flood my mind. I swipe my cheeks with the back of my hand. The last room is the living room. I stand and stare at the corner where we always placed our Christmas tree. Christmas was Mom's favorite holiday; the house was always decked out with decorations and so many baked goods you would gain ten pounds from just looking at them. I close my eyes and commit everything to memory: the smells, the colors, and the many moments we shared. With a deep breath and one more swipe to rid my face of tears, I walk out the door, closing it tightly, ensuring that it's locked. I know that my decision to leave is the right one. I can't deal with being here without them. Not right now anyway.

I make my way over to the Jones's and leave the key in the mailbox just like Mrs. Jones asked me to do. They are at a family graduation party today. This is better really; I don't have to see the pity in her eyes. I know she doesn't mean it. I get it from a lot of people who know me and knew my parents. They feel sorry for me. Just another reason moving away is a good idea. I need to be surrounded by people who treat me normal. Not like the girl who just lost her entire world. I need to get my life back on track, need to move on.

The drive takes us about eight hours. Of course, we make a few stops. Leah and I keep Brent entertained with our musical styling. At one point, we are laughing so hard, Brent has to pull over so we can pee on the side of the interstate. Not our proudest moment, but for me it's freeing. Just the thought of being away from a town where I will have to see my parents everywhere I look, lifts my spirits. I will never forget them and I will forever love them until my last breath, but being there with that constant daily reminder, yeah, the move is a good idea. *I hope.*

As we pull in front of our new home, Brent pulls out his cell and sends a text.

"Who you texting, babe?" Leah asks him.

"I hired a moving company to unload the truck. I knew we would be beat from the drive, and tomorrow is my only day of rest before I start my new job. I thought it would be best," he tells her.

Leah leans over and kisses him. "I love you, so much," she says softly.

There is an ache in my chest, but it's not for Josh as much as for the intimacy. I have come to terms with Josh being a cheating scumbag and the fact he had been going behind my back the entire time we were dating. Accepting this has killed any and all feelings I ever had for him. Losing my parents at the same time also played a part. Life is too short to dwell on what you cannot change. Leah's theory is I really must have not been that into him not to notice. We did spend a lot of time apart, but we were both busy with school. I've learned my lesson. No more relationships for me, at least not for a while. I want to get settled and get my life under control and adjust to all the changes before I include another person and emotions into the mix.

Leah elbows me. "Let's go," she says, reaching over me and trying to open the door.

"Stop, I have to pee." I say through my laughter. Brent just shakes his head and smiles at us. He hops out the driver's side and shuts the door. This leaves Leah pushing me out the passenger side and grabbing my hand. She pulls me behind her, racing up the sidewalk. Brent is standing at the door holding it open with a big smile on his face.

"Ladies, welcome home," he says.

He and Leah made a trip up here a few months ago to check out the place and signed the lease immediately. At the time, they didn't know I would be tagging along. I feel an ache deep in my chest. *Am I doing the right thing?* I feel as though moving is disrespecting my parents and their memory. But living in that town, seeing them everywhere, and constantly getting sympathetic looks and pats on the back, it was slowly killing me. I need to start over. They would want that; want me to find happiness. Of that I am certain.

"Come on. Let me give you the tour," Leah says excitedly. She is pulling on my arm, dragging me from room to room. After we see the main part of the condo, she drags me upstairs to the bedrooms.

"This is your room, and ours is at the end of the hall," she tells me.

I step into the room and take in the deep purple walls. I look over my shoulder at Leah, raising my eyebrows in question. I don't need to say anything; I know she can read my mind. We have best friend superpowers like that.

"We had the painters paint it last week. Brent and I wanted you to feel like this is your home. I know this is your favorite color," she says.

I turn around and walk back to the door where she is still standing. I wrap my arms around her and hug her tight. I feel the moisture on my cheeks, but don't bother to hide it, not from Leah.

"The movers are here," Brent yells up the steps.

I slowly pull away and wipe my tears. "Thank you, Leah. I love you. You are my family, my sister, my best friend." I shake my head, trying to keep from totally breaking down. "What you and Brent have done for me…I will never be able to repay you."

Leah wipes at her tears and grabs my hand. "You are a part of me, a part of our family. You belong here with us. Now, let's go see if the movers are worth watching. Hopefully, they are all beef and brawn," she says, wagging her eyebrows at me. I laugh though my tears as I allow her to pull me back down the stairs. This girl, my best friend, always knows what I need. I can only hope I provide the same comfort for her.

We reach the bottom of the stairs and Leah burst into laughter. She turns to face me and motions her head toward the living room. I turn my head and join her in laughter. The movers are both men in their late forties and both are sporting beer bellies with t-shirts so tight they leave nothing to the imagination. I place my hand over my mouth to stifle the laughter. I follow Leah into the kitchen and we both bust loose, not able to contain it any longer. Brent walks in with a grimace on his face.

"Hey, babe," Leah says after getting herself under control. "What's up?"

Brent shakes his head. "I'm trying to get that image out of my head," he mumbles.

Leah and I share a look, we have no idea what the hell he's talking about.

"Okay, what image is that?" she asks him.

Brent points to the living room, and grimaces again. "Hairy ass crack. Do they not know their shit is hanging out? No pun intended," he says. His voice is stern and serious. Leah looks at me, and again we crumble into a fit of laughter. "Laugh it up you two; I may be blind." He rubs his eyes as to wipe away the memory.

CHAPTER 6

BLAISE

"All right, man, you're all set. Stop and make an appointment for four weeks from now and we will finish the second half of your sleeve," I tell Mark, a longtime client. Asher did his first piece the week we opened the shop, and here we are six years later, and I'm giving him his second sleeve. Ink is an addiction for many.

I'm busy cleaning up my station when Ember walks in. She helps us out here and there between classes and during the summer. We are going to have to hire someone now that she will be teaching full-time in the fall. "Hey, Blaise, got time for one more?" she asks.

I roll my neck from side to side. I just spent the last four hours working on Mark's sleeve. "What is it?" I ask her.

Ember rolls her eyes, so I know it's something I could probably do in my sleep. "I have a girl who wants a rose on her hip." She hands me a picture that was printed out on the internet.

Yep, this will take me twenty minutes, tops. I hate to turn away customers so, of course, I agree. Asher is on call tonight, so it's just me at the shop. "Yeah," I sigh. "Just give me a few minutes to finish sterilizing the station and to get a quick drink."

Ember nods in agreement and walks back to the reception desk. I hear a squeal and roll my eyes. My sister's bad habits are rubbing off on me. Just what I need, another co-ed vying for my attention. At first, Asher and I got a thrill from it. We had more female clients than we did male. The ink was also the typical rose, a heart, or even a butterfly. The result was always the same, "What are you doing later?" Of course, we were all over that shit, especially me after the Beth incident. Neither one of us ever have to work for female companionship.

Eventually that gets old. I know, I know, every man's fantasy. Well, not really. Men want the same thing women want; well, at least some of us do. Asher fell hard and fast for Grace, and he makes it known to every female who comes through the door that he is taken and is a one-woman man. That leaves me to fend off the piranhas.

Finished with the station, I head back to the break room/office and grab a bottle of water. I tilt my head back and finish it off all at once. Twisting the cap back on the bottle, I toss it in the recycle bin and head back to my station. I stop and yell down the hall to Ember that she can bring back my next client.

I settle myself into my chair and begin prepping my gun. From the picture of the rose, I have a good idea of the colors I will need, so I set that up as well. I hear the clank, clank, clank of high heels marching down the hallway. Rolling my neck from side to side, I take a deep breath. It's been a long ass day.

"Well hello, handsome," I hear a southern twang from the doorway.

I stand up and reach out my hand. "Blaise. It's nice to meet you," I say in my most professional voice.

"Courtney," she says, her voice lowered like she's trying to seduce me. Great, I so do not want to deal with this right now. However, a customer is a customer, so I grin and bear it.

"Have a seat." I motion to the table with my free hand. "Ember showed me the picture." I hold up the print out. "Is this exactly what you want, or did you want to make any changes?"

"No, I want that exact thing, right here." She pulls her pants down to expose her hip.

Without meeting her eyes, I continue getting everything ready. "Okay, let me get this sketched out real quick and we'll get stared."

"No rush, handsome." She winks at me.

UGH!

I make quick work of the sketch and prep the site. Courtney giggles as I place the transfer on her skin. "That tickles."

I smile and nod. I hate being rude; but really, can she be any more obvious? "All right, here we go. I'll have you out of here in no time,"

I tell her. Hopefully, she doesn't hear the hidden meaning behind my words; *I want you out of here.*

"Am I your last customer?" she asks me. I can tell she is trying to mask the discomfort of the needle against her skin.

"Yes," is my reply. This chick is starting to get on my nerves. It's nothing that she's done. I'm just over it, over chicks like her. A vision of Asher and Grace pops in my head. I can admit to myself that I'm envious of what they have. I would never admit it out loud; well, not sober anyway.

Courtney wiggles her hips, and luckily, I lift my gun before her tat turns into a larger fucking rose. "Hold still," I tell her.

"Sorry," she giggles. "So, what are you doing after? Want to get a drink?"

I'm shaking my head no before she is even finished. "Sorry, can't. I have to be up early in the morning, family thing," I tell her. It's not a complete lie; I promised Ember I would help move some new furniture into her condo. Apparently, Mom decided they needed a new dinette and gave Ember her old one. I smile thinking about my mom. She did the same thing to Asher and me, only it was a living room suite.

"Oh, well maybe some other time," she says.

I continue to keep my eyes focused on her tattoo and don't even bother to reply. A few more swipes of shading on the stem and I'm done. Finally. Seems like the longest twenty minutes of my life. I clean her up and cover the tat, all while going over the care instructions with her.

"Ember will take care of you out front. Have a good night," I say as I tear off my gloves and walk out the room. I'm so sick of the stereotype. Just because I'm a decent looking guy covered in tats, who just happens to own a tattoo shop, doesn't mean I'll sleep with anyone who is willing to spread her legs for me. I'm just not wired that way.

I hear the bell above the door, and I know that she's gone, so I head back to clean up my station. Ember follows me in. "What's up, Blaise?"

I shrug my shoulders. "Nothing," I snap.

"Liar," she fires back.

"I'm just tired."

"You're not just a piece of meat," she says, reading my mind.

"And I thought Asher and I were the ones with the freaky twin thing going," I retort.

She smiles. "I know my big brother. You'll find her. The one girl who will steal your heart. When you do, you will want to latch on and never let her go," she says in a soft voice.

My sister, always the romantic. "You hungry?" I ask her, changing the subject.

"Yes, you buying?"

I smile and throw my arm around her shoulders. "For you, little sister, always. Give me a few to finish and lock up."

Within ten minutes, Ember and I are in my truck and headed toward the local pizza joint. The same one our parents used to take us to when we were little. It's been around for as long as I can remember and the food is the best. It's always been Ember's favorite place to eat.

Ember leads us to an empty booth in the back. There is no need to look at the menu, we always get the same thing. Large Pepperoni and banana pepper with breadsticks. The waitress arrives and we order our drinks and food at the same time.

"So, Mom is still working like crazy," she says as the waitress returns with our drinks.

"I thought I heard her and Aunt Ruth talking about a candidate?"

Ember nods her head. "Yeah, I guess the new doctor that's starting at Aunt Ruth's office next week recommended her. It's a friend of his fiancée or something like that."

"I hope she's a good fit. I hate that Mom is working so many hours, along with the time she also spends doing paperwork for the department," I reply.

"Me too. I offered to help out, so I may be splitting my time between there and the shop for a while."

"No problem. We need to work on finding a replacement for you anyway. You start your new job in a couple months. I'm really proud of you by the way," I tell her.

I see tears pool in her eyes. "Thank you, Blaise."

Our pizza arrives and disappears just as quick. I, for one, have not eaten since early this morning and Ember loves her pizza. I drive her back to the shop to get her car and wait to make sure she gets off okay, before I head home as well. It's been a long ass day.

My cell rings as I pull into my driveway. Glancing at the screen, I see it's Mom calling. "Hey," I answer.

"Blaise, are you busy tomorrow?" she asks me.

"I don't have anything at the shop until the afternoon, what's up? Is everything okay?" I ask, concerned.

"Oh, yes, everything is fine. I just merged some files, which need to be carried downstairs to storage, and I was wondering if you could stop by the office and help me?"

"Sure, I don't want you throwing your back out like you did last time. You should have asked then," I remind her.

"Psh, well, I'm asking now. Your father is on call so I can't ask him, and Asher said he has an appointment at the shop first thing," she rambles on.

"Mom, it's fine. I'll be there; it's no trouble at all. What time do you need me?"

"How about nine? I'll bring breakfast for you. This way it won't keep your entire day locked up."

"Even better, I'll be there at nine," I tell her.

"Thank you. I love you. See you tomorrow," she says, and the line goes dead.

CHAPTER 7

"So, today's the big day. Are you ready?" Leah says, walking into my room.

"Yep, ready as I'll ever be." I continue tucking my shirt into my skirt before grabbing my blazer from the bed. "I dread the question, what brings you to Tennessee? I know they can't ask personal questions; I just hope I can keep my emotions in check to not look like a blubbering idiot during the interview," I tell her.

Leah stands up and adjusts the collar on my shirt. "Relax, Tate. You'll do great. As a matter of fact, I already have our night out to celebrate all planned," she says, pointing to her head.

I laugh at her. "Don't put the cart before the horse. Let me get through my interview first."

"Nah, you got this. I wouldn't be surprised if they hire you on the spot," she retorts.

I don't argue with her; I don't really have the mentally capability at this point. I barely slept last night, worried about the interview. I need this job; it's crucial to my plan of starting over. The plan to learn how to live without them.

"Well, how do I look?" I ask as I spin around, allowing her to take in my appearance.

"Professional and beautiful as ever. Good luck today," she says, giving me a hug.

With that, I'm out the door and on my way to my first job interview that actually coincides with my education. I'm a college graduate. I take a deep breath to hold back the tears. I reach my car door and stop. I tilt my head back to the sky. "I know you're up there watching over me. I miss you every day and I love you," I whisper. Wiping the lone tear that escapes, I climb in behind the wheel and head toward what I hope will be the start to my future.

I arrive at the city offices fifteen minutes early. I actually drove here yesterday, just to make sure I knew where I was going. Leah rode along with me. I'm glad Brent talked me into having my car shipped. It was kind of expensive, but worth it. I would not have wanted to make that drive by myself. Grabbing my purse and my portfolio, I make my way to the front door. Just as I'm about to reach for the handle, a very muscular, very tattooed arm reaches in front of me.

"Allow me," he says with a deep voice. He has a small southern drawl to him as well. I can feel how close he is to me, so I don't risk turning around and getting myself into an awkward situation. Instead, I slightly step to the side, allowing him to open the door.

"Thank you," I say softly. I don't bother to wait for him or look back. I continue on my journey to the receptionist desk.

"Good morning, may I help you?" the receptionist asks. I notice she glances over my shoulder and her smile grows even bigger.

"Good morning. I have an appointment at nine with Mayor Hamilton," I tell her.

"Oh, you must be Tatum. Have a seat, dear. He's running a little late. Can I get you anything, coffee?" she asks politely.

I shake my head no. "No, thank you," I reply, and walk to the other side of the reception area to find a seat.

"Well, hello, my handsome son," I hear the receptionist say.

"Hey, right back. You ready for me?" I hear that deep, masculine voice say. My curiosity is killing me, but I don't want to be obvious. I open my portfolio and raise it, pretending to study what's written in front of me. Instead, I let my eyes wonder to him.

Holy shit!

Standing before me is the most beautiful, yes beautiful, man I have ever seen. Tall, dark, and handsome, covered in colorful intricate artwork. He appears to be about six foot three or so. Close to Brent's height. His hair is jet black and a little long, but not so long that he looks like he lets himself go. Chiseled cheekbones encased in a five o'clock shadow. My eyes travel down to his arms. At first, all I notice is his tattoos, but now that I'm really taking him in, I see all that ink is displayed on a shit ton of muscle. I know it's rude to stare, but I can't look away. Wow!

"Tatum." I hear my name being called. I jerk my head up to find the kind receptionist, and tattoo guy who appears to be her son, watching me.

I clear my throat in an attempt to gain my composure. "Yes." I'm able to respond without sounding breathless, how I'm not real sure.

"Mr. Hamilton can see you now. Right this way," she says. Stepping around her desk, she stops in front of me and waits for me to stand up and follow her.

As I stand, I make eye contact with the tattooed Adonis. His eyes, they captivate me. Silver eyes. A color unlike any I've ever seen before. Shining so bright they appear to sparkle when he smiles. Which he's doing at me this very minute. I offer him a shy smile in return and quickly turn to follow his mom to Mr. Hamilton's office. I can't help the smile that crosses my face. At least he helped rid me of my nerves.

I follow Mr. Hamilton's receptionist down the hall. She stops at the last door and knocks. "Mr. Hamilton, I have Tatum Thompson for you," she tells him.

"Yes. Thank you, Nancy. Ms. Thompson, it's a pleasure to meet you, please have a seat."

Taking the seat in front of his desk, I remove another copy of my resume along with letters of recommendation from professors and a list of references.

I'm ready.

"It's a pleasure to meet you, Mr. Hamilton," I say politely.

Mr. Hamilton is an older man, probably late fifties to early sixties. His smile is kind and further relaxes me. "Well, Ms. Thompson—"

"Tatum, please," I tell him.

He smiles. "Well, Tatum. You come highly recommended. Nancy has been my administrative assistant for twenty years now. Her family and mine are all close. Her sister Ruth works with a friend of yours." He consults the paper in front of him. "Dr. Brent Wethington," he reads from the paper, and then lays it back on his desk.

I smile. "Yes, sir. Brent is engaged to my best friend Leah. Leah and I have been inseparable since kindergarten." I take a breath and decide to get it out there so I can control the conversation. "Brent, Leah, and I just moved here from Ohio. Brent is starting private practice, as you already know." I offer him another small smile. Here come the emotions. I take a deep breath and push through. "I lost both of my parents in a tragic car accident." I stop to fight back the tears. Shit! I thought if I led with this, I could control the pain, the hurt. Clearing my throat I continue. "Leah and Brent were moving and offered for me to come with them. I needed a change," I say, and drop my gaze to my lap. I try to discreetly wipe at the tears that are fighting to fall. I hear the squeak of his chair and the clearing of his throat.

I look up to find Mr. Hamilton holding a box of tissues out for me. Speaking in a quiet voice, he says, "I'm so sorry for your loss. You're about the same age as my Holly, and I can't imagine what you are going through." His words are sincere and spoken from the heart. He reminds me a lot of my father. He was the most kindhearted, gentle man.

My tears begin to flow, not only from the thoughts of my father, but from the kindness of the man sitting before me. This is going down in the record books as the worst job interview ever!

Finally, getting my emotions in check. I feel like I can talk without sobbing. "Thank you, Mr. Hamilton. I miss them terribly," is my reply.

"So tell me, Tatum. Why marketing and public relations?"

Finally, moving toward safer ground. "I enjoy the work, taking a product or brand and helping to get others interested. As far as public relations, I enjoy working with people. I added a double major with the mindset that my marketing skills would come in handy for working with the public and selling the brand or product and vice versa," I tell him.

"We have been looking for a new public relations person since Lucy left over a year ago. We just haven't been able to find anyone. Most are interested in big city life, like Nashville. You think that you can be happy here?"

I nod my head. "Yes, sir, I do. Leah and Brent are making a life here, and they are my family now, all that I have left. I just want to live again," I tell him honestly.

"Tatum, I'm not sure how much you've heard about the position, but we are actually looking for a part-time person to do some marketing. So you see, your double major has piqued my interest. The workload will be heavy at first. Nancy has been attempting to do her job and that of PR for the last year. She has been juggling two full-time positions. I feel confident that once you get the hang of things, you will be able to utilize both your marketing and PR skills," he says.

I stare at him, trying to understand what he's saying. "Mr. Hamilton, I would be honored if you would consider me for the position. I know I'm right out of school with limited extern experience, but I'm a hard worker and I need this. I promise you, I won't let you down."

He smiles at me. "I like to go with my gut instinct; it always steers me in the right direction. My gut is telling me you will make a great addition to our team. So, Tatum, I would like to offer you the position."

My mouth drops open. He just offered me the job on the spot! "Thank you, sir." I stand and reach my hand out to shake his. "Thank you so much." I feel the tears start to well behind my eyes and I will them not to fall. My future starts here, in Tennessee.

Mr. Hamilton shakes my hand. "Let me take you back to Nancy and she can get you squared away with all of your new hire paperwork."

I don't hesitate to follow him out of his office and down the hall back to the front desk. "Nancy, Tatum will be joining our team. Can you please get her set up with the necessary paperwork, background check, and drug screen that goes along with the new hire process?" He turns to face me. "Nancy will get you set up. One of us will call you when we have all the results to set your start date."

I reach out and offer my hand again. He quickly shakes my offered hand, and heads back toward his office. As I turn to Nancy, a single tear slides down my cheek. I squeeze my eyes shut willing the rest to not fall, at least not until I'm alone.

"Are you all right, dear?" Nancy asks, her voice laced with concern and motherly love.

That thought alone causes my chest to ache. I take a deep breath and open my eyes. Nancy is looking at me, worry in her eyes. Behind her is her son, the tattooed Adonis. I don't look at him long enough to try and figure out what he must think of me. My embarrassment won't allow it. I feel my face heat as I reach up and wipe the escaped lone tear.

"Yes, I'm fine. I've just had a lot going on these past few months and this job…" I pause, reining in my emotions. How much do I tell her? I don't want her to think I'm too much of an emotional wreck to handle the job.

I need this.

"This job, well, it's my future, and I couldn't be happier to be a part of your team," I tell her. That is as close as I can get without spilling my woes. She reminds me so much of my mother that it wouldn't take much for me to let the words fly. I bite down on my bottom lip to keep from doing just that.

Nancy reaches over and places her hand on top of mine. "Well, we're glad to have you."

CHAPTER 8

BLAISE

I arrive about fifteen minutes early to meet Mom. I hate to make people wait on me, and I know she's busy. Besides, she offered me breakfast. As I'm walking toward the building, I see a girl headed for the same door as me. I quicken my step to get the door for her. My parents raised me right. I catch up to her and reach out to open the door. "Allow me," I say next to her ear. I didn't plan it that way. She is closer to the door than I realized. My height makes it possible for me to easily reach around her.

I can hear that she is softly replying to my southern hospitality, but I can't comprehend what she says. The sweet scent of her hair invades my senses. I follow her into the building where she heads toward my mother's desk. Mom greets her with her ever pleasant smile. I stand close behind her for a multitude of reasons. One, her scent is intoxicating, and two, I want to know her name, who she is. Shaking my head to break this sudden trance she has me in, I focus on their conversation. I hear her tell my mom her name is Tatum and she is here for an interview with Mayor Hamilton. She must be the candidate Aunt Ruth was talking about.

The girl, Tatum, takes a seat against the wall. I force myself not to watch her every move. As soon as she walks away, Mom greets me. I wrap my arms around her and hug her tight. Because, really, is there any other way to greet your mother?

Pulling out of our embrace, I ask her, "So where do you want me?"

"Well, go on back to the break room. I brought freshly baked cinnamon rolls. Make sure you save some for Harry or he'll never let you live it down," she tells me.

"Don't have to tell me twice," I say, already headed toward the break room. The smell of freshly baked rolls greets me halfway down the hall, and I pick up the pace. Nothing beats Momma's homemade cinnamon rolls.

Mom joins me a few minutes later and I've already had two rolls. She just smiles at me and shakes her head. "Good thing I made a double batch," she chuckles.

Yep. Best mom ever!

I finish off my bottle of water and toss it in the trash as I walk to the sink to wash the cinnamon goo from my hands. "I'm all yours. Where are these boxes?" I ask her.

"Well, all right then." She leads me to a file room where an entire wall is lined with boxes. These need to be carried downstairs to storage.

"Any particular place I should put them?"

She nods her head. "Yes. I'll follow you down and show you."

I lean down and pick up two boxes and turn to face her. "Blaise, you're gonna throw your back out," she scolds me.

I playfully roll my eyes at her. "Mom, I'm a firefighter. The gear I wear weighs more than this." I then wink at her for good measure.

Mom stomps her feet all the way down to the basement. All the while, mumbling about stubborn cocky men. My grin widens. I love getting her worked up.

Mom shows me were to place the boxes, and then goes back to her desk. It only takes me about twenty minutes to carry everything downstairs and organize it the way she wants it. The time actually flies by. My mind is occupied with the dark haired beauty upstairs. When I'm finished, I head back to the break room and wash my hands. The basement is dusty. I grab another bottle of water from the fridge and head back to the reception area.

What I find when I get there stops me in my tracks. Mom and the dark haired beauty, Tatum, are in what appears to be a deep conversation. Mom has her hand on top of Tatum's and her eyes are glossy with tears. Tatum looks up and catches my stare. Her eyes, green, peridot green, the same color as the birthstone charm Momma has for Asher and me. Mesmerizing eyes filled with sadness. I can tell I'm making her uncomfortable as she tries to continue her conversation. With one last glance, trying to commit her gem colored eyes and sweet scent to memory, I turn and head back to the break room to allow them some privacy. Besides, Mom would be harping on me for not being a "gentleman" if I didn't.

I'm not sure how much time passes before Mom appears at the door of the break room. I busied myself with my phone, updating the shop's facebook and twitter status, checking e-mails, and going over my schedule for the next week.

"Thanks for your help," she says as she leans against the door jam.

I stand up and stretch. "No problem. Is that all you needed help with? I didn't want to leave in case there was anything else you needed done."

She shakes her head no. "I'm good. Thank you for helping; you're a life saver."

I tower over her at my six foot three height. Leaning down, I kiss her cheek. "Anything for your cinnamon rolls," I say, barely able to hold in my laughter as she pokes me in the side.

"Shush, you. Get out of here and enjoy the rest of your day," she laughs. "I have work to do. Harry hired that girl and I have to set up all of her pre-employment testing as well as the rest of my work and what will soon be hers. Finally, there is light at the end of the tunnel."

"So, she's the new PR rep?" I ask. Trying to be casual. If Mom suspects I'm the least bit interested, she will start her matchmaking.

She nods her head yes. "And, she has a double major in marketing. We get two for the price of one. She just moved here from Ohio."

I want to ask her more. I want to know everything she knows about the dark haired beauty named Tatum with the captivating green eyes. Instead of asking and letting my attraction to her over take my common sense, I say goodbye to my mother and head to the shop.

Every damn time I walk through the door of Self Expressions, our tattoo shop, I can't help but smile. Asher and I always dreamed of this, and here we are living the dream. Life doesn't get much better than this.

Ember is at the counter, eyes glued to her laptop, no doubt shopping online for her new apartment. I hear the hum of a tattoo gun so I can only assume Asher is hard at work. I don't have a client until three, but this place is home to me. Ember looks up from her laptop. "How was mom?" she questions.

"Good. I carried all the boxes down to the basement for her. Harry hired a new PR rep while I was there, so hopefully her work load will decrease," I tell her.

"That's awesome. She has been carrying the load for so long, she won't know what to do with herself," she replies excitedly.

Asher appears with his client and hands Ember his cash out slip. "What's awesome?"

"Harry finally hired a PR rep, so now maybe Mom can cut back and relax a little."

"About damn time," he says, turning to his client. "Let me know when you want to get started on that other piece," he tells him. They fist bump and the guy in on his way.

"Another satisfied customer." Asher grins.

Before I have a chance to reply, my cell rings. I pull it out of my pocket and see Heather's name flash across the screen. I turn my phone so my siblings can see who it is. I'm already walking down the hall and out the back door before answering.

"Hey, stranger," I say into the phone. I lean my back against the building with one foot propped up against the wall.

"Hey, yourself. How have you been?" she asks.

Heather and I dated after Beth and I broke up. It was a short-lived courtship. We have nothing in common well, except the sex. We dated for about three months and mutually decided it wasn't working out and parted as friends. Heather is a model and flies all over the world. About six months later she called and said she was in Nashville for a video shoot and would love to get together. I didn't have anything else going on, so I drove to Nashville to have dinner with her. One thing led to another and we ended up back at her hotel room. We spent the night together. The next morning, we went to breakfast, and then she went her way and I went mine. Neither of us has been in a serious relationship since. So, when she's in town, she calls and we hook up. Heather is a beautiful girl. She and I both just want to be able to relieve some tension without a bunch of random hook-ups. It works for us. Hell, we have given each other dating advice. We talk about everything. She's one of my closest friends, with benefits. We both have vowed when that special someone comes along, we will remain close friends and no hard feelings. It works for us.

"I'm good. Shop is busy as ever," I reply. "How about you?"

"Doing well. I'm in Nashville shooting another music video. You busy tonight?"

"Yeah, I have a full schedule here at the shop. How long are you in town for?" I ask her.

"I fly back to London tomorrow afternoon. This is just a short trip to do a few stills for the video."

"I wish I would have known you were coming to town. I could have made arrangements in my schedule," I tell her. I miss my friend.

"Yeah, actually I…um…I met someone," she whispers.

"Wow, who's the lucky guy?" I'm happy for her.

"His name is Antonio. We met at a shoot about four months ago. He was the photographer. We've been texting and calling. We don't see much of each other, but I really like him, Blaise."

"I'm happy for you. So when do I get to meet him?" I ask her.

Heather laughs into the phone. I feel absolutely no jealousy or heartache over her revelation. As one of my closest friends, I want her to be happy.

"Not sure. I'm actually flying to London to spend two weeks with him. I'm nervous as hell. I've only seen him one other time in the last four months and we were at a shoot. It's weird though. I feel like I already know him. Talking and texting all the time, it helped," she tells me.

Heather is beautiful, and once you get to know her, she is one of the nicest people that you will ever meet. However, she is very standoffish to those who don't know her. Her upbringing was rough and she's lived some hard times. She's worked her ass off to be where she is, and I couldn't be more proud of her. I consider what she's telling me. The way she's forced, due to their distance, to communicate and get to know Antonio, may be what she needs. This might just be it for her, the one.

"Just relax and be yourself. You're amazing, but I'm sure Antonio already knows this."

"So what about you? Anyone new in your life?" she asks.

My mind immediately travels to the dark haired beauty from Mom's office this morning. "Nope. Asher and Grace are pretty serious. I think he's going to propose," I tell her.

"Wow. Good for him." I hear voices in the background. "Listen, Blaise, I have to go; they're calling for me. I'll call you in a few weeks and let you know how London goes," she says.

"Sounds good. Be safe and have fun. Just be yourself," I tell her.

Hitting end on my phone, I slide it back into my pocket. I push off the wall to go back into the shop. As I pull on the door, Asher comes tumbling out.

"Shit!" we say at the same time.

"Hey, how's Heather," he asks.

"Good, she met someone," I tell him.

Asher studies me. "You don't seem bothered by that," he says matter of factly.

I shrug my shoulders. "Why would I be? We tried the dating thing; it didn't work for us. She's a great girl and I want her to be happy," I tell him.

Asher seems to accept my answer and drops it. "Hey, Ember left to grab a pizza. You got a minute?" he asks.

"Sure." I don't hesitate.

Asher tilts his head and motions toward the door. I follow him back into the shop and down the hall, back to our office. He walks over to the safe we have hidden in the wall for the deposits. I watch as he enters the combination and opens the door. He reaches inside and pulls out a small, black, velvet box. My mouth drops open.

Holy shit!

Asher hands me the box. "Open it," he says. I don't need to look at him to know he's smiling. I can hear it in his voice.

I open the velvet box and inside is an engagement ring. I don't know much about engagement rings, nothing really. But this one is big and there are a lot of diamonds that encase a larger one in the center.

"Congratulations, man," I say as I reach out and hug him. Handing the ring back to him I ask. "So when are you gonna ask her?"

"I have to talk to her dad first. After that, as soon as possible."

CHAPTER 9

"Shit!" I do not need this today. I steer my car to the shoulder of the road, barely making it before I lose all power. "Shit, shit, shit!" I say, beating my hands against the steering wheel. Why me? This is only my second week on the job and it looks like I'm going to be late. I have no power at all. My car didn't want to start this morning; I should have known something was wrong. Releasing a sigh, I reach for my phone in the cup holder and call Nancy.

"Good morning, Mayor Hamilton's office," she says in greeting.

"Hey, Nancy, it's Tatum. I'm going to be late," I say, my voice defeated.

"Oh my, what's wrong? Are you all right?" she asks. I can hear the concern in her voice. This woman is just too sweet.

"Yeah, my car died. I was able to steer it off the road, thankfully. Do you know of a tow agency I can call?" I ask her. "This happened a few years ago and it was the alternator."

"Oh, dear. That does sounds like your alternator. That happened to me a few years back. Where are you?"

I tell her where I am as best I can. I am still new to the area.

"All right, let me take care of it. You just hang tight and lock your doors."

"Nancy, you don't have to do that, really. Brent is already at the hospital and he's on call so I can't call him, and Leah is taking her boards for her Tennessee license today, but I can call a tow truck. "

"Nonsense. Just hang tight and I'll take care of it," she says, hanging up.

I throw my phone back in my cup holder. I swear I couldn't draw good luck with a pencil these days.

The car has no power, so listening to the radio is not an option. I don't want to use my cell battery just in case. You really never know. I reach for my purse and pull out my Kindle. I'm reading *Let Me Love* by Michelle Lynn and a little bit of Trey is exactly what I need.

I reach over and lock my doors, just like Nancy asked and settle in with Trey. I don't know how long it'll take the tow truck to arrive. I'm thankful it's early morning, otherwise I would be roasting by now.

Completely engrossed in my reading, I scream when there is a knock on my window. *Sheesh.* I look in my rearview mirror and see a big truck. Who is that? I can feel my heart racing, kick started from the adrenaline of window knock. I reach for the door and hit the lock button to reassure myself that I did indeed lock my doors. I take a deep breath before turning to look out my window at my visitor.

My mouth drops open in shock…Blaise.

He leans down, smiles and waves before standing back up. I take the opportunity to look my fill. He's wearing faded blue jeans that hang on his hips just right. How do I know this? His black fitted t-shirt conforms to his muscles, all of them including the V at his hips. Yeah, the jeans are looking good.

I'm startled when Blaise bends down and peers into the window. I'm caught; he knows it and I know it. His cocky smile is confirmation.

Deciding to act like I didn't just get busted, I open the door and stand with him on the side of the road. The next thing I know, there is a huge gust of wind and I'm up against the side of my car with Blaise's masterful body molded against mine. I feel his arms around me. He gently lifts my chin with his free hand. "You okay?" he asks, concerned. "That guy was driving way too fast," he says as he studies my reaction.

Ah, that explains the blast of wind. Thoughts of my parents' accident flash in my mind. I feel my body become rigid and my hands are starting to shake. Will I ever be able to get past this? Will I ever be able to hear about a car accident or potential accident in this case, and not turn into a basket case? I miss them so much, and the visions of how I lost them float through my mind. I still have nightmares; I'm just better at hiding them from Leah and Brent.

Blaise assumes it's our current predicament that has me shaking. In a way, it is, but it was really just a trigger of the painful memory of the loss of my family. He pulls me tight against him. One hand placed on the small of my back, the other holding the back of my head against his chest. "I got you," he whispers softly.

I allow myself to relax against him and focus on slow even breaths. Once I get my emotions under control, I pull away. Blaise again gently lifts my chin; his silver eyes capture me. "You good?" he asks.

I shake my head yes, which causes him to lose his hold on my chin. He grabs my trembling hand and leads me to the rear of the car, out of the danger of oncoming traffic. Gah! He probably thinks I'm crazy.

CHAPTER 10

BLAISE

I've been in enough intense situations to recognize fear when I see it. Tatum was scared. Pulling her into my arms and pushing her against the car out of harm's way was instinct. Once she was there, molded against me, let's just say other instincts were forefront in my mind.

I grab her hand and lead her to the back of her car. This is my attempt to make her feel safe. I can still feel the tremble in her hands. At first, I thought she was just startled, but now, I know it's more than that. I kinda feel like an asshole. When her tight little body was pressed against mine, I…let's just say there were inappropriate thoughts.

Lots of them.

Now that she is safely behind the car, I gently lift her chin so I can really look at her. Her green eyes stare back at me. "You good, sweetheart?" I ask her.

She nods her head yes.

"All right, well, Mom called and said you were having car trouble, so here I am," I say, holding my arms out.

"Thank you," she says it so softly that I almost missed it. "I'm sorry to bother you. I told her I could call a tow truck," she says, her voice stronger.

I wave my hand in the air. "It's no problem at all. I'm happy to help," I say as I study her. Her big green eyes seem…sad. That look makes me want to wrap her in my arms and make it better. *What the hell is wrong with me?*

I'm not sure what's got me thinking like a chick, but I feel like distance is the answer. I walk along the right side of the car, the one opposite the road. I open the passenger door, reach over the console and pop the hood. I make my way to the front of the car and lift the hood. I don't see anything amiss from a quick glance. I'm leaning over the engine when I hear her soft voice.

"I started losing power: lights, radio, things like that. I think it might be my alternator," she says.

I slowly stand, trying to hide the affect her soft voice has on me. Shit! What is it about this girl? "You know cars?" I ask her.

She shrugs. "This happened a few years ago and my dad had to replace the alternator. I just assumed it was the same thing. Your mom also said it sounded like the alternator," she shrugs.

I nod my head in agreement. "You're probably right." I step back and close the hood of her car. "I'll call Larry's and have him tow it to my house. I can have a new alternator on in an hour tops. While I do that, why don't you call your dad and see where he bought the last one. There may be a warranty, and if it's a store we have here in Tennessee, we can have it transferred," I tell her as I remove my cell from my pocket and call Larry.

Larry answers on the first ring and says he is on his way. I turn to relay the information, and what I see has my feet moving double time to get to her. Tatum is standing at the back of her car. Both of her hands are placed on the trunk, holding her up. Her face is white as a ghost and tears are streaming down her cheeks. *What the fuck?*

I'm at her side in an instant. I hesitate at what my next step should be. I don't know what has her so freaked out, and I don't want to make it worse. Before I realize it, my hand is on the small of her back. I'm not so sure touching her is a good idea for me, or for her, but my hand apparently has a mind of its own.

"Tatum?" I say softly.

She jumps and her legs wobble. I use the hand on the small of her back to pull her against me. "What happened, sweetheart?" I softly whisper in her ear.

She's shaking again.

I gently rub her back as I hold her tight. I want her to know she's safe. I don't think it's me she's afraid of from the way she's holding onto my shirt. I briefly take a few seconds to relish the feel of her in my arms. She's beautiful and she fits perfectly. I instantly feel like a prick…again. She is obviously upset and here I am thinking inappropriate thoughts about her…us.

I stand there and hold her, giving her time to get her emotions under control. I realize I'm going to be the talk of the town. I'm not exactly known for being affectionate, at least not in public, and yet here I stand, holding a beautiful woman in my arms on the side of the road. I see Larry in the tow truck heading our way.

"Tatum, the tow truck's here," I say gently. She slowly lifts her head and looks at me.

"I'm so sorry," she says, her face flushing with embarrassment.

I place my hands on her waist and gently squeeze. "Nothing to be sorry for. Are you all right?" I ask.

She exhales. "Yeah."

I don't want to upset her, so I nod my head and step away as I see Larry climbing out of his truck. I introduce him to Tatum and tell him to tow her car to my house. Once the car is loaded, I usher Tatum to the passenger side of my truck and open the door for her. She is so tiny she has to climb in using the running boards. My hand's itching to touch her. I place both hands on her hips and give her a boost. She sucks in a breath at my touch. I smile at her and wink. Glad to know she's just as affected by me as I am by her.

I make my way to the driver's side of my truck and settle in behind the wheel. "I don't want to push you." Yes, I do. I really really do, but more than that, I want her to feel safe with me, so I won't do it. "But are you okay? I won't push for you to tell me what happened back there, but you're safe with me," I tell her. My eyes bore into hers, willing her to understand I'm being serious.

Her eyes go wide at my admission and then they focus on my hands, which are currently gripping the wheel so tight they're white. I will myself to release my grip. This girl has me tied up in knots. I hate that she was frightened. What happened to her?

"I know that," she says softly. "Thank you for coming to get me, and calling Larry to tow my car. I'll find a garage and get it out of your hair."

"No need, sweetheart. I'll have it fixed in no time. I don't have to be at the shop until five, so I have all day."

She fidgets in her seat. I don't say anything more. I start the truck and wait for Larry to pull out so I can follow him to my place.

I turn on the street that leads to my house. "Where are we going?" Tatum questions. "The office is the other direction."

I nod. "Yes, but Mom said you are to take the day off. She said the office is slow, and she checked your calendar, you don't have any appointments," I tell her.

"I can't miss work. I've only been there a couple of weeks. I can't lose this job," she says, her voice getting louder.

I reach over and grab her hand, which is resting on her leg, and give it a gentle squeeze. She doesn't pull way.

"Relax. Harry is great to work for. He understands. It's not a big deal. Let's get your car fixed," I say in a soothing tone.

"But—" My ringing cell phone cuts her off. I retrieve it from the cup holder. "Hey, Mom," I say in greeting.

"Yes, I called Larry and he's taking it to my place. I think she's right, it's the alternator. She said her dad replaced it a few years ago, so that could be the issue again. Sometimes you get refurbished parts and they don't last as long. Yes, I told her and we were just discussing it. I know. All right hold on." I hand the phone to Tatum. "She wants to talk to you," I tell her.

"Hello," she says, and I can hear my mom talking. Tatum can't get a word in edgewise and I smile. I love my mother.

"Yes, but—" She stops to listen. "Okay, thank you. I'm so sorry," she tells my mom.

I can hear Mom chastising her for apologizing. I hear Tatum say goodbye. She hands me the phone. "She wants to talk to you."

Mom tells me to take care of Tatum. She says she's had a rough couple of months, and her friend Leah and her fiancé Brent are all she has. I want to drill her for more information, but I won't. At least not in front of Tatum.

KAYLEE RYAN

I glance at her out of the corner of my eye. I can still see the sadness in her expression. I have the urge to make it better, to make her smile. Her hands are clutching her purse like it's her lifeline as she chews on her bottom lip. I can't help but wish it was me biting that lip.

I say goodbye to Mom as I pull into my driveway. I hop out and rush around to the passenger side to help Tatum. Again, feeling like I need to touch her, I grab her hips and lift her from the truck. I let her body slide down mine slowly. I'm torturing myself, but fuck is it worth it. I see her face turn pink in embarrassment. Fuck, this girl is beautiful.

Once she is steady on her feet, I release her. "I'm going to help Larry unhook; then we can go get the part we need," I tell her. "Why don't you take a seat on the swing and wait for me." I motion to the swing on the front porch.

She nods her head in acceptance and walks off toward the front porch. I watch her walk away of course. I hear the grinding sound of the tow truck wench and snap back to reality. I help Larry unload the car and pull my wallet out of my back pocket. Of course, he refuses to let me pay, telling me my service on the department is payment enough. *I love this town.*

I wave to Larry as he pulls out of the drive. I walk toward the front porch where Tatum is sitting. As soon as I see her, I stop dead in my tracks. Tatum is sitting on the porch swing, legs propped up, with her Kindle in her hand. The gentle breeze is blowing her hair. I have to adjust myself. My reaction to her is surprising. It's been a long time since a woman has held my interest like this. I'm not sure it's ever been like this.

I continue my approach. Tatum hears my footsteps and looks up from her Kindle. She would get along great with Ember and Grace. Those two are glued to their Kindles. Tatum sits up and swings her legs around. I assume it's so I can sit next to her, and there is no way in hell I'm going to pass up the opportunity to be close to this girl. Nope.

I sit down on the swing and give us a gentle push with my feet. Tatum closes her Kindle case and smiles at me. *Wow!*

"My parents…" She clears her throat. I have no idea what she's trying to tell me, but from Mom's earlier speech and what I have

59

witnessed from her today, I know it's big. I reach over and lace our fingers together while controlling the motion of the swing with my feet planted on the porch.

"My parents passed away a few months ago," she whispers.

I tighten my grip on her hand. I can hear the heartbreak in her voice. *Fuck!* I told her she needed to call her dad. I'm the one who caused her to freak out earlier.

"I'm sorry for your loss," I say, my voice low. I know my words are just that to her, words. I'm sure she's heard them a million times since the loss of her parents. She doesn't know me well enough to know that I am. I'm truly sorry for her pain, her loss. I feel a tightness in my chest.

"Thank you. I'm sorry I freaked out on you. They were killed in an auto accident and well…" she trails off.

I pull one leg up on the swing as I turn to face her. I keep one hand laced with hers, while I wipe her tears with the other. "Never be sorry for that. Not to me. I can't even begin to imagine what you've been through. I'm sorry I caused you pain," I say. The tightness in my chest intensifies at the thought of hurting her. What is going on with me?

Tatum's beautiful green eyes hold mine captive. "Thank you, but it wasn't you. I still have triggers." She smiles softly. "That's what Brent calls them."

I tuck her hair behind her ear. The thick locks feel like silk. "I'm a good listener if you ever need to talk," I tell her.

She nods. No words are needed.

I lift her hand to my lips and place a gentle kiss on her knuckles. "Okay, well how about we run to the parts store and get that alternator. We can stop and grab an early lunch while we're out. Then we can come back here and I'll have you fixed up in no time," I say, trying to distract her.

I stand up and feel her grab my wrist. I look down at her.

"Thank you, Blaise," she says softly.

I smile and pull her to her feet, and lead her to my truck.

CHAPTER 11

The last month has flown by. My job is great. Nancy, who has taken it upon herself to mother me, has been showing me the ropes. She and I have become close in such a short time. She found out I was looking for an apartment and suggested her daughter Ember was looking for a roommate. She insisted I come to their family's Fourth of July barbeque to meet her daughter. I was reluctant at first, but she even invited Leah and Brent. Her sister Ruth is Brent's office manager.

"We are all one big happy family," she told me. "Besides, you and Ember will hit it off and I worry about her living alone."

The guilt trip did it and is why Leah, Brent, and I are currently loaded in Brent's SUV headed toward Nancy and Steve Richards' house.

Leah turns around in her seat to face me. "Tate, we like having you with us. You don't need to move," she pouts.

I smile at her. "I know that, Leah. I need to do this. I need to start moving forward. I appreciate you guys for bringing me with you and being there to support me, but I need to let you live your lives so I can start living mine again," I tell her.

My words sound way more brave than what I really am. The thought of being on my own scares me, even living with a roommate. My world is about to once again shift, but it needs to. I need to let Leah and Brent start their life as true newlyweds would. Living alone. I need to start mine as well, moving forward.

One day at a time.

"Nancy is great. If Ember is anything like her mother, we'll be fast friends. I'll be fine, promise," I reassure her.

Brent and Leah share a look before she turns back to face me again. "You are a part of our family, Tate. You will always be welcome and have a place with us. Never forget that," she tells me.

Tears prick my eyes. My best friend, my savior. "I love you for that, both of you. I need to do this."

Leah nods her head, letting me know she understands. She may not be happy about it, but she gets it. The rest of the ride is filled with chatter of our work weeks. Leah started working part-time as a school nurse, just filling in here and there. She and Brent want kids right away, so working for the school system is the perfect job for her.

Brent pulls into a packed driveway. Nancy lives on the outskirts of town, but still within the city limits. This is a requirement for her husband, Steve, since he is the fire chief. Their twin boys, Asher and Blaise, also work for the department. Nancy says they are volunteers. The department is a big part of their life. You can tell just by the way Nancy speaks of her husband and kids she's very proud. Hell, their names, Ember, Asher, and Blaise, alone speak volumes to the family's dedication to the department.

Climbing out of the SUV, I grab the cake I made this afternoon. I found the recipe on Pinterest. I used strawberries and blueberries to make it patriotic. Leah grabs the cookies she made and Brent grabs the cooler with our drinks. We head toward the big white tent in the side yard. We don't make it ten feet before I hear my name being called.

"Tatum!"

I turn my head to follow the voice, and I see Nancy headed toward me. She takes the cookies from Leah and tells her and Brent the drinks are at the other end. "Follow me," she says, and I oblige.

"Tatum, I'm so glad you and your friends made it. I can't wait for you to meet Ember," she says excitedly.

We make a stop at the dessert table and drop off the cake and cookies. Nancy slips her arm through mine and leads me to a picnic table filled with people. I notice Blaise immediately, tracking me with his silver eyes.

"Everyone, this is Tatum. Tatum is the PR/Marketing person Harry hired last month. Tatum, this is my family. That handsome devil there is my husband Steven. Beside him is my son Blaise, who you've already met." I offer Steve and Blaise a small smile and a wave, working hard not to let my eyes roam over Blaise and get lost in his mesmerizing eyes. "This is Asher and his girlfriend Grace, and this is Ember."

I wave and smile at each of them. I can feel Blaise watching me, but I don't dare look at him. He is too sexy for his own good. I do not need to embarrass myself in front of these people.

Ember stands up and offers me her hand. "It's nice to meet you. Mom says you might be looking for a roommate?" she asks casually.

I nod in agreement. "Yes. I moved here with my best friend and her fiancé from Ohio. They are planning their wedding, and I want them to be able to enjoy their home as newlyweds," I explain.

"We told her it's not necessary, but she's stubborn," I hear Leah say behind me. I turn and smile at her before turning back to the group.

"Speak of the devil. This is my best friend, Leah, and her fiancé, Brent." I step to the side so Leah and Brent have a clear view of the group. "This is Nancy, and her husband, Steve, and their children."

Leah and Brent exchange pleasantries. "Thanks for inviting us," Brent says.

Nancy waves her hand in the air to say it's no big deal. "Ruth and Tom are here somewhere. Make yourselves at home."

"So, Tatum why don't we go chat about this roommate business," Ember says to me.

"Absolutely," I say. I turn to Leah and Brent. "I'll catch up with you guys." Leah waves us on with a smile.

"We're going to grab some food. Did you see the spread?" Leah asks, already pulling Brent in the direction of the grill.

Ember leads me to a bench that has been strategically placed under a shade tree.

"So, the apartment is a three bedroom. It's bigger than what I need, but the lease was a great deal. Besides you can never have too much space, right?" she asks.

"Think of the closet the third bedroom would make," I say, mostly kidding. Ember's eyes light up.

"Why didn't I think of that?" she laughs. "Anyway, I propose we just split everything fifty fifty: rent, utilities, etc. We can take turns on groceries, unless you're particular about that sort of thing.

"No, not really. I've only ever lived at home; well, until I moved here with Leah and Brent." The words slip so easily from my tongue. Ember and Nancy are so kind; it's easy to share a part of myself and my past with them. I know eventually I'll have to talk about my parents, but I don't want today to be about that.

"I can see the pain in your eyes. I won't badger you with questions, but when you need a friend, I'm here. No questions, just support."

I work hard to swallow back the emotions begging to break free. "Thank you, that means a lot to me."

Ember places her hand on my arm and gives it a gentle squeeze. "So what do you think roomies?" she asks.

I can feel a grin taking over my face. "Roomies." I hold out my hand and we shake on it. I don't need to see the place. Nancy and her family are good people. I'm sure it's great.

"Great, you can move in as early as tomorrow. I can have my brother's help move your things."

"Oh, that won't be—"

She waves her hand in the air cutting me off. "Really, they won't mind. Besides, if I don't ask them to, Mamma and Daddy will. That's the way we do it here in Tennessee." She winks at me.

We both break out in laughter. It feels good to make a new friend, and try to begin picking up the pieces of what my life has become. It's time to mend them back together.

CHAPTER 12

BLAISE

I'm sitting at the picnic table with my family. It's Mom and Dad's annual Fourth of July get-together. I'm keeping a close eye on Asher, wondering if tonight will be the night he pops the big question. He met with Grace's dad earlier this week. Dad and I are discussing a field fire we had last night when I hear my mom greet a newcomer. I lift my eyes, and it's her. Tatum. The girl who has been in my head since the day I met her. I have no idea why, but something about her…she intrigues me. I will myself to look away, but I can't. If I'm being honest, I don't want to. I haven't seen her since the day I fixed her car; well, not in person. She's been haunting my dreams.

Tatum is sexy as hell. Those green eyes of hers are shining bright today. The image of her eyes filled with tears flashes in my mind. I feel that same tightening in my chest at the thought of her in pain. Her sweet voice rings out as she says hello and introduces her friends. I briefly take my eyes off her to glance at them. I spot an engagement ring on the girl's finger and the guy has his hands on her waist. I feel a rush of air leave my lungs. The thought of her being here with someone doesn't sit well. She told me about her best friend and her fiancé, but I still needed proof. I have Beth to thank for that.

I continue to watch her, uncaring really if anyone realizes it or not. Her long, dark brown locks are pulled up into a twist. Her tanned legs are encased in a pair of short denim shorts. Her green tank is the same color as her eyes. I love her eyes. She looks to be about five foot five or so. Almost a full foot shorter than me. She's beautiful. I allow myself another long glance from head to toe. Yes, even her bright red toenails are sexy. My minds flashes back to me holding her on the side of the road. Yes, I was trying to comfort her, but damn she felt nice up against me.

I watch as she walks off with her friends and my sister. I vaguely remember Mom mentioning she might have found the perfect roommate for Ember. By the looks of it, she was referring to Tatum. A smile graces my lips. I'll have to make sure I drop in to visit my little sister a little more often.

"Dude!" I hear Asher say. I blink to clear my head.

"What?" I ask him.

Asher reaches over and hands me a napkin. "I think you need to wipe the drool, brother," he chides.

I scowl at him. "Shut it," I say in reply.

I hear my dad's deep belly laugh. "Son, you couldn't have been more obvious. I don't think I've ever seen you that enamored with a young lady before," he says as he places a hand on my shoulder.

I shrug my shoulders. "Are you two blind? Did you see her? Of course I'm going to stare; she's gorgeous." I have nothing to hide.

"Yeah, you and the rest of the single guys here," Asher says, pointing to where Ember and Tatum are now standing near the edge of the tent. "Hell, even the ones who aren't single can't seem to tear their eyes away from her," he laughs.

"Asher," Grace admonishes him.

He kisses her cheek. "Everyone but Dad and I, of course," he says with a wink.

Grace just chuckles and rolls her eyes. "Leave him alone. Tatum seems like a really sweet girl. She's just what Blaise needs in his life," Grace says.

They continue to talk, but I tune them out. My attention is all hers. She's standing at the edge of the tent talking to Jackson Johnson and Cade Chapman. She and Ember both seem to be enjoying the company.

"Hey, you guys up for some touch football," my cousin John asks.

I'm up and walking toward the girls as I throw an answer over my shoulder. "I'll round up the troops," I say. I walk with purpose to where Ember and Tatum are standing.

"Hey," Jackson says, reaching out to shake my hand. He's the one who has been flirting nonstop with Ember. Jackson and I graduated together, and have been friends for years. He's a good guy; I won't stand in his way...but if he hurts her, he will have both Asher and me to answer to. I give him the look; he nods his head. Glad to see we're on the same page.

"Glad you could make it," I tell him. I turn to face Cade and stretch out my hand to shake his.

Cade smiles and shakes my hand. "Long time, no see, my man," he says.

"Yeah. How you been, man?" I ask him.

"Good. I just moved back. Dad finally convinced me to come home and practice with him."

"Good for you," I say. I try not to snarl my words, but he's standing really close to Tatum, and well, I don't fucking like it.

Cade then turns to Tatum. "I'm an attorney. I've been practicing in Chicago since I passed my boards. I missed home and Dad has been pestering me for years to come back home. So here I am." He smiles coyly at her.

"So, we're getting a game of touch football together and you know the rules. Male to female ratio and all," I say to Ember. Of course, there is no need to remind her of the rule. It exists because of her. She used to whine when Asher and I refused to let her play with our friends. So Dad created the equal male to female ration on special occasions for when we play. Fourth of July is such an occasion.

Right now, in this moment, I am so glad I have a baby sister who caused that rule to be in place. It means she will most likely convince Tatum to join the fun; this leads to me spending more time with her. I need to get this attraction worked out of my system. Sure, she's gorgeous and her eyes captivate me, but shit, I'm acting like the fifteen-year-old version of myself with this girl.

"EEEK!" Ember reaches out and grabs Tatum's arm. Tatum's eyes go wide at Ember's excitement then she smiles and her face lights up. If I thought she was gorgeous before; now well, I can't even find the words to describe her.

"Tatum, you have to play. It's so much fun." Ember then proceeds to tell her about how Asher and I used to refuse to let her play so she whined to Dad and he made the male to female rule on special occasions.

Tatum bites her bottom lip. My eyes watch in fascination and, well, jealously. "I've never played," she says shyly.

My lust-filled brain is slow on the uptake. Once her words register in my brain, I open my mouth to tell her I can teach her anything she needs to know. *Anything*. But Cade beats me to it.

Cade places his arm around Tatum's shoulders. "I would be happy to show you the ropes." He winks.

Not wanting to try to decipher why I feel rage over Cade touching a girl I have only spent a minimal amount of time with, I interrupt him. "Well, let's get moving," I say snidely. I turn and walk to the other side of the yard where John and the others are assembling to pick teams.

I don't bother to look behind me and see if they're going to follow. I know my little sister, and no way will she pass up this opportunity.

I reach the side yard and John tells me he and I are going to be team captains. I smile because I want Tatum on my team. I contemplate telling John to pick Cade and Tatum is mine, but I stop myself. My mind races with the thought of her being mine. I quickly shake my head and observe my family and friends who have created a huddle to join the fun.

John goes first and chooses Asher. Good choice. I choose Jackson first. I wanted to scream "Tatum," but I've been obvious enough for one day. John then picks Tatum. *Fuck me!* I scowl at him, and he looks at me like I've lost my fucking mind. Well guess what, I have. Tatum is now controlling my thoughts. I need to shake this girl. I choose Ember as my next pick; she's just as good as most of the guys. Asher and I taught her well. To my dismay, Cade and Tatum do end up on the same team.

I stalk off to the center of the field while each side lines up. We have already done the coin toss, and John's team gets the ball first. I'm standing on the imaginary line when I feel a hand on my arm. I look down to see its Ember. She's smiling at me like I just gave her a million dollars. She motions with her finger for me to come closer. I bend down and she whispers in my ear. "Just think, you get to tackle her," she says with a laugh. Instantly my mood is a little brighter.

"This is touch," I tell her.

Ember shrugs her shoulders. "Who says you can't accidentally fall into her. Accidents happen," she quips.

Did I mention I adore my little sister?

Mom, who is on the sidelines, blows the whistle to start the game. She has been our referee since we were little. Some things never change.

On the line, I am directly in front of Tatum. Yeah, I did work to make that happen. I stand with a scowl on my face as I watch Cade with his arm around her explaining the basics.

John snaps the ball and I put my arms out to keep Tatum from getting by. She smiles shyly and places her hands on my chest to push me out of the way. I don't move. She looks up and our eyes lock. I hear Mom blow the whistle. Tatum backs away and takes her spot on the line. The whistle blows and she's in front of me again. John hikes the ball. Tatum sprints forward and tries to duck under my arm. I reach out and grab her around the waist and swing her body against mine. Her back is pressed against my front and my senses are assaulted with her sweet scent. I can feel her chest rise and fall. The whistle blows and I don't want to let her go, but I know I have to. I'm starting to have a little issue in the land down under and I'm glad I have on loose fitting cargo shorts. I shift my stance, trying to make myself more comfortable.

The game goes on for another hour, until we are all too hot and too tired to continue. I think I'm really the only one that's jazzed. This has everything to do with Tatum. I continued to find ways to touch her, and hold her, longer than was legal or necessary for the game. I'm standing at the cooler under a shade tree when Asher joins me.

"What's with you, bro?" he asks.

I continue to chug my bottle of water, my eyes finding his over the bottle. "What?"

"I've never seen you this way. All flirty, and did I hear you growl during the game?" he asks, amused.

"Don't," I say, my words clipped.

Asher laughs and walks back to the tent to find Grace. She opted out of the game and instead played rummy with our grandma. Asher is one lucky SOB.

CHAPTER 13

"Holy Shit!" Ember says as we sit in the grass chugging bottles of water.

"What?" I ask her.

"What do you mean what? My brother, that's what," she says, smirking.

"Which one?" I ask, playing dumb. I know she can see right through me. Ember is like Leah and I in so many ways. The more time I'm around her, the more excited I get about living with her.

"Pretend all you want, roomie, but I know you know what I'm talking about," she laughs.

Instead of responding, I twist the lid off my water and sip slowly. I feel her watching me. Ember clears her throat and taps her finger on her leg, waiting impatiently for me to admit there was something going on out on the field between Blaise and me. I can't admit it. I have no fucking clue what was happening out there. My mind is still trying to piece together the puzzle.

Ember releases a sigh, like I'm inconveniencing her by not telling her what's going on between us, but there is no us. I'm just as clueless as she is.

"Really," I tell her. "I have no idea."

"Well I do. My brother wants you. He had his hands all over you," she laughs. "I have to hand it to him; he gives a whole new meaning to the phrase 'touch football'."

I can't help but join in her laughter. Part of it is because I'm at a loss for words, and the other part is the thought of an Adonis like Blaise wanting me is rather hilarious.

"I'm going to run to the restroom. You need anything?" Ember asks.

"Actually, I think I'll go with you. I need to wash my hands," I say, showing her my dirt covered digits.

Ember leads me into the house and up the stairs. "I'll use the one in my bedroom; you can use the one down the hall. Second door on the right."

"Thanks," I say as I continue down the hall. I stop in front of the second door on the right. I reach for the handle, but the door swings open, causing me to lose my balance. I'm mentally prepared for the fall, but strong arms wrap around me.

"You okay, sweets?" a deep timbre asks me.

I look up and find silver eyes watching me. Blaise. He has one arm around me, his hand resting on my back and the other hand resting on my hip, holding me tight against him.

Oh. My.

"Yes, sorry. I wasn't expecting you," I tell him. Fighting to keep my voice from revealing that he is leaving me breathless being this close to him, his hands on me.

Blaise studies me for what seems like a lifetime; in reality, it's only mere seconds. He bends down and places his lips next to my ear. "I wasn't expecting you either," he whispers.

I can feel the blush cross my cheeks. Blaise notices because his smile gets bigger.

"I'm sorry," I say, and place my hands on his chest to push him away. His chest is tight and ripped. This does nothing to tone down the blush, which I'm now sure covers my entire upper body.

Blaise chuckles, moves his other hand to my hip, and turns me so I'm now in the bathroom and he's standing in the hallway. "Great game," he says with a wink before he releases me, turns and walks away.

I quickly shut the door and lock it. I brace my hands against the sink and bow my head. My heart is racing. I turn on the faucet and wash my hands. I then turn the water to cold and splash my face. I need to get myself together. Blaise, as tempting as he is, is not what I need right now. I need to focus on my job and my new home. With Ember, Blaise's sister. I briefly re-think my decision to move in with her, but quickly squash it. I need to learn to resist temptation. Josh has put me off men for a while, even sexy walking sin like Blaise.

Walking out of the bathroom, I see Ember standing in the hall waiting for me. "Did I hear you scream?" she asks me.

Shit. I must have screamed when Blaise opened the door. I was too entranced to even notice.

"Um, yeah. When I went to open the bathroom door, it opened on its own," I tell her. I'm purposely being evasive, although Ember is too much like Leah and me. I know she's going to pry it out of me.

"And? I grew up in this house, so I know it's not haunted. Who was it?" she questions.

"Blaise," I say as casually as I possibly can.

Her only reply is to laugh.

I follow her back down the stairs and outside. Grace and Asher, along with Leah, Brent and Jackson, are all sitting on the deck. We join them. Grace suggests we play battle of the sexes, but we need one more player. Before anyone else can make a suggestion, Asher has his phone to his ear.

"Bro, meet us on the back deck; we need another for battle of the sexes," he says into the phone. I can only assume from the "bro" comment that he's talking to Blaise. "Me, Gracie, Ember, Jackson, Leah, Brent and Tatum." He pauses. "Cool," he says and hangs up.

"Blaise is in," he tells us.

Ember jumps up from her chair. "I'll go get the game. Ladies on one side, guys on the other," she says over her shoulder.

CHAPTER 14

BLAISE

Asher called to tell me they needed another player for battle of the sexes. I was about to bow out until he listed the other players.

Tatum.

As soon as I heard she was involved, I stopped and headed back toward the house. My long legs make my trip short and sweet. I climb the stairs to the deck and plop down beside Asher. Ember comes out and starts setting up the game. Behind her is Tatum. She's carrying drinks. She hands everyone a beer. I watch her as her eyes fall on the only empty seat around the table. The guys have assembled on one side and the girls on the other. The table is made to seat four comfortably so we are all sitting close. The only remaining chair is the one right next to me. I can't contain the broad smile taking over my face. This is turning out even better than I could have imagined.

"Let's go, girl, time's a wasting," Ember scolds Tatum.

I watch as her shoulders drop in defeat and she rounds the table, taking the seat next to me. My southern hospitality gets the best of me and I reach over and pull the chair back for her. She offers me a shy smile and a soft "thank you."

I nod my head; no words are needed at this point. Tatum takes the seat and I slide her in. Her sweet smell wraps around me and I take a deep breath. That smell, it's like vanilla and sweet honey all wrapped into one. Sweet.

The game starts, and we're all laughing and having a great time. Well, I am for sure. Tatum and I are sitting so close we are constantly bumping our legs into one another and touching arms while reaching for the same thing. We've all taken turns going and getting another round of beer, and by this point, the ladies are all starting to feel the effects of the alcohol. I have a slight buzz, but it would take several more for me to reach their state of drunkenness.

Tatum, when's she's relaxed, is a hell of a lot of fun. Her green eyes sparkle, and it's taking great effort on my part not to just make her the center of my attention.

"Okay, time for a bathroom break," Ember says, jumping up. Leah, Tatum, and Grace stand to follow her. Jackson, Brent, Asher, and I stay behind. It takes them longer than it does us. Besides, we can walk to the side of the house if we need to.

Asher leans back in his chair and takes a long swig of his beer. "She's nice, bro," he says to me. It still unnerves me sometimes how well my twin brother and I can read each other's thoughts. I shrug my shoulders, not committing to anything.

Brent clears his throat and I look up to meet his steady gaze. "Tate is amazing." He takes a drink of his beer. "She's been through so much in just the last few months," he tells us.

The image of Tatum in my arms on the side of the road comes front and center in my mind. I want to ask him for details. I know she lost her parents in an accident, but I can't help but think the accident is not all the haunts her. What else? I'm not sure. What makes those beautiful green orbs fill with such sadness? Who? Who hurt her? My gut clenches at the thought of someone hurting her in any way. Before I can form the questions running rampant through my buzzed brain, the girls stumble out the patio door. All four of them carrying two beers. Ember hands her extra to Jackson so I can only assume Tatum's second beer is for me. My pulse begins to race just thinking of her being my girl. The thought of she and I being here as a couple. *What the fuck?*

What is she doing to me? I haven't had thoughts like this since… well, since Beth and I parted ways. No one has ever piqued my interest enough for me to imagine more. I shake my head and scoot back my chair. I head into the house to use the bathroom. I hear the guys file in behind me. I need a minute to clear my head. I don't even know this girl, not really. Maybe I should slow down on the alcohol. I'm obviously more buzzed than I originally thought.

Once we are all back in our seats, Mom comes walking up on the deck. "It's starting to get dark. The fireworks will be starting soon," she says, clapping her hands with glee. We all smile and laugh. She is just like a kid when it comes to fireworks. She's always loved them. When we were little, she used to say there is nothing more romantic than watching fireworks with that special someone.

As that thought enters my mind, I turn my head to look at Tatum. She's laughing at something Leah and Ember are saying. Leah motions her eyes toward me. It's obvious she is trying to be discreet, but details are my life. On the department, even the smallest missed detail could be my life or the life of one of my fellow fire fighters. At the shop, details are key to what we do. Who wants something permanent on their skin that was just slopped on? No, details are key. Tatum turns her head and she catches me staring. I'm good with it. I smile at her, and I can barely tell from the glow of the tiki torches and candles, but I can see a slight blush cross her face.

I remember that blush.

She quickly looks away.

Asher stands up. "Let's get this cleaned up before the show starts," he tells us.

We all stand and start cleaning up our empty bottles while Tatum and Ember put the game away.

Ember grabs Jackson's hand and tugs him toward the steps. "Let's go watch by the dock."

Without a word, the rest of us follow them. My parents have a decent sized pond with a dock. As kids, we would always lay on the dock and watch the fireworks. We live right on the edge of town. Our property just so happens to run against the town's land. The exact spot the fireworks are lit every year. This is how the Richards' annual Fourth of July celebration began. We have a front row seat to the action right in our backyard.

Once we reach the dock, we all take a seat. I notice Ember is sitting close to Jackson, his arm wrapped around her. Leah and Brent as well as Asher and Grace are also cuddled close. Makes this moment a little awkward for Tatum and me. I'm not really sure it is for her, but for me, my arms ache to hold her.

CHAPTER 15

When Ember suggested we watch the fireworks from the dock, it sounded like a great idea. Little did I know everyone would be paired up. I mean, I should have guessed with the way Ember and Jackson have been acting all night, but really, that thought never crossed my mind; that is, until we got here.

I sit on the edge of the dock in the shadows, hoping to go unnoticed to all the lovebirds. I hope Blaise sits…well, somewhere else. Sitting next to him all night, sharing glances and touching him, my nerves are shot. The temptation to be held again, to feel safe in a man's arms, is tearing at me. I can still feel Blaise's arms around me. Until I think about Josh and what he did. I needed him and he betrayed me at the worst moment of my life. It's going to take some time before I can trust again.

I feel a brush against my leg. Turning my head, I see Blaise is sitting beside me, even deeper in the shadow than I am. His leg brushes mine.

"You like fireworks?" I ask him. Lame I know, but holy shit, I lose all brain function when he's this close. This feels intimate, the two of us sitting in the shadows of the night. The others are too wrapped up in each other, literally, to pay any attention to us.

A soft smile graces his lips. "Yeah. Growing up here was great. All of our friends would gather around and we would lay out here just like this." He surveys our group and looks back at me. "Well, not exactly like this. Mostly just Asher and a few of our friends. Ember would always have a friend or two here as well. We always have the front row seats," he says.

I glance around at our group as well. "What, you never brought your girlfriend here to cuddle and watch the show?" I question.

Blaise chuckles. "No, believe it or not. I've really only had one steady girlfriend, and she never came to many family functions. She always claimed she had family functions of her own and we should each be with our families. It was either that or I was working. Back then, I was putting a lot of hours in at the department covering for a guy," he says.

We're quiet for a few minutes before he continues. "Looking back now, I guess that should have been a telltale sign that she was cheating on me," he deadpans.

"Blaise," I say his name softly. I don't really know what to say. I've been cheated on and it sucks ass. I also know nothing anyone says can make it better.

He reaches his hand over and rubs my knee. "It's fine, really. It was several years ago."

I nod my head even though I'm sure he can't see it in the darkness. I swallow the lump in my throat that's keeping me from speaking. My eyes are focused on my knee. I can't see his hand in the darkness, but I feel it. I feel the heat from his calloused fingers rubbing against my knee. I should tell him to stop, that him touching me like this will not get him anywhere...but I don't. Not just because my words are locked tight in my throat, but because I'm enjoying it more than I know I should.

I'm so focused on the sensations from Blaise's caress, when the first spark is ignited and the colorful designs take up the sky, I jump. I immediately feel a blush coming on. I expect to hear Blaise laugh at me, but he doesn't. Instead, he scoots his body closer to mine. He places one hand behind my back, resting it on my other side against the dock. He's so close, and it feels like he's holding me even though he's not. His left hand reaches over and grabs mine. "You okay, sweets?" he whispers in my ear.

Holy Shit!

I nod my head yes. I know he can feel it this time, even if he can't see it, because he's sitting so close. A shiver runs through me just from his touch.

"You cold?" he asks, scooting even closer; how that's even possible, I'm not sure.

"N—no," I manage to say. I clear my throat and attempt to get my hormones under control. "Just a cold chill, but I'm good," I whisper back.

He doesn't move away. Instead, he sits leaning into me, his hand still holding mine. I focus on taking deep, even breaths. It takes extreme effort to not give into the temptation to let him wrap me in his arms, the arms that are bulging with muscles and sexy ink. The man attached to them isn't helping either.

We sit in silence, heads slightly tilted back watching the show. I keep telling myself that I need to move. I need to shift away from him, but I can't. It feels…nice.

Blaise takes his right hand, which has been behind my back holding his weight, leans into me, and rests it on my hip, gently pulling me against his side. Switching our positions, my back is now resting on his chest. His left hand still holds mine, while his right hand remains on my hip, holding me to him. I should pull away. The alcohol flowing through my veins is preventing me from thinking clearly. It has nothing to do with the sexy man with the silver eyes, nope, not a thing.

It's taking all of my concentration to not snuggle deeper into his embrace. This isn't me. This isn't what I'm looking for right now. It's amazing and, oddly enough even though we barely know each other, it feels…safe.

I feel his warm breath against my ear as his deep timbre whispers, "Relax."

Relax! Really? How in the hell am I supposed to relax when the sexiest man I have ever laid eyes on has me in his arms. Not to mention, said sexy man is virtually a stranger to me, well, not really, but still. There will be no relaxing.

I'm not sure how long the fireworks show lasts. I looked toward the sky the entire time, but I don't remember any of it. Before I know it, the show is over. I'm brought out of my trance when Blaise again whispers in my ear, "Show's over, sweetheart."

I pull away from him and jump to my feet. I survey our group and see no one is paying any attention to us. I sigh with relief. That's all I need is for Ember to get it in her head to play matchmaker with her brother and her new roommate. Not to mention Leah and Brent. They both are constantly telling me I need to get back on the horse. They avoid talking about Josh and the day I found him cheating on me. They choose to ignore the entire day, but they do remind me daily, well Leah reminds me daily, I need to put myself back out there and Josh is a douche. She gets no arguments from me on that account.

"Dad's going to get the fire going," Ember says, stepping up beside me. She throws her arm over my shoulders, oblivious her brother just had me wrapped in his arms. "Please tell me you like S'mores," she begs.

I can't help it. I laugh at her. This girl is so carefree and fun. "Yes, I love S'mores. To not like them would be un-American," I tell her, still laughing.

Ember hugs me tighter. "This is a beautiful friendship in the making," she says before releasing me and running to catch up with Jackson.

I shake my head as I watch her go. I see the others have walked on as well. I breathe a sigh of relief. No matter how damn tempting Blaise Richards is, I will resist him. Josh was not even in the same caliber as Blaise and he hurt me. I can only imagine my shredded heart after a guy like Blaise is through with it.

Must. Resist. Temptation.

CHAPTER 16

BLAISE

Holy fucking shit! I'm not sure what has come over me, I think Tatum has some kind of secret voodoo and she has cast a spell on me. I've had a few beers, but that's no excuse. I don't cuddle, not since Beth, and even then, that just wasn't our thing. There is this connection, this pull that Tatum has. She draws me in. It's like if she is anywhere close, I need to be next to her. This is all new to me. I know I sound like the biggest pussy, but I don't know any other way to describe it.

When she sat down in the shadows on the dock, I didn't even hesitate. I sat down beside her. If that wasn't bad enough, I couldn't seem to get close enough. I moved closer. In my mind, I was sure she would pull away, and then I would have a reason to think logically about the situation. She didn't. The longer I sat next to her, breathing her in sweet scent, holding her hand, the more I wanted.

I was supposed to be watching the fireworks display. Instead, I was thinking of how it would feel to really hold her in my arms. The next thing I know, I'm tugging her close and pulling her back against my chest. She's cast a spell.

The show's over, so I slowly stand and follow the group to the fire. I hear Ember asking Tatum if she likes S'mores and my heart skips a beat at her laughter. I'm walking behind Asher and Grace, and watch as she snuggles next to him as they walk. I've never been jealous of my twin, but right now, I am.

I roll my neck and my shoulders, trying to shake off some of the tension I feel. The universe is playing tricks on me. I need another beer.

Everyone is paired up, but Tatum and me. This makes it harder for me to focus. There are a lot of single guys here, Cade being one of them. Any minute now, one of them could waltz up to her and latch on. That thought alone doesn't sit well with me. Needing a distraction, I help Dad with the fire.

"Thanks, son," he says to me as I throw another log on the fire. "What did you think of the show this year?" he asks.

I clear my throat. I didn't see much of it; I was distracted. "Good," I reply.

Dad watches me. "You all right, son?"

I sigh. Should I bother telling him Tatum has me in knots? Dad has always been good at listening and helping us through any issues. "Well, I didn't really watch much of the show." I decide to go with honesty. Obviously, he can see right through me.

"I see. Are you going to elaborate on that statement?" he asks.

"Tatum."

He smiles. "Yes, she is a very beautiful girl."

"Yes, she is. She's also cast a spell on me," I mumble.

I can tell he wants to laugh; he's trying hard to hold it in.

"I mean it. I met her at Mom's work the day of her interview and again the day her car broke down. I helped her fix it. I think about her a lot." All the time is more like it. "When girls come into the shop, I compare them to her. Now today, I got pissed off when Cade was talking to her." I take a swig of my beer. "That's not the worst of it. We all went down to the dock to watch the fireworks. Just like we have for as long as I can remember. Out of the eight of us, everyone was paired off except for Tatum and me."

Dad holds up his hand. "Wait, wasn't Ember with you?" he asks.

Shit! I hope she didn't want to keep Jackson a secret. "Yeah, she and Jackson were watching together."

Dad shakes his head and smiles. Shew! Jackson is a great guy; looks like Dad approves.

"Anyway, Tatum sat off by herself in the shadows. This is where the spell comes into play. She pulled me to her."

The grin on Dad's face gets even wider. I continue with my story, telling him how I couldn't get close enough and how I held her. Once I finish, Dad doesn't say anything. He continues to poke at the fire.

"Well?" I say. The suspense is killing me.

Dad walks over to the cooler and pulls us both out another beer. He hands me mine. We both twist off the tops and throw them into the fire. "You really want to know what I think?" he asks me.

"At this point, yes. I'm at a loss," I say, sitting down on a log.

He walks over and sits down beside me. "I had this same conversation with Asher about a year ago. I was wondering when your time would come."

I watch him, not saying a word. What the hell is he talking about?

"I met your mother the first day of school, senior year."

"I know. High school sweethearts, yada, yada, yada."

He chuckles, "You know that's when we met, but you don't know I knew then that she was it for me. We were young, but I knew there would be no one else." He takes a sip of his beer. "It's not something you plan; it's not something that you can control. It just happens."

"So, why did you tell Asher a year ago and not me?" I ask.

Dad shakes his head. "Your brother had just met Grace and was feeling a lot of what you are now, I suspect."

He's watching me, waiting for my reaction.

"Wait. You don't think?" Is he saying what I think he's saying?

Dad nods his head yes. "I do think. It's in our blood, son. When you find 'the one', you can't control it. Instead, you need to embrace it and hold on with everything you've got."

"I just…I don't even…" I stop and take a deep breath. "Beth." I say. "You didn't have this talk with me when I told you I was going to ask Beth to marry me."

"Nope," he says. "I didn't. Do you know why?"

He doesn't give me time to answer.

"She wasn't the one. When you talk about Tatum, even though you're fighting what you feel, your eyes light up. I bet your heart even races at just the thought of her, or even from just hearing her name. That didn't happen with Beth." He shrugs.

I'm stunned speechless. What do you say to that? My dad just schooled me, and even though I hate to admit it, he's right. "I never felt half of that with Beth. I cared about her, but she never—"

"Life is all about choices, Blaise. You can choose to take the next step in a situation because it's what you think is the right thing to do. You can also choose to follow your heart. Let it lead you."

Finding my voice, I ask, "Is that what you did? Followed your heart?"

"Yep and look where it led me. I have the most amazing wife who blessed me with three amazing children. I wouldn't change a single day."

"I barely know her," I try to reason.

"I'm not saying you have to marry the girl tonight. Just let your heart lead you. Spend some time with her. If the feelings remain the same—" laughter from the other side of the fire interrupts us.

We both look to see what's going on. Ember, Tatum, Leah, and Grace are all dancing around the fire with S'mores in their hands. They all look so happy and carefree. I zero in on Tatum. Her green eyes shine with laughter in the firelight. The sight of her takes my breath. I can't tear my eyes away.

It's not until I feel Dad slap my shoulder and chuckle that I do, reluctantly.

"She just took your breath away, son. Do you need any more confirmation than that?"

Wait? What? "How did you—?" I ask his retreating form. I watch him as he walks over to Mom and wraps his arms around her, kissing her cheek.

My eyes drift back to Tatum. I still think she's cast a spell on me.

CHAPTER 17

Walking into work the next day, Nancy greets me with a warm smile. That same warm smile I've grown accustom to since I started here. "Good morning, Tatum," she says brightly.

"Good morning, Nancy. Thanks again for inviting us to the party. We had a lot of fun," I tell her. "I didn't want to get out of bed this morning, but duty calls."

"I'm so glad you made it. We can be a lively bunch," she says with so much affection in her voice. "So, Ember tells me the two of you are going to be roomies."

I shake my head in agreement. "I'm moving in this weekend. Brent is off all weekend, so he and Leah are helping me."

"Oh, well I'm sure one or all three of the Richards men would be happy to help." She holds up her finger while dialing the phone with the other. A brief pause and she starts talking into her headset. "Steve, honey, can you tell me what y'all's schedule is for this weekend?" She smiles at me. "Well, Tatum is moving in with Ember and I was wondering if any of you had the weekend off to help her move."

"Nancy, I—" She thrust her finger up again, telling me to wait a minute. I can't help but smile.

"Okay, dear. Would you please? Great! I'll see you at home later. Love you," she says before hitting end on the switchboard.

"Blaise is off. He was in Steve's office and said he would be happy to help you move," she says, beaming.

"Oh, no, that's not necessary. Brent and Leah—" She holds up her finger.

"Nonsense. Brent and Blaise can do all of the heavy lifting while you girls supervise." She winks.

I don't bother to argue any further. If I've learned anything these past few weeks, if Nancy sets her mind on something, there is no talking her out of it.

Instead, I say, "Thank you. You didn't have to do that."

Nancy motions me away with her hands as she answers the next incoming call.

As I walk to my office, I can't help but be a little excited to get to spend more time with Blaise. After the fireworks were over, I didn't see much of him. He was there by the fire, but he spent most of the time talking to his dad. After that, he just sat around the fire, sipping his beer and taking it all in. I know because I watched him from afar. Several times our eyes met, and I had to dig deep to turn away from him.

Must. Resist. Temptation.

Easier said than done with those sexy silver eyes and a smile that causes butterflies deep in the pit of my stomach.

The day flies by. I'm staying busy getting up to speed and working on marketing programs for different areas of the city. I might have also been thinking about tattooed arms and silver eyes.

Shutting down my computer, I turn out the light and head toward the main lobby.

"Tatum, wait just a second. I have something for you."

Nancy walks from around her desk carrying two cardboard boxes. "I cleaned out the storage closet and thought you might be able to use these."

"Thank you, that's perfect."

My boss, the Mayor, or Harry as he insists I call him, is leaving as well. He studies Nancy and me; then looks at the boxes. "Going somewhere?" he asks, concern lacing his voice.

Surely, he doesn't think I'm leaving Tennessee already? Nancy answers before I do.

"Tatum is going to be Ember's new roommate."

I can visibly see him relax. "Well, that's great. Since tomorrow's Friday, why don't you take the day off to pack? It'll give you an extra day to get settled. This has been an off week with the holiday anyway. We'll hit the ground running on Monday.

"Oh, that's not necessary," I tell him.

"I insist. Take the day. I'll see you on Monday," he says to me. Turning to Nancy he says, "You too. You work too hard and need an extra day. I'll have Donna come in with me tomorrow and she can cover the phones."

Donna is his wife. Nancy mentioned that sometimes she covers when Nancy needs the day off. I offered for her to train me and I would be happy to cover for her as well.

"That's very thoughtful of you. Thank you," Nancy says.

"Yes, thank you. Are you sure?" I ask.

"Positive, now be gone," he laughs. "Enjoy your weekend. I'll see y'all Monday."

With that, he turns and walks out the door. I turn to Nancy. "Wow. That was nice."

She smiles. "He's great to work for. This is truly a family environment," she says, placing her hand on my shoulder. She knows there is something in my past. She knows my parents are gone, but I didn't tell her how. I can't think about that day for a multitude of reasons. My nightmares are less frequent, but still there. I don't try to decipher why I told Blaise, well not everything, but he knows about the accident. I haven't told anyone the details. That's a conversation I don't think I could live through.

CHAPTER 18

BLAISE

I'm sitting in Dad's office discussing my schedule for the next few weeks when his cell rings. I watch as he checks the screen and a smile breaks across his face. Mom.

He answers. I continue to look at the schedule and compare it to the Self Expressions client schedule in my phone.

"Can you help Tatum move into your sister's this weekend?" he asks me.

My head snaps up.

Tatum.

I've tried unsuccessfully to not think about her since the party yesterday. "Sure," I say, shrugging my shoulders. I'm trying to hide the fact that the thought of spending the day with her excites me.

Dad passes the information along to Mom. I hear him tell her he loves her too and put his phone back on the desk.

I focus my attention on the schedule. I can feel him watching me. "Have you thought any more about what we talked about last night?" he asks.

"Nothing but," I say with a sigh.

Dad nods his head in approval and resumes our conversation about the schedule.

After Dad and I get the schedule worked out, I quickly say goodbye and head to the shop. I have a full client load today.

Walking into the shop, I see there is no one at the counter. We really need to hire someone to replace Ember. I head back to my station and set up for my first client. The schedule says Misty and rose tattoo. I hear the chime over the door, and Asher's voice greets the visitor. I continue my setup.

"Hey, man, your client's here," Asher says in the doorway.

"Thanks. I'll be up in a minute."

Asher chuckles, "Good luck with this one, bro. I can already tell you're going to have your hands full. Your last client is at five, just in case you need to make plans," he says, wagging his eyebrows at me.

I don't know why, but that irritates me. Unless a five foot five beauty with locks of silky dark hair and sparkling green eyes is on my schedule, it's not going to happen.

I finish setting up my gun and walk out to the reception area to call back my client, Misty with the rose.

"Misty," I say to get her attention.

She licks her lips as she walks toward me. Great, here we go. I really don't feel like dealing with her, but what choice do I have? I'm just glad Asher is in the next room and we're not here alone.

"Have a seat." I motion to the table. "So it says here you want a rose. Do you have anything in particular in mind, and what location were you thinking?" I ask, getting right down to business.

Misty pulls a small piece of paper out of her bra and winks at me. Yeah, that's not really doing it for me. In the past when this kind of thing would happen, I would just chalk it up to another easy lay. They're all the same. Things have changed; I don't want an easy lay. I refuse to think about why that is.

I slip on my gloves before taking the paper from her hand. I can tell by the look in her eyes and the small pfft sound she makes that I've offended her. I'm not going to be losing any sleep over it.

I take the paper to my desk in the corner and begin to draw up a design. We get a lot of request for roses, so this is a quick process for me. Once I'm finished, I show Misty the design.

"I love it. It's sexy, just like you," she says with a purr.

Really? I ignore her statement and begin to cup up the ink colors I'll be using. Once I have everything ready, I turn to Misty. "All right, so where do you want it," I ask her.

Misty licks her lips and trails her hand over her crotch, up her stomach, and onto her right breast. "How about right here," she purrs.

I have to fight against rolling my eyes at her. She's not sexy; she's easy. Easy used to be enough; not anymore. Visions of Tatum last night flash through my mind. I push them down and regain my focus on Misty and her rose tattoo. The sooner I get her out of here, the better.

Unfortunately for me, Misty wants the rose placed on her left breast. This means I will have to touch her...there. Normally this would be a good thing. I've never minded touching the many women's body parts that come through the shop, but tonight, I'm just not feeling it. Thank God, it's a small piece and I can have her out of here in less than thirty minutes.

Misty pulls her tank top over her head. She reaches to unhook her bra and I stop her.

"That's not necessary for the placement," I tell her.

Again with the pfft sound. Whatever.

I place the transfer paper and hand her a mirror. She agrees with the placement and I get right to work.

"So what time do you get off tonight?" she asks me.

"Not until later. Asher and I have a family thing," I tell her. I wish she would just not talk. That wish goes unanswered.

"What about after?"

"It will be a while," I reply without looking at her.

"Hmpf. I was told you were a sure thing," she scoffs.

My temper is flaring by this point. Who the hell is this chick? "Well, you were given false information. I'm taken." The words spill out of my mouth before I even realize what I'm saying. Asher clears his throat behind me.

I lift my gun from Misty's breast and turn to look at him. "I'm going to run next door, want anything?" he asks, smirking.

Great, he heard me.

"Yeah, pick me up a sweet tea will you?" I ask him, ignoring the fact he heard me tell Misty I'm taken.

I turn back around and resume Misty's tattoo. She doesn't try to make conversation and neither do I. Asher walks in just as I give her the care instructions.

"What about you, sugar, you free tonight?" she asks in what I can only guess is a voice that is meant to be sultry. Yeah, it's not.

Asher throws his head back in laughter. "Hell, no. I'm unavailable," he tells her.

Misty smirks. "I won't tell if you won't," she tells him.

"All right, this one's on the house; time for you to go," I say, standing up so she can get off the table.

Misty stands and her mouth is gaping open. She looks like a fish. "Well, whatever!" she says as she storms out of the building.

Asher finally composes himself and plops down on the table.

"Dude, I just cleaned that," I tell him.

"Chill out," he replies. "So you're a taken man, huh?"

I give him the look. You know the 'shut the fuck up, you're on my last nerve' look. "I had to shut her up," I tell him through gritted teeth.

"Hmmm," Asher says, tapping his index finger against his chin. "Are you sure this has nothing to do with a dark haired beauty who seems to have attracted your attention?" he says slyly.

"This has nothing to do with Tatum," I grit out.

"How do you know I was talking about Tatum? There is a harem of dark haired beauties who come through these doors," he quips.

"Shut it," I tell him.

"Bro, she seems like a great girl. She's not like the harem; she's different," he says, growing serious.

"Yeah, she's my Grace," I mumble under my breath.

Asher sits up. "What did you just say?"

"Nothing."

"Come on, dude. What did you say?" he asks again.

I shake my head no and continue to clean up.

"You don't have to repeat it because I heard you. I just wanted to hear you admit it again, louder," he says.

I remain silent, still just cleaning up my area.

"Blaise," Asher says my name in a tone where I know he's being serious. "If what you said is true, if Tatum is your Grace," a huge grin crosses his face from just speaking her name, "hold on tight with everything you've got. That doesn't happen twice in a lifetime."

I take a deep breath and exhale. All this shit has got me tied up in knots. Tatum is always front and center in my mind. The shit my dad was saying last night intertwined with the feelings I've been having and now Asher, too. "Dad said some stuff last night," I say. I don't look at him as I continue to clean up. I can feel him watching me.

"Really? Was it the story of how he knew when Mom was the one?" Asher asks.

"Yep."

Asher walks over and places his hand on my shoulder. "Bro, don't fight it." And with that, he leaves me to myself.

CHAPTER 19

Rays of sunshine seeping through the blinds wake me from my slumber. I stretch my arms above my head and look over at the nightstand; it's six thirty. Today is the day I start yet another new chapter in my life. I'm moving in with Ember. Leah and I were up late last night. She was trying to convince me not to go. I know she understands why I'm going. She just doesn't agree.

I will never be able to thank her or Brent for what they have done for me. They picked me up when there were just pieces of me. They molded me back together. They are my family.

I survey the boxes in my room, and my heart starts to race. Ember called yesterday and said Blaise was going to be helping me move; of course I already knew this. She informed me the two of them would be here at eight sharp to start loading boxes. According to Ember, she was too excited to wait any longer for me to move in. She is such a sweet person and reminds me so much of Leah; I have no reservations for the move. Still, my heart is racing, but that's all because of Blaise. I haven't seen him since the party. That doesn't really matter, because I can still feel his arms around me and I could describe his silver eyes in detail.

Throwing off the covers, I make my way to the bathroom, washing my face and brushing my teeth. I pull my hair up into a messy bun and throw on gym shorts and a tank top. No point is getting all dressed up to move. Maybe this look will keep Blaise and his advances at bay. Sometimes he looks at me like he wants to devour me, and well, that's not really helping me resist him.

"Knock, knock." I hear Leah say at my door.

Tempting Tatum

"Hey, you."

"Brent's making breakfast. Biscuits and gravy, your favorite," she says with a sad smile.

I wrap my arms around her and hug her tight. "I love you, Leah," I whisper. I feel her arms wrap around me as she returns my embrace.

I slowly pull away. "Now, lead me to the goodness that is Brent's biscuits and gravy," I say with a wink.

Leah smiles and I know she understands. I grab her hand and pull her behind me to the kitchen. As we walk in, Brent snags Leah around the waist and nuzzles her neck. "It's ready, beautiful," I hear him whisper.

I try not to impose on their moment, but it's hard. This is what I miss. Intimate moments with that one person who completes you. Well, in my case, the one person you thought completed you. I know now what Josh and I had was in no way in the same league as what Leah and Brent share. He was never really intimate and sweet. On the rare occasion he was, I held onto those moments as if they were my lifeline. I always just chalked it up to him showing his emotions differently. I was consumed by him and the love I thought we shared. After he...did what he did, Leah suggested maybe I didn't love him like I thought I did. I was not as torn up about it as I should have been. Josh and I had been drifting apart, hardly spending much time together. Again, I chalked it up to school and getting ready to graduate. Now I'm not blinded by what I thought we had. As I watch Brent with Leah, I'm envious.

"Come on, guys, I'm trying to eat," I say as I fill my plate with the mouthwateringmeal that Brent has created.

They laugh as they pull apart, but not before Brent places a kiss on her cheek.

"So, I talked to Blaise. He and Ember will be here around eight," Brent says.

"What? You talked to Blaise? Since when did you two become close?" I ask.

Brent smiles at me knowingly. "Well, if you must know, we exchanged numbers at the party."

98

Great. If Blaise and Brent become friends, then that increases my chances of running into him. Of course, I'm going to be living with his sister. For a minute, I think about backing out. No, I can't let this attraction, if that's even what you call it, keep me from forging ahead. Brent and Leah need this as much as I do, and I would do anything for them.

Brent and Leah join me at the table as we scarf down breakfast. Just as we are finishing up, Brent's phone chimes; he has a message.

"It's Blaise; they are about two minutes out," he tells us.

I jump up and start cleaning up the kitchen. Today marks the beginning of another major change for me.

Leah and I have just finished with the dishes when I hear his deep voice. Composing myself, masking what his voice does to me, I follow Leah into the living room.

Blaise is talking to Brent, but as soon as I enter the room, his eyes find mine. He continues to talk to Brent, but he's watching me. I'm following Leah on autopilot, and before I realize it, I'm standing right in front of him. Ember launches herself at me.

"EEEEK! I am so freaking excited!" she says happily.

All three of us laugh at her enthusiasm; you can't help but love her.

"Me too," I tell her. "I'm ready to go; just need to load everything up. I left a lot of my furniture back in Ohio, so I don't have a lot." I shrug my shoulders.

"Don't worry about that. I have everything we need," Ember says.

"Well, I guess we should get moving," Leah says. She grabs Ember's arm and leads her down the hall to my room. Brent follows them. I remain standing in the same spot.

I feel his hand reach for mine. His are rough and calloused in comparison. I look down at our hands as he laces our fingers together. He lifts my chin with his index finger so I'm now looking at him. "Hey you," he says softly.

"Hi," I manage to croak out.

"Let's get you moved," he says as he places a gentle kiss on my forehead.

What. The. Hell.

Blaise, with our fingers still laced together, leads me toward the bedroom. Once we reach the door, he gives my hand a gentle squeeze, then lets it go. Before I have the chance to miss the feel of his touch, his hand is on the small of my back leading me into the room.

CHAPTER 20

BLAISE

As soon as she walks into the fucking room, my eyes are glued to her. Her hair is bunched up on the top of her head in a mess of curls. She has on a pair of work out shorts and a tank top, nothing special, and to me she's never looked better.

Brent is talking. I think he's thanking me for helping him move Tatum today. I'm trying to listen to him, but it's not working out too well. I can't pull my eyes away from her.

As soon as she's close enough for me to touch her, I have to shove my hands into the pockets of my shorts to keep from reaching out and pulling her into me. Ember helps as she wraps her arms around Tatum, yammering on about how excited she is. I know it's irrational, but I'm jealous of my baby sister right now.

Once Ember finally releases her, Leah grabs Ember and leads her down the hall. I'm hoping Brent goes as well so I can be alone with her for even just a few seconds.

Lady luck is on my side. I smile as Brent follows Leah and my sister to start loading Tatum's things. I reach out and grab her hand. This girl…I've never been like this before, needing to touch someone, needing the connection. I lace our fingers together. I've missed her. I know it makes no sense, but it is what it is.

Tatum is looking down at our entwined fingers. She doesn't retreat, so I take that as a good sign. Lifting her chin I say, "Hey you."

She replies with a croaked hi. The crack in her voice calms me. She feels this, too. She has to. This can't be one-sided. "Let's get you moved," I whisper. To my surprise as much as hers, I kiss her forehead. I lead her down the hall to join the others. I don't trust myself to be alone with her. I gently squeeze her hand and let go before placing it on the small of her back. I'm not ready to not have that connection with her.

I'm at a loss as to why I'm acting this way. And right now, in this moment with Tatum right next to me, I couldn't give a fuck. I'm going with it. Isn't that what Dad and Asher both said to do?

"Brent and I will get the furniture and the heavier boxes and put them in my truck. Why don't you ladies load up Brent's SUV," I say. I don't understand why, but I want to feel like I'm taking care of her.

Brent shakes his head in agreement. "Sounds like a plan."

In no time, we have all of Tatum's things loaded in my truck, her car, and Brent's SUV and we're ready to head to Ember's place.

"So Ember and I will meet you there?" I say to Tatum. I know I sound like a dumbass. Of course she's going to be there; she's moving in.

"Uh, yeah. Sounds good," she replies.

We are standing beside her car, so I open the door for her. She hesitates before finally getting in. Brent and Leah head off to theirs while Ember and I climb into my truck. The door is barely shut before Ember bursts out.

"Holy shit, Blaise"

"What?" I ask her. I know damn well what she's holy shitting about, but I play dumb anyway.

"What do you mean, what? Don't think I didn't see you touching her every chance you got. Hell, you were devouring her with your eyes," she exclaims.

I don't respond. I don't want to outright lie to her, and well, she's right. I reach over and turn up the radio. Thomas Rhett's "It Goes Like This" is playing. It makes me think of Tatum; hell, what doesn't make me think of her?

Ember reaches over and turns the radio off. "You're different with her," she says.

"Yeah," I say. I decide since Ember is going to be living with Tatum, she should know what's going on in my head. "I really like her,

Em. I haven't been able to spend a lot of time with her, but what little bit I have…" I shake my head. I can't really put into words what I'm feeling.

"I saw you, you know, on the dock. I saw you sit beside her. I kept glancing at you out of the corner of my eye. I watched you move closer and then pull her into your arms," she says softly.

"Yeah."

Thankfully, the drive to her apartment is a short one. We pull into the lot, so Ember doesn't have the opportunity to badger me anymore. I know I'm different with her. I need to figure out what it means, what I want it to mean, and either shit or get off the pot as Grandpa used to say.

"Jackson said he and Cade may stop by and help," Ember says as she reaches for the door.

I growl.

Ember chuckles. "Exactly. You need to figure out what you want. Tatum is beautiful, and I would hate to see you lose someone who you obviously care about because you can't get your shit worked out," she scolds me, and then climbs out of the truck.

I tighten my hold on the steering wheel at the thought of anyone else touching Tatum. My mind flashes to Cade with his arm around her at the picnic.

Nope, not happening.

Tatum's mine.

I step out of my truck just as Tatum is pulling up. She parks beside me. I rush to her door so I can open it for her. I want her. She's different than anyone I've ever met. Now I need to show her. Show her what we can be.

As Tatum gets out of her car, I see Ember is already inside and Leah and Brent are not here yet. Perfect.

As soon as she's standing, I grab her waist and pull her into me, wrapping her in a hug. This shit is not me, but I need to touch her. She's stiff at first. After a few seconds, which seems like a lifetime, she hugs me back. Just like that, all is right in my world.

Reluctantly, I pull away. I drop a kiss on her temple. "Let's get you moved in, sweets." She smells so fucking good.

I slowly step away as Brent and Leah pull in. Brent and I get to work moving all the furniture in first. Tatum instructs us on how she wants it. Once that's done, it doesn't take long to have everything in the apartment.

"Hey! Why don't we throw some burgers on the grill?" Ember says, looking at me. "Maybe you and Brent can run out and pick up the necessities for a cookout while we girls get Tatum settled."

Spending more time with Tatum.

I'm in.

I look over at Brent. He nods his head, then leans down and kisses Leah. My gaze travels to Tatum and I want more than anything to kiss her goodbye as well. I've never been that guy. In this moment, with Tatum…I want to be. Not only do I want to be, I'm good with it.

CHAPTER 21

Ember and Leah are the best! By the time the guys are back from the store, we have all of the boxes unpacked and everything put away. We carry the boxes down to the dumpster and settle into the living room to take a break and soak up the air conditioning.

This is where the guys find us.

"Good help's hard to find," I hear Brent say, laughing at us.

I'm sure we're a sight. We all three are sprawled out. Ember is on the floor, right by the vent. Leah is laying sideways in the recliner, and I'm kicked back on the couch. We worked our asses off getting everything organized and put away. We deserve a break.

I can hear Blaise and Brent laughing in the kitchen. I assume they're putting everything away. I'm too hot and too tired to really care at the moment.

I hear a knock at the door, but don't bother to move. Ember and Leah remain where they are as well. The guys will take care of whoever or whatever it is. I hear lots of male laughter and it's getting closer.

"Ember, you have a guest," I hear Blaise tell her. I can tell by the tone of his voice that he is still highly amused by our lack of interest.

I open my eyes to see Jackson sitting down beside Ember on the floor. He pulls her head onto his lap. "It's so hot," Ember whines, making Jackson laugh.

"I told you, man," Brent says. "They're beat. We were only gone for like an hour, and this is how we found them."

"Hmph! We unpacked all the boxes and got everything organized. Then we hauled them down to the dumpster. Tate is officially a resident of this fine establishment," Leah explains.

This causes another chuckle from all three guys. Although I can't see him, I can hear him. It's like my body is in tune with him, so I know Blaise is close. The next thing I know, I feel big strong hands on my ankles as he lifts my legs and plops his fine ass down on the couch. I try to move my legs and sit up, but Blaise has other plans. He pulls my feet into his lap and starts to massage gently. He continues his conversation with Brent and Jackson like it's no big deal, like he's not driving me freaking crazy right now.

"So who has the most talent on the grill?" Blaise asks. His hands continue to caress, and it takes everything in me not to moan at how great it feels. I'm overwhelmed. Is it the massage itself that has me feeling this way, or is it Blaise? Hell, maybe it's both. Either way, I don't want it to stop.

Jackson raises his hand. "I got this," he says. He bends down and kisses Ember on top of the head before gently laying her head on a pillow he pulled off the chair. It must have fallen off when Leah plopped herself down.

Jackson seems like a great guy, and from what I can tell, he's really into Ember. I can only assume I'll be seeing a lot of him with my new living arrangements.

"It's my night to cook. Burgers okay?" she asks us.

"Sure. I'll help," I say starting to get up.

Jackson raises his hand to stop me. "I got this. You just relax," he says, pulling Ember from the floor and leading her to the kitchen.

Blaise leans his body toward me so that we are closer. I can't help but stare at him. Today he's sporting a five o'clock shadow. He's scruffy and his hair is a mess; he is so damn sexy. Strong broad shoulders, and I can see his sculpted chest through his tight ass t-shirt. Blaise is a living breathing temptation. His silver eyes catch me checking him out. I don't pretend otherwise. He knows what he's got going on.

"Hey you," he says with a soft smile, kissing my temple.

Melt. I could melt into a fucking puddle. Hell, my panties are proof of that. Blaise affects me like no other. I can't help but wonder what it would be like to be with him. To have all those muscles above me. To feel the scrape of his five o'clock shadow between my legs. Lord help me!

Quickly, so I know Blaise won't have time to stop me, I swing my legs off his lap and jump off the couch. "I'm gonna go see if Ember needs any help," I say as I travel down the hall toward the kitchen.

I find Ember in the kitchen staring out the glass doors onto the small patio. She's watching Jackson.

"Hey, need any help?" I ask, bringing her out of her Jackson trance.

"Uh, yeah you can cut up the tomatoes," she says.

"So," I motion my head toward the door, "you and Jackson?" I ask with a smile.

Ember blushes and shrugs her shoulders. "No…I mean, yes…hell, I don't know. Jackson has been friends with my brothers for as long as I can remember, and I've always kind of had a thing for him. I'm afraid to get my hopes up."

"He seems like a great guy. He's into you," I say, voicing my observation.

Ember smirks. "Oh, yeah? Well, I know a great guy," she raises her eyebrows, "and he's into you," she says sweetly.

Shaking my head, I'm ready to debate the "he's into you" statement. I know Blaise is a great guy. He's proven that. He may also be "into me" as Ember says, but guys like Blaise don't get into relationships. They play the field, and that doesn't work for me. Guys like Blaise are flings. Even if he was the settling-down type, after what happened with Josh, I'm better off single. "He's—" I stop when Blaise, Leah, and Brent enter the room.

Blaise walks toward me. He places one hand on my hip while he reaches up with the other and grabs plates out of the cabinet over my head. His strong muscular body is pressed up against me. The smell of his cologne surrounds me. He gives my hip a gentle squeeze before releasing me and taking the plates to the table.

Ember clears her throat, which draws my attention. When I look up at her, she winks at me. I roll my eyes and continue slicing the tomatoes. I want more than anything to seek out Blaise, to ask him what all of these small caresses are for. Instead, I focus on slicing so I don't cut off a finger.

CHAPTER 22

BLAISE

I quickly step away from Tatum and busy myself setting the table. The main reason is so I can hide what she does to me. I'm in a constant state of arousal when she's within fifty feet. It's the spell, I'm sure. When I leaned over her, I had to touch her. It couldn't be prevented. One touch and I'm granite. Any other time, I would have pushed the evidence into the girl's back so she knows the score, but not with Tatum. I want her to be mine. I don't want the "wham bam thank you ma'am" with her.

I want it all.

My grand plan is to touch her whenever I can, let her know I'm here, and I want her. Obviously, I didn't think the plan through like I should have. Turns out I'm torturing myself. I had to dig down deep for the will power to not take her there on the couch in front of everyone during her foot massage. Her silky smooth skin... *Fuck!*

Jackson strolls in carrying a plate full of grilled meat. My mouth waters. The stars must be in alignment because once everyone takes their place around the table, Tatum has to sit next to me. Everyone must be starving, not much is said as we all fill our plates and scarf down the food.

"I'm stuffed," Brent says.

"Well, we're not done yet. I made strawberry shortcake last night," Ember says as she stands up.

Jackson reaches over and touches her hand gently. "I'll get it." He leans over and kisses her cheek before retrieving dessert. I smile. I'm glad my longtime friend is treating her right. I warned him if he didn't, he would be answering to me. Maybe I should have done more, like punched him or something? Asher and I have always taken a laid back approach with Ember. We warn the men who sniff around her that we are her big brothers. It helps that we are both well over six feet tall and pack around two hundred and forty pounds of muscle. We want her to have a life, but at the same time, whomever she's involved with, and anyone who is interested, needs to know who we are and where we stand if they fuck with her. Jackson is a good guy and he obviously likes her. She could do worse, that's for sure.

I glance at Tatum watching Leah and Brent who are sharing an intimate moment. I can't describe the look in her eyes, longing maybe? Before I can decipher the meaning, Jackson is back with the dessert.

Tatum hands her plate to Ember. "This is my favorite." She smiles.

Ember laughs. "I know. You mentioned it at the picnic. It's kind of a welcome treat for moving in day," she says cheerily. My sister, such a good heart.

After dessert, we all pitch in to clean up. Jackson settles in on the chair in the living room with Ember on his lap. Leah and Brent announce it's time for them to head home. I watch as Tatum's eyes fill with tears. I want to wrap my arms around her and tell her everything will be fine. I've never had that desire before well, unless you count Ember. As her brother, that's my job. Even then, this is different. I slip quietly into the living room, giving the three of them some privacy. Besides, if the tears start to fall, I don't think I could stay away from her. The pull now just at the thought of her being upset causes an ache deep in my chest.

I sit down on the couch.

Ember smiles softly. "How's she holding up?"

I shake my head no. I can't talk about it or I will march right back in there and wrap my arms around her.

"Hey!" Ember yells into the kitchen. She stands up dragging Jackson with her.

"Yeah?" Tatum calls back. I can hear the emotion in her voice.

"Why don't we all meet up at Backwoods tonight for a drink?" I hear Ember ask.

"Sounds good," Brent replies.

"Great. We'll meet you guys there around eight," Ember tells them.

I hear a few low murmurs and then a door closing. Ember and Jackson must have gone to her room. I shudder at the idea of hearing my little sister in any form of, well…that.

Another door closes; this time it's the main door to the apartment. Tatum joins me in the living room. She is standing beside where I'm sitting on the couch. I'm sure she feels out of place no matter how hard we tried to make her feel welcome. This is all new to her. I reach over, then gently lace her fingers with mine.

Tatum stares down at our hands, and then those beautiful green eyes seek out mine. "Hey you," I say softly.

She doesn't respond again, she doesn't pull away. I tug on her hand and lead her to sit down with me on the couch. She sits down and I pull her hand to get her to move closer.

"What?" she laughs. Music to my ears.

I gently tug her hand again, fingers still laced together. "You're too far away," I tell her.

Tatum just laughs. She thinks I'm playing with her, flirting. Nope. She is really too far away from me. She's not moving any closer, so I slide next to her. I rest our joined hands on her leg. I pull the remote from the coffee table and settle in.

"Uh, Blaise…What are we doing?" Tatum asks with hesitation.

I wink at her. "Watching a movie," I say. I can't tell her I'm grasping at straws to spend more time with her. Nope, if I tell her that, she will run and I don't want her to run.

Tatum kicks off her flip-flops and brings her feet up on the couch, settling in against me. "So what are we watching?" she asks.

"You choose; tell me when to stop," I say, flipping through the channels.

Tatum surprises me when she tells me to stop as I reach the comedy channel. "I love Jeff Dunham," she says.

There is a sparkle in her eyes; the sadness from earlier is gone. I did that. I made her smile, and I want to every fucking day. I want to make her face light up. "Jeff Dunham it is," I say, laying the remote on the arm of the couch.

Not able to control myself with her being so close, I gently rub my thumb across hers. Tatum doesn't act like she even notices my touch and me. With the exception of her eyes, so expressive. She glances at me and smiles, then settles further against me.

Best. Day. Ever!

CHAPTER 23

Holy Hell! Blaise is confusing me. His touches, his words. He's not treating me like a playboy would treat his conquest. Then again, what do I know? Josh treated me well, and look how that turned out.

As soon as Leah and Brent leave, I feel a little out of place. Blaise must sense my unease. When his fingers lace through mine, it feel as though I have been shocked by the connection, the same one I feel every time he touches me. Maybe I should consider a fling with Blaise. He's a decent guy. I'm sure he knows his way around the bedroom. Actually, the more I think about it, the more the idea appeals to me. Why continue to resist temptation? Why not jump into bed with the most beautiful man I have ever laid eyes on?

Blaise runs his thumb across mine, my fingers still tightly entwined with his. I relax my body and sink closer to him. His touch does that to me, calms me. Again, why am I trying to resist him?

I hear a throat clearing. I slowly open my eyes and see Ember standing at the end of the couch, arms crossed with a smirk on her face. It takes me a minute to realize my situation. I'm lying on the couch; I must have fallen asleep.

Blaise.

I feel his strong arms around my waist. I try to break free.

"Don't move. I'm not done holding you," he mumbles into my hair.

Ember is now smiling from ear to ear. Jackson walks up behind her and places his arm around her waist. He winks at me.

"Blaise, you're giving your sister a show and I have to pee," I whine.

"I don't care," he says sleepily.

I release a heavy sigh. "Fine, I'm up," Blaise says, releasing his grip on my waist. "What time is it?" he asks.

I look at Ember and Jackson for the answer. I have no idea how long we were asleep.

"It's six thirty, big brother. You need to get ready. I called Asher and Grace; they are going to meet us at Backwoods as well," Ember tells him.

"I'm gonna run home and change. I'll be back in an hour," Jackson tells Ember as he gives her a chaste kiss.

Ember walks him to the door.

I stand from the couch and start to walk away. Blaise is up and grabbing my arm. He pulls me against him with one hand while the other lifts my chin so he can see my face. "Thank you," he whispers.

I take him in. He's got this sleepy look on his face, his hair is tousled from sleep, and his five o'clock shadow is more prominent. He's sexy as hell. It doesn't help that I can still feel him wrapped around me.

"For?" I ask, my voice soft.

Blaise leans down and places his mouth next to my ear. "For letting me hold you," he says as he kisses my neck. "Best sleep ever."

He stands back to his full height without releasing his hold on me. "I'm going home to change, too. I'll be back before you know it," he tells me.

He kisses my forehead before releasing me and walks out the door.

I hear him talking to Ember and Jackson. I have to walk past them to get to my room and I really need to use the bathroom. I decide to act as though nothing happened. I walk through the kitchen and head down the hall.

"See you guys in a few," I say over my shoulder. Nothing like avoidance.

I take a quick shower, and shave my legs. I am barely dressed when I hear a knock on my bedroom door.

"Can I come in?" Ember asks.

"It's open," I yell through the door.

"Wow, great outfit," she says. I'm wearing a denim skirt with a teal, off the shoulder shirt with a black tank underneath. "What shoes are you wearing?" she questions.

"I don't know yet." I point to my closet. "What do you think?" I ask her.

Ember studies me for a minute. "Hold on, I'll be right back," she says as she dashes out of the room. I can only assume she has shoes she wants me to wear.

Ember comes back holding a pair of teal cowboy boots. "These will set that outfit off," she tells me. I have to admit, she's right. "Are we the same size?" I ask her.

"Eight," she says, holding up the boots.

"Yep," I say, taking them from her hands.

"So, are we going to talk about earlier?" Ember questions.

I shake my head no. "There's nothing to talk about. We were watching TV and fell asleep."

"Okay. How do you explain my brother wrapped around you like a pretzel? Not to mention, he was refusing to let you go," she taunts me.

"I guess we just gravitated that way in our sleep." I shrug my shoulders. "It's no big deal, really."

"If you say so," Ember says with a smirk. "I'm going to finish my hair. The guys will be here soon," she says as she walks out of my room.

Is it too soon in our friendship to tell Ember I want to seduce her brother? I want a no strings attached fling. I no longer want to resist the temptation that is Blaise Richards. I think I'll start tonight.

I braid my bangs to the side and pull my hair up into a ponytail. I hear deep voices mixed with Ember's. Jackson and Blaise are back. I grab my wristlet and make sure I have my license, cell, and cash before joining the others.

I follow the voices and end up in the kitchen. The sight of Blaise causes my heart to race. I wipe my sweaty palms against my skirt. He's wearing a pair of jeans that hang just right on his slender hips. His black form fitted t-shirt molds to every line, every muscle. I lick my lips. It's then Blaise looks up and our eyes meet.

Hunger.

His takes me in slowly, every inch. I feel as though he's undressing me with his eyes. This fling might be easier to initiate than I originally thought.

CHAPTER 24

BLAISE

I'm standing in the kitchen talking to Jackson and Ember, and I feel her. I know she's watching me. I give her time to take in her fill before I raise my gaze to hers. I pull in a breath. Holy shit, she's fucking stunning. I shove my hands deep in my pockets to keep from rushing to her and pulling her into my arms, where I want her. Tatum is wearing a short jean skirt and a shirt that is hanging off one shoulder. Her hair is pulled up and I can see the creamy skin of her neck exposed, for me. I want nothing more than to bury my face in the crook of her neck and taste her, consume myself with her sweet scent. I allow myself another pass to make sure I'm not missing one single inch of her body. My eyes flow past her short skirt to her legs that end up in cowboy boots that match her shirt.

I'm hard as a rock. I shift my weight from one foot to the other, trying to relieve the tension she's created just from walking into the room.

Jackson's laugh pulls me out of my Tatum induced trance. He slaps a hand on my shoulder. Leaning in he whispers, "Dude, you're drooling." He chuckles.

"I'm good with it," I tell him. I am. I don't care who knows I want her. I want her to be mine.

Ember and Tatum are turning off lights and making sure the patio door is locked. When Tatum is finally close enough for me touch, I snake my arm around her and pull her into a hug. "Hey you," I whisper in her ear.

I feel her relax into my embrace. She doesn't say anything, and she doesn't need to. Her body is telling me everything I need to know.

I keep Tatum in my embrace as I lead her to my truck. Jackson and I had already talked about who would drive. Since my truck is four door, I volunteered. My only stipulation was that Tatum was to be up front with me. Considering my sister has him by the balls, he was eager to agree.

I lead her to the passenger door, opening it for her. I turn her so she's facing me. I ache to kiss her. Those big green eyes of hers watching, waiting. She knows I have to lift her in, which is a big part of why I wanted to drive. I place my hands on her hips. I kiss her forehead before gently lifting her into my truck. I try like hell to ignore the way she shudders as soon as I touch her. I pretend that as soon as I touch her that I don't feel the electric current. Instead, I shut the door and make my way to the driver's side.

Tatum's eyes are on me as soon as I open the door. I climb in and start the truck. I see Ember and Jackson walking toward us. I reach over the console with my right hand and caress her cheek. She leans into my touch.

"You're stunning," I tell her.

I watch as a light blush takes over her face. "You're not so bad yourself," she replies with a wink.

Holy shit! Tatum's flirting with me. Maybe convincing her to be mine won't be as hard as I had originally thought.

I lean over and place a quick kiss to her forehead. I can't help myself. I pull away just as Jackson is opening the door for Ember. I place both hands back on the wheel and wait for them to get in. I need something to do with my hands, something to keep me from pulling her into my lap and kissing the hell out of her.

The drive to Backwoods is only ten minutes. During the drive, I keep one hand on the wheel while the other rests on her knee. I feel goose bumps break out on her skin and I smile. She's just as affected as I am.

Tatum takes care of the radio with the direction of Ember. My sister claimed we could only listen to "dancing" music to set the mood for the evening. I'm not really much of a dancer. I'm more of what you would call a head bobber. I like to kick back with a beer and enjoy the music. I tend to bob my head to the beat, but dancing…I don't really.

I can, I just don't do it. The female population seem to think dancing and romance go hand in hand, so yeah, it's not really my thing.

As I go to lift Tatum out of the truck, her phone alerts her of a new message. I nod my head toward her hand for her to check her phone. I plan to attach her to me as soon as she is out of this truck. Everyone here is going to know she's mine; well, that I want her to be mine. I hope they assume she already is and stay the fuck away from her.

Tatum swipes the screen on her phone and smiles. "Leah and Brent are inside," she tells me.

I nod my head in understanding. I reach for her and my phone alerts me of a message. I growl and Tatum smiles. I leave one hand on her hip, because really, I need to touch her. I can't explain it and I don't really understand it, but I'm going with it. I reach into my pocket with my other hand and pull out my phone. Swiping the screen, I see its Asher. "Asher and Grace are inside, too," I say.

I place my phone back in my pocket and my hand immediately finds her other hip. I grip her waist and lift her from the truck. I let her body slide against mine. My cock thinks it's time to party and my heart feels like it's about to bust out of my chest. Her feet touch the ground, but I don't let go of her. Instead, I wrap my arms around her waist and pull her tight against me.

This…us, is a perfect fit. Nothing and no one has ever felt this good. The feeling intensifies when Tatum moves her hands from my shoulders to place them around my waist.

"I hate to interrupt, you look like you're having a moment; but are you coming inside?" Ember asks sweetly.

I feel Tatum stiffen in my arms, and just like that, the moment is lost. Without answering Ember, I slowly ease out of the grip I have on Tatum. I place my hands on her shoulders and gently run my hands down her arms. When my hands reach hers, our fingers lace together. I lean down and rest my forehead against hers.

"What are you doing to me?" I whisper.

Tatum doesn't answer; she doesn't need to. I know she's just as mixed up about this as I am. I pull back, gently kissing her forehead.

Releasing my left hand, I keep hers clutched tight in my right and lead her into the Backwoods.

Ember and Jackson went in without us after my darling sister ruined our moment. I spot them heading toward the back. I look ahead of them and see Leah, Brent, Asher, and Grace are sitting at a large table in the back.

As we reach the table, all eyes are on us. Asher is smirking, while Grace, Ember, and Jackson are smiling. Leah and Brent both are staring at our hands. I don't care. I'm not letting go.

"Hey! I didn't think you all were ever going to get here," Leah says, standing up to hug Tatum. She tries to let go of my hand; I grip her tighter. She gives Leah a one armed hug. As soon as she releases her, I gently tug her back to me.

I can feel the eyes of my siblings; they're watching me. I'm not a big public display kind of guy. It's different with Tatum. I don't even think about where we are or who is watching. It's just her; all I see is her. But I know others are watching her, watching us. I know there are at least a dozen or more guys here that are checking her out. How could they not? Her long dark locks and those green eyes, she takes my breath away. There's not a guy in this room that can deny that. I know they see what I see. I smile because she's mine, or at least she will be.

Tatum relaxes her stance and leans against me. I smile. Those assholes can look, but not touch. Tatum is mine; she just doesn't know it yet.

CHAPTER 25

Blaise has stepped up his seduction tactics. He's constantly touching me, giving me sweet gentle kisses. His attention has me on fire. I'm ready to take him to the nearest storage closet or bathroom and take full advantage of what he's offering.

He's marking his claim for the night, and really, he doesn't need to. I plan to allow him to seduce me. My earlier thoughts coming to mind. I know I shouldn't since he is Ember's brother, but I want him. I want to know what it feels like to feel his weight on top of me. To be able to trace his ink with my tongue. I can no longer resist his charms, or seduction techniques, whatever you want to call it. I just don't want to resist him any longer. I want one night with him. One night of passion and no thoughts of what I lost. I just want him. With that thought, I relax against him. Blaise releases my hand and slips his arm around my waist to hold me against him. I need a drink!

"All right, ladies, what'll be?" Asher asks.

We all call out our drink orders. We all request a beer. Nothing special, just a nice ice-cold beer to cool me down. Maybe if I relax a little, my libido will, too.

"Come on, man, you can help," Asher says to Blaise.

I look up and his eyes are on me. I try to pull away, but Blaise tightens his hold. He leans his lips down to my ear. "I'll be right back, sweetheart. You're mine tonight," he whispers, and then kisses my neck before pulling away and following Asher to the bar. Jackson and Brent follow them.

I watch him walk away, because really, why would I willingly miss that? His ass looks so good in those jeans. I can't wait to take them off of him. The thought of what I want to happen, what I hope happens, brings a smile to my face.

Once Blaise and his fine ass are out of sight, I turn back to the table and my three companions are all watching me, each of them wearing a shit-eating grin. "What?" I ask innocently. I know what they're smiling at. I'm busted. I shrug my shoulders when they don't answer.

Grace breaks the silence. "So, Asher and I have been talking about marriage a lot lately. Well, Asher has," she tells us.

Thank you, Grace, for the change of subject!

"He loves you," Ember says. "It wouldn't surprise me if he proposes soon. I've never seen him with anyone like he is with you. Besides, you guys have been dating for a while now."

Grace nods her head. "Sometimes it's still hard for me to believe that the once former playboy wants to settle down. I know he loves me." She shrugs. "I guess it's surreal, all these emotions. I want him to be my forever. The thought of him really wanting the same is..."

"Reality," Ember says. "You know he worships you. When the Richards men fall, they fall hard." Ember winks at me.

"I know, I guess it's just nerves. I want it to happen. I'm nervous it won't."

Grace looks at Leah and me. "Before I moved here to live with my dad, I didn't have a lot of good in my life. Hell, nothing really, except for my dad. Asher is, well...he's my dream, and to spend the rest of my life with him would make that dream come true. I'm worried things are going too smooth and I'll lose him."

Ember places her arm around Grace. "Ash loves you. I know your past was rough, but you have us. We're your family," she tells her.

"And us," I say, motioning my hand between Leah and I. Leah voices her agreement.

Grace doesn't have the chance to respond before the guys are back at the table with our beers. There is a waitress right behind them carrying a tray holding eight shot glasses. The guys give us our beers while the waitress passes out the shots.

"All right," Jackson says. "On three." We all lift our shots in the air. "One, two, three," Jackson counts off. On three, we slam back our shots. I chase mine with a long drink of my beer.

Ember does the same. Sitting her mug down on the table, she says, "All right, ladies, let's hit the dance floor."

Immediately, Grace and Leah are out of their seats. I go to stand and Blaise's hand lands on my thigh. He leans in, his breath hot on my cheek. I squeeze my legs together at the sensation it's causing as he whispers, "Remember your mine tonight," and places a kiss on the corner of my mouth.

I feel a tug on my arm; it's Ember. "Let's go, girl," she says over the music.

Blaise lets me go; although, he looks reluctant. I follow the girls out to the dance floor and let the music take control. One song leads to another, and the four of us are having a blast. The only time we leave the floor is to take another shot or visit the restroom.

I don't know how many shots we've had, but we are all feeling really good. Pitbull's song he does with Ke$ha "Timber" blares over the speakers and all four of us scream. It's scary how much we are alike.

I lift my hands in the air and sway my hips. I see Jackson, Asher, and Brent join our group and start dancing with their girls. I feel a pang of jealousy because I don't have that. Then my mind wonders to where Blaise might be. Earlier we tried to get the four of them to join us. Blaise was adamant that he doesn't dance. I feel strong hands grip my hips and pull me against a rock hard body. I don't have to turn around to know it's Blaise; it's as if my body is in tune with him. Not to mention, the look of surprise on our friends' faces, especially his siblings, to see him out on the dance floor.

I lean back against his chest and arch my back. This causes my ass to grind into his crotch. Looks like he's happy to see me. I lift my right arm and place my hand on the back of his neck. Blaise follows suit, tilts his head, and buries his face in my neck. He grinds his hips and I can't help the moan that escapes. I'm grateful for the loud music drowning me out. Although with my current state of inebriation, I'm not sure I would really care.

Our friends may not have heard me, but Blaise did. He nips at my neck in retaliation. I turn to face him, and his arms are immediately tugging me as close as he can get me. There is no space between us. I can feel every hard ridge of his muscular body. Blaise sways his hips and I mirror his movements, our bodies in sync. My eyes find his, and the look in his eyes causes a tidal wave of warm sensations to pulse through my veins. My pulse quickens at the thought of him on me, inside of me. I lick my lips at the visual.

I hear a growl. I can actually feel it in Blaise's chest right before his lips crash with mine. I don't even hesitate to open for him. I want him. Tonight, I want to feel young, careless, and free. I want that with Blaise, just for tonight. I need that for tonight.

I lean up on tiptoes as my hands find their way to his hair as I pull him closer. There is no such thing as personal space between us; it's our space. It's Tatum and Blaise consumed with desire. In this moment, I can't tell where he ends and I begin.

CHAPTER 26

BLAISE

This song, "Timber," it's fitting. I'm falling hard and fast for this girl. I feel like I should be yelling "Timber" at the top of my lungs. Tatum is grinding her ass into my crotch and any willpower I may have had, just flew out the fucking window. I love the feel of her body next to mine.

She turns in my arms. I hold her close as I sway my hips, grinding to the beat. Her eyes catch mine. I see what I'm feeling reflected back at me, lust and longing. I can't wait any longer. I crash my lips to hers. She willingly opens for me. The taste of her on my tongue fuels my desire. I nip at her bottom lip, then plunge back in. She gives as much as I take.

Every part of Tatum is pressed tight against every single fucking part of me. My hands are all over her. One is caressing her cheek while I use the other to go back and forth between holding her close to me and caressing her back. Her fingers run through my hair, and I lose control. I grip her hips and eliminate all space. I want to lift her thighs and wrap her legs around me; with the skirt she's wearing that's not possible. No one is going to see her, no one but me.

Holding her in my arms, her scent and her taste, my senses are on overload and my cock thinks it's time to come out and play. I know she can feel me, how hard I am. There is no controlling it with our bodies fused together.

I know I need to put a little space between us so she doesn't think I just want to fuck her.

I do.

I want her.

I want all of her. I want her smiles and her laugh. I want to be the one she leans on, runs to. I want to be the one who can make the sadness is her eyes disappear. I want to build a life with her.

The song changes to a slow one and I slowly end our kiss. Tatum tries to step away. I'm not having that. I want her in my arms, as close as I can get her. It doesn't escape me that I'm not only dancing, but I just had a very public make out session. I can't find it in me to care.

I tighten my grip around her waist until I feel her relax in my arms. She rests her head against my chest as Hunter Hayes sings about making his girl feel "Wanted." I can relate. I don't want a day to go by that she doesn't know how much I want her.

I hold her tight with one hand while the other gently strokes her back. I've never felt this...this need for another person. I know I'm coming in fast and strong, but dammit, I can't stop it. I've always been known for going after what I want. Hell, Asher and I dreamed of Self Expressions and busted our asses every day to make it happen.

I look down at Tatum, her eyes half closed, wearing a lidded look of satisfaction. I want to give her that look every single day.

I'm going to fight with everything in me to make her mine.

For the rest of the song, I hold her tight. I listen to the words and vow to myself that I will make Tatum feel wanted every day.

Once the last note is sung, Tatum lifts her head. "I need a drink," she says softly.

I nod my head and grab her hand, lacing our fingers together. There is no way I can go without touching her after that. Holding her in my arms, she's a perfect fit.

I lead her back to the table and pull a chair out for her. Leaning down, I whisper in her ear, "What do you want, sweetheart?"

She turns her head to answer me and her mouth is mere inches from mine. All I have to do is lean in just a little to have my lips on hers again. So, after she tells me she wants water, that's exactly what I do. I lean in and give her a chaste kiss on the lips.

At the bar, I order Tatum and I both a water. I've only had two beers tonight and one shot. I am driving after all. I feel Asher's hand land on my shoulder.

"That was some show back there." He motions his head toward the dance floor. "I don't think I've ever seen you like that," he says.

Because I've been waiting for Tatum. "Nope," is my reply.

Asher laughs, "I hear you brother, loud and clear." He squeezes my shoulder and heads back to our table.

I'm right behind him. I reach the table and Cade is sitting in my seat. I try to remain cool. Technically, Tatum is not mine, but she will be.

I stand beside Tatum and reach for her hand. I gently tug to get her to stand up. Once she does, I sit down in the chair and pull her onto my lap. I hand her one of the waters. "Here's your water, babe."

She smiles at me and takes the bottle of water. "Thank you."

Take that, Cade. I don't want to be a possessive ass, but really, he needs to understand it's time for him to move on.

A few more minutes of small talk and Cade is still the odd man out. I try not to smirk each time he looks at us, but it's really hard not to. Especially since Tatum has taken it upon herself to lean against my chest. I have one arm around her waist holding her to me while the other is resting on her thigh. I'm in the middle of discussing the upcoming UFC fight with the guys when she adjusts her position and is now sitting sideways on my lap. During a break in the conversation, I hear her soft voice. "I'm ready for us to go home," she says.

My heart soars. Not only did she associate me with home, she insinuated we are together. I know I'm reaching. I did drive her here, but in Cade's eyes, she's with me, we're an us.

I kiss her forehead. "Sure thing, sweetheart," I tell her.

Tatum has had a lot to drink and I can tell she's ready to fall asleep. I take the half-full water bottle from her hands and place it on the table. I look at Jackson and Ember. "Tatum's ready to go home." I don't bother asking them if they are. They rode with me and my girl is ready to leave. I lift her in my arms, nod my head at Asher and Brent, and head out to my truck.

"I can walk," she says over a yawn.

"I would rather you be right where you are," I tell her. No way am I passing up a chance to hold her. Not going to happen.

I reach my truck and realize I'm going to have to put her down in order to get the door open. I don't want to.

"Tatum, can you pull the door open, sweetheart?" I ask her.

She opens her eyes as she reaches for the door. She opens the door; I walk around it and place her gently in the passenger seat. Tenderly, I brush her hair out of her eyes.

"Thank you for the dance," she says in a soft sleepy voice.

I don't respond. Instead, I lean over her and latch her seatbelt. My face is close to hers and her eyes pop open. I freeze. Locked in place, I take her in.

Tatum reaches up and places her hands on both cheeks, holding me still. "You kissed me," she says, almost in question.

"I did," I say, my voice thick with emotion. This girl, she has me.

"Do it again," she says right before her lips touch mine.

Holy. Fucking. Shit.

No hesitation. I slowly caress her lips with mine. Tatum tries to take the kiss deeper, but I pull back. Jackson and Ember should be here any second, and if I let this go any further, they will see more than they bargained for. I want to, God, how I want to.

CHAPTER 27

I'm drunk. I'm drunk and trying to make a move on Blaise. He shuts me down. He kisses me back, but not like he did on the dance floor. Instead, he shuts my door and walks to his side of the truck. I should have known better. I should have known a sexy specimen such as himself wouldn't want me. This…everything these past few weeks has been a game for him. He must have chickened out because I'm Ember's new roommate. Even with his rejection, I can't help but wonder what it would feel like to be with him. That's my last thought as I drift off to sleep.

It's not until Blaise lays me down on my bed do I wake up. He slips off my boots, or Ember's boots rather, and pulls the covers over me. Leaning down, he kisses my forehead.

"Sweet dreams," he whispers.

Before he has the chance to get away, I reach out and grab his arm. "Stay." One word can change it all. If I'm successful at seducing him, I may have to find a new place to live, if we can't get past it. My alcohol induced brain is screaming for me to ravish him, damn the consequences. I have resisted him as long as I can; now I want him to give me what he gives all those other girls. I want a night with the infamous Blaise Richards.

Blaise sits on the edge of the bed. His hand sweeps my hair away from my eyes. "I can't stay. I don't trust myself with you," he says softly.

I place my hand on his thigh and inch closer to his goods. He places his hand over mine to stop me. "Don't."

The rejection hits me like a wrecking ball. What's wrong with me that turns men away? First Josh, now Blaise. I'm humiliated, again. I can feel my lip start to tremble. I bite down hard, tasting blood. Maybe Blaise will assume the tears are from the pain in my lip and not his rejection. I roll onto my side so my back is to him. I don't want him to see me cry.

He places his hand on my back and begins to rub soothing circles. I hate how his touch still ignites a fire within me even though he doesn't want me. Damn hormones. I don't respond. I bite down harder on my lip and curl into a ball, fighting off the tears that are pushing to the surface.

I hear him stand up. I listen with baited breath for the door to close. It doesn't. Instead, I hear shoes softly tumbling onto the hardwood floor. I feel the bed dip with his weight and then I feel Blaise. He's lying behind me. I can feel his body heat seep into me. I'm instantly pissed off because I want him. I wanted a night of passion. I wanted to forget the pain. Unable to hold them in any longer, tears begin to flow and my shoulders begin to shake.

Without hesitation, Blaise wraps his arms around me and pulls me back against his chest. He doesn't say anything; he just holds me. I don't understand why he's being so nice. The only reason I can come up with is he feels sorry for me. Maybe he feels bad for leading me on?

I focus on taking deep breaths and get my emotions under control. Blaise notices and speaks for the first time since he laid down. "You want to talk about it?" he asks as he continues to hold me tight.

Really? A laugh escapes me. "Sure, Blaise, let's talk about how I practically threw myself at you and you rejected me. Let's not," I say dryly.

His arm tenses around me. "What? No, baby. I didn't reject you. I was protecting you," he excuses.

I roll over to face him. He keeps his arm locked tight around me. We're now face to face and he can see the evidence of my tears.

Blaise removes his hand from my waist and gently wipes my tears away with his thumb. As soon as he's finished, his arm goes back around me, holding me to him.

We lie there, watching each other. Blaise finally breaks the silence. "Baby, I could never reject you. I want you, I do. What I don't want is for you to think I used you for a quick fuck when I want all of you," he tells me. His eyes are boring into mine, trying to convince me he means what he says.

Holy Shit!

It must be the alcohol. There is no way I comprehend this correctly. My face must show my confusion because Blaise starts to further explain.

"I want you. All of you. I want your smiles, your laughs. I want to be the one person in the world you know you can always count on. I want to be the one you run to. I want to be able to fall asleep like this every night and wake up to you every morning," he tells me.

"Blaise," I whisper his name.

"Shh, just rest. We can talk more tomorrow," he says softly.

"Will you…?" I stop myself before I ask him to stay. His words confuse me, but I also know while lying here in his arms, I feel at peace, and it's been a while for me. So, yes, I want him to stay, but I won't allow myself to ask him.

Reading my thoughts, he says, "I'm not going anywhere." With that, he pulls the cover over us.

I relax into his hold. I never thought I would feel loved and protected again, like I belong here, in his arms. After losing my parents, I felt…out of place. After what Josh did, I was sure that I would never feel safe with another man. As I lay in his arms, I feel completely safe, loved and cherished. This is where I belong. This is my last thought as sleep claims me.

CHAPTER 28

BLAISE

I'm not sure what caused Tatum's tears. I hate she's upset. Her lip quivers and she bites down hard. I can see her eyes are glassy from the dim light of the moon shining through the window. She rolls over, trying to shut me out. This girl has seen so much pain. I don't know all the details, but what I do know is I never want to be the one who causes that look in her eyes, that causes her tears to flow.

Decision made, I stand up and close her bedroom door. I walk back to the bed and remove my shoes. I crawl in next to her and align my body with hers. I gently rub her back, letting her know I'm still here. Her shoulders begin to shake and so does my heart. I wrap my arms around her and hold her tight, letting her work through whatever it is that caused this. I have a good idea she thinks I rejected her, when that's not the case. I don't want to take advantage of her. She's had a lot to drink and I don't want her to feel used. Selfishly, I also want our first time to be memorable for both of us.

I feel her breathing even out, so I decide to ask her if she wants to talk. She confirms my suspicions. She actually thinks I don't want her. *Fuck!*

I try to explain to her the best I can without scaring her away that I wasn't rejecting her. I know that in her current state of mind it will be hard to reason with her. I tell her how much I want her anyway, knowing she probably won't remember any of this in the morning. I'll wait until she's asleep, then slip out to the couch. I want to be here when she wakes up. We need to talk about this.

"Will you…" she starts to ask me something. I know deep down she wants me to stay. I can feel it in the way her body relaxed in my arms. I may have made her cry, but she feels safe with me. That's all I can ask for right now.

I reassure her I'm not going anywhere and wrap her tight in my arms. I listen as her breathing evens out, her soft breath against my chest. No way am I moving to the couch, and no way am I falling asleep. My heart is hammering against my chest. This feels right. Tatum in my arms, our bodies fused together as we lie here in the darkness. I want to commit this to memory. When Tatum wakes up and she still thinks I rejected her, who knows how long it will take for me to get her back in my arms like this. I plan to savor the moment.

I'm lost in thought. My mind reliving every moment I've shared with her when she begins to be restless. She's whimpering in her sleep. She calls out, "No…they're not gone…they can't be gone." I watch as a tear rolls down her cheek.

I take my thumb and gently wipe away her tears. "No," she says again. Her voice soft and broken. My heart breaks at the sound.

I bring her head against my chest. "It's okay, baby. I'm here. I got you," I whisper these words to her over and over while rubbing her back, trying to soothe her. If I could take away her pain, I would. There is an ache in my chest and a lump in my throat as I fight back my own emotions. She's scared. It's breaking my heart to watch her.

"Blaise," my name falls from her lips. I wait to see if she'll say more, but she doesn't. She still sleeping. My name on her lips helps ease my own turmoil. She's either asking for me, or feels me here with her. I'll take either.

Tatum stirs in my arms as the sun starts to rise. She rolls over and we are face to face. Slowly she opens her eyes. I wait for panic or anger. Instead, I get a sleepy smile.

Her hair has fallen in her eyes; I tuck the thick locks behind her ear. "Hey you," I say, my voice gruff. This is a surreal moment for me, waking up with her. I hope she's ready for what I'm about to bring. I'm going to fight for her, for us. I want this moment with her every fucking day.

"Morning," she says in her sleep-laced voice. "You stayed."

"Yeah," I say, my eyes not leaving hers.

Tatum holds my stare. A slight blush crosses her face. "I had a dream you were here. I guess that was real," she says, finally looking away.

Is she embarrassed? I use my hand to gently guide her head back to face me. "I was here. I am here. I will always be here," I tell her. My voice is firm but soft.

She doesn't say anything; she just stares at me. Since I have her full attention, I keep going.

"Tatum, how much do you remember from last night?" I ask.

She takes a deep breath. "I remember throwing myself at you and you rejecting me. I remember you telling me you were doing it for me." She breaks our connection and looks up at the ceiling. "I remember you saying you want me. In my dream…" She swallows hard. "In my dream, I was, um, having a hard time. You were holding me, telling me you were there for me." Her eyes find mine. "I assume that part was real as well?" she asks.

I nod my head. "Yes, you were upset. I'm here if you ever want to talk about it," I tell her.

"Thank you, but I'm good," she whispers.

"I'm glad you remember. I was afraid you wouldn't. However, I still want to clarify in the light of day when we both have clear heads." I raise up and rest my weight on my elbow so I am looking down at her. Her body is close and I can feel the stirring of desire. By the look in her eyes, she can as well. "I want you, Tatum. You have consumed my thoughts since the day I met you. The more time I spend with you, the more I want. I swear you've cast some kind of spell on me." I kiss the tip of her nose. "I just want you to let me in. Let me be a part of your life. Give me the chance to show you what you mean to me. I know it's fast, but I feel it in here." I pull her hand and hold it against my chest, right over my heart.

Tatum closes her eyes. When she opens them, I see the sadness has returned. "Blaise, I'm a mess. I'm trying to find out who I am, where I belong. I lost my parents and my ex…" She stops, collecting her thoughts. "He cheated on me the day my parents died. I'm afraid to open myself up again. My parents' death was tragic and Josh's betrayal deepened the wound. I don't know if I can let you in."

I nod my head in understanding. "Take your time. I'm not going anywhere," I tell her.

She chuckles and I relish the sound.

"What? What's so funny?" I ask her.

"This…us. Last night my plan was to seduce you. I wanted one night with you. I wanted to forget the pain."

Her words elate me and piss me off all at the same time. "One night?" I ask.

She blushes. "Yeah, I mean, I never would have thought you would want me, you know, for more than just one night. In my mind, it was a solid plan, until you turned me down."

I try not to let her words hurt me. I know I have the reputation of a ladies man, but she's different. I'm different with her. I remind myself Tatum doesn't really know that. She only knows what she's seen and heard. I'll just have to prove it to her.

"Yeah, one night is not an option. When I have you," I place the palm of my hand against her cheek "and trust me, I will have you; when I finally get you in my bed, I'm never letting you go."

Tatum licks her lips. "And when will that be exactly?" she asks, her voice husky.

I move in close. "When you understand you're mine. When you're ready to commit to this chemistry and the feelings between us. When I know this," I place my hand over her heart, "is mine."

Enough talking. I capture her lips with mine slowly. I lick her bottom lip, then gently bite. Our tongues are in a slow battle of passion. I put my every emotion I have for her into the kiss. I hope she gets used to this, because kissing her is my new favorite thing.

Tatum releases my lips; her chest is heaving with exhilaration. Good, looks like I got my point across.

"Blaise, I don't know if—" She tries to speak, but I stop her by placing my finger to her soft lips.

"I'm not going anywhere." I flash her a cocky grin. "I'm going to make it hard for you to resist me." I kiss her once more, before hopping out of bed. "Now, I'm going to go make us some breakfast. Jackson and Ember will be up soon." Leaning down over the bed, I kiss her forehead, then turn and walk out of the room.

CHAPTER 29

My eyes follow Blaise as he walks out of my room. So much has happened. Blaise says he wants me. The look in those silver eyes of his says he does. His actions say he does. Can the playboy commit? Can I? It's only been four months since my parents' death and the death of my relationship with Josh. UGH! Why does life have to be so damn complicated? Last night, I wanted one night with him. Just one night to forget the pain. Do I get that? No! Instead, I get Blaise and his gentle caresses begging me to let him in.

My heart wants that, wants to let his sweet words and gentle kisses take over. My head is telling me it's a bad idea. Sighing with frustration, I head for the shower; maybe that will clear my head.

After my shower, I feel refreshed, but my head is still a jumbled mess and my heart is still screaming to trust Blaise. I make my way to the kitchen and find Blaise at the stove making pancakes. Ember and Jackson are sitting around the table, already eating.

"Good morning, roomie," Ember says cheerily.

"Good morning," I say.

I stop at the counter and pour a glass of orange juice. Blaise reaches around me and sets a plate full of pancakes in front of me. He leans down and kisses my cheek. No words are said. He goes right back to the stove and continues making breakfast. My face is burning with embarrassment. I'm not used to the attention, not publicly; that wasn't Josh, at least not with me.

I grab the bottle of syrup and douse my plate before joining Ember and Jackson at the table. I know they're watching me. I don't make eye contact. Instead, I focus all of my attention on the mouthwatering pancakes Blaise has created.

Ember bumps her shoulder with mine. "I don't know what you did to my brother to bring that smile to his face, but whatever it was, keep it up." She sits back in her seat and cuts a big bite of pancake. Her hand stills in the air. "I hope he makes breakfast every time he stays over. We may have to move him in," she teases.

"Hey! I can make a mean pancake myself." Jackson fake pouts.

Blaise joins us at the table, taking the seat next to me. "Good, next time it's your turn so Tate and I can sleep in," he says without missing a beat. He looks at me and winks.

He did say he was going to make it hard for me to resist him.

The pancakes are as delicious as they smell and soon all four of our plates are empty. Jackson cleans the kitchen since Blaise cooked. Ember and I try to help, but he pushes us away.

"Let us take care of you," he tells us.

Ember smiles sweetly at him and pats him on the ass. I, on the other hand, am having a hard time accepting it all. Brent and my father are the only two men I know who treat the women in their lives like precious gifts. I know men like that are out there. However, what are the odds of Ember and I having found them. Of course, it's her brother and his friend, but still. To find a man like that, it's a rarity. My mom always used to say I needed to hold out to find a man to love me like Daddy loved her, and mutual respect and love were key ingredients to a relationship. Tears spring to my eyes at the thought of them. Would my parents approve of Blaise? Would I have ever met him if not for the move and the events leading up to it?

Suddenly, I need air. I can't let them see me cry. Let him see me cry. Not again. I grab my keys and cell from the hall table. "I'm going out for a walk. Be back in a little while," I say as I walk out the door.

The apartment complex is amazing. Not only do we have a pool, we also have a garden area. I make my way to the garden and find a shade tree, a weeping willow. Fitting. I rest my back against the tree. There is a slight breeze blowing; that with the shade of the tree, is relief from what is looking to be a hot July day in Tennessee.

I hear footsteps and I know it's him. I don't have to look; the connection we share is so strong it's scary. I've never had that.

Blaise sits down beside me and leans up against the tree. He holds out his hand for me to take. "Come here," he says quietly.

I scoot closer to him. The next thing I know, his hands are on my hips and he has me between his legs, my back against his chest. His arms wrap around me and I settle against him. Blaise kisses the top of my head. We sit there in the quiet, just being. He doesn't try to make me talk; he just holds me.

Breaking the silence, I say, "I was in class when I got the call. It was a nurse from the hospital. All she would tell me was my parents were involved in an accident. I had no idea what happened or even if they were okay." I pause to rein in my emotions. This will be the first time I've ever told the entire story, and I want to tell Blaise. "The college was close to the hospital so it didn't take me long to get there. I went straight to the ER and asked for them. I could tell by the look on the receptionist face that it wasn't good. I was scared. She led me into a room and said she would get the doctor. I didn't have to wait long. I remember he tried to get me to sit down, but I couldn't. I kept my back against the wall and my legs were trembling. My parents were traveling home from settling my grandmother's estate. They were a day earlier than I expected. Dad was driving on a winding road. They were on an uphill stretch going around a curve when a semi coming the opposite direction lost its load. The trailer swung over into my parents' lane." I stop to compose myself. My tears are causing a lump in my throat at the thought of what my parents went through. Blaise doesn't speak. His arms remain tight around me, holding me to him. His embrace brings me comfort. "The detective said it happened so fast that Dad didn't have time to react. Their car hit the tractor trailer head on. He also said they didn't suffer; they died on impact. They were pronounced dead at the scene, but they had to bring them to the hospital to the coroner."

Blaise lifts me in his lap. I'm sitting sideways. He guides my head to rest on his shoulder while gently rocking me. He still doesn't say a word. His s

My throat is sore and my eyes burn from the tears, but I want to finish. "I remember being on the floor, feeling the walls closing in on me. My parents were gone. I'm an only child and so were my parents. I had just lost my last living grandparent two months prior. All I could think about was getting to Josh." I feel Blaise stiffen, but he still doesn't say anything. He just holds me tight, allowing me to draw from his strength. "I ran out of the hospital. The doctor was yelling for me, but I didn't stop. I needed to be with someone who cared about me. I drove to Josh's apartment. I don't remember much of the drive. He wasn't supposed to be there. I knew he had class, but I wanted to be there when he got home. He had been trying to convince me to move in with him, but I just wasn't ready. Our relationship was different. Anyway, he had given me a key. I didn't have to use it because the door was unlocked. It didn't dawn on me at the time that the door was actually unlocked." I pause allowing him to process what I've said so far. I nuzzle closer to him and I feel his muscles relax for the first time since I mentioned Josh.

"I opened the apartment door and got the second dose of tragic events for the day. Josh was in the living room having sex with some blonde bimbo. He had her leaned over the back of the couch. What happened after that is really inconsequential. I yelled, and he tried to tell me it wasn't what it looked like. As I was leaving, he tried to stop me. His neighbor heard the yelling and stepped out into the hall. He stood in Josh's way so I could leave."

I sit up and sit on my knees beside him, facing him so I can seek out his silver eyes. "That brings me to now. Leah and Brent were moving here for Brent's new job. Leah has been my best friend since kindergarten. There was nothing left for me in Ohio. Leah and Brent sat me down and convinced me to move here with them. I closed up my parents' house, and here I am."

Blaise reaches for my hand. I take it. "Stand up, Tatum," he says, his voice low and gruff. I do as he asks without question. He tugs on my hands and guides me so I'm now sitting on his lap facing him. He places his hands on my cheeks and wipes away my tears with his thumbs. "Thank you. Thank you for trusting me, for letting me in."

I'm speechless. He's right. I haven't even told Leah the entire story. It was always too painful; I didn't want to relive it. Today, well, I just needed to talk. Blaise was there for me.

He moves one hand to the back of my neck and pulls me close. "Hey you," he says, a soft smile gracing his lips. "You might want to close your eyes for this."

"For what?" I ask, confused.

"For this." He leans forward and his warm breath caresses my lips. Slowly tracing them with his tongue, gently nipping. All I can do is close my eyes and relish the sensation his lips and tongue are causing. His hold on me is gentle, yet firm. He wants me to know he's not done with me yet. His free hand slips under my shirt as he softly traces my side, causing my body to shiver from the sensation. His hand comes close to my breast and I long for him to touch me, but he doesn't. His touch is driving me insane. He moves his lips from mine and slowly kisses a soft trail down my neck. I tilt my head, allowing him access. His soft lips cause a shiver of pleasure to run through me.

Way too soon for my liking, Blaise ends his assault on my senses. He rests his forehead against mine. "Best day ever," he says.

I can't help it, I laugh. I know he's trying to lighten the mood and I'm grateful. I lean forward, place my arms around his neck, and hug him. "Thank you," I whisper, my lips next to his ear.

Blaise squeezes me tight. "Ready to head back?"

Pulling back, I say, "Yes." I hop off his lap. He gets to his feet and laces his fingers through mine. We walk back to the apartment without speaking, no words are necessary after what we just shared.

CHAPTER 30

BLAISE

Today is Monday and I'm starting a twenty-four hour shift at the firehouse. Yesterday, after Tatum told me about her parents and the dickhead Josh, we spent the day together. We watched a few movies, and later that night, Jackson and I put some steaks on the grill. Jackson seems to be really into Ember. I'm happy for them. Things with Tatum are good. I didn't hold back yesterday. I constantly found reasons to touch her. When I left, she walked me to the door and I stole a quick kiss. Nothing like the one under the willow tree, but a kiss from her sweet lips all the same. My ass is dragging today. I tossed and turned all night, and after not sleeping Saturday night, I feel like a zombie. I couldn't stop thinking about Tatum. What if she had a bad dream and called out for me? I wasn't there to hold her.

As a volunteer on the department, I'm not required to report until they actually need me. Most of the time, I spend the day here and hang out with Dad. We clean the trucks, inspect equipment, and things like that. The full-time guys have other duties, but not me. I'm going to check in with Dad and the guys, then hit the bunks. Hopefully, I can get a few hours of sleep.

I walk into Dad's office and stop in my tracks. Tatum is sitting across from his desk.

She looks up when she hears me walk in and a smile lights up her face. That smile, all for me. I want to push my chest out and spread my feathers like a proud peacock. That smile makes me feel as though I can conquer the world.

I walk straight to her, thoughts of saying hi to Dad and catching some sleep forgotten. Once I reach her, I bend down and place a kiss on her cheek while whispering in her ear, "Hey you." This day just got a whole hell of a lot better.

143

Dad clears his throat.

I stand up to my full height and move to stand behind Tatum. I place my hands on her shoulders and begin to gently rub.

Dad smirks. He knows the deal. He's the one who told me to go for it. "Harry sent Tatum over to talk about fundraising ideas for the department," he tells me.

Tatum looks over her shoulder at me. "We were just brainstorming ideas."

Dad's phone chimes. He picks it up and swipes the screen. "Shoot. I forgot some of the guys and I are supposed to be doing a presentation at the local YMCA to the summer camp. I'm sorry, Tatum. Can we reschedule this?"

Tatum waves her hand in the air. "It's fine. I just popped in at the suggestion of Harry. Call me when you get back and we can reserve a time to meet," she tells him.

"Thank you," he says as he grabs his phone and keys before heading out the door.

I walk in front of Tatum and pull her up out of the chair. As soon as she's up, I have her in my arms. "I missed you," I tell her.

She laughs. "Blaise, you left last night at ten o'clock. We spent the day together. How could you miss me already?" she asks me.

"I missed this," I tell her, pulling her back into my embrace. "I didn't sleep last night. I wanted to be with you." I'm not going to hold back with her.

Tatum sighs. "Blaise, we're not…I'm not sure I can do this."

"Take all the time you need. I'm not going anywhere," I say with conviction.

Tatum reaches up and places her soft hand on my cheek. I didn't shave today. She runs her hands over the stubble. "You look tired, B.," she says.

I nod my head yes. I'm exhausted. I just need to be able to actually fall asleep, and then I would be good to go. That's when the idea hits me. "What time do you have to be back?" I ask her.

She shrugs her shoulders. "No rush. There's not a lot going on today. I don't have any other meetings. Maybe a couple hours or so."

"Can you do something for me, with me?" I ask.

"Yes," she answers with no hesitation whatsoever. She has no idea what I'm even going to ask and she said yes.

"I'm on call, but since I'm volunteer, I'm not required to be here. I just have to report if there's a run." She nods her head in understanding.

"Would you mind following me home and laying with me until I fall asleep? No funny business, I promise. I just…want you to stay until I fall asleep." I don't say I need her next to me or how after only one night of her in my arms, I ache to have her there again. No, I won't tell her that. I want her to agree to this.

"Just until you fall asleep?" she clarifies.

"Yes. I just want you to lie with me, and then you can go." I turn my head and place a soft kiss on the palm of her hand.

"Okay. I'll just follow you there?"

I immediately embrace her against my chest. "Thank you, baby," I say before releasing her and walking her to her car.

As I'm opening her door for her, I yawn. Damn, I'm beat. I wait for her to get inside before I shut the door. I watch as she buckles her belt before walking away. I've seen too many accidents from being on the department. Safety first.

Even though I'm exhausted, I practically run to my truck. Tatum in my arms, in my bed. I can't get there fast enough.

CHAPTER 31

As I follow Blaise to his house, I call Leah to take my mind off what I'm about to do.

"Hey girl! Aren't you supposed to be at work?" she says in greeting.

"Hey. Yeah, I am, but Harry asked me to meet with the fire chief to discuss fundraising," I tell her.

"So did you see Blaise while you were there, or is he even there? He's only volunteer right?" she fires questions at me.

"Uh, yeah he was there. I'm actually on my way to his place." Might as well get it out there. Maybe she can talk some sense into me before I get there.

"Okay…And why are you on your way to his place?" Leah asks.

"Funny story. Steve had a meeting; I just popped in at Harry's insistence. Blaise was there and he asked me to stop by for a while." I'm being vague and I know she can tell. She's about to call my ass out. I can tell by the sounds she's making.

"Are you going to share with me the meaning of this little field trip?"

"Uh…well…Blaise, he said he didn't sleep well last night and he sorta said it was because he slept with me the night before."

"Holy shit! You're gone two whole days and I miss all the good stuff. Start talking missy," she instructs me.

"When we left the bar Saturday night, I fell asleep in the truck. I tried to seduce him; he shot me down. I cried at his rejection. He said it was because he wants more from me and then I asked him to stay.

He held me all night; the end," I say in a rush. Partly because I want to get it out and over with and partly because I'm afraid Leah will interrupt me and we're getting close to his place.

"And?" she asks. Leah knows me so well.

"And last night, he claims he couldn't sleep. He asked if I would come home with him and lie with him just until he falls asleep. I said yes," I mumble the last part.

"I knew I liked that guy," Leah gloats.

"Wait. What? You're supposed to talk me out of this. Tell me I'm crazy and this is all too soon."

"That is so not happening. Tate, you have been through so much these last few months. You've spent time with him. You work with his mom. You live with his sister. I have a good feeling about this. Blaise is one of the good ones."

"I thought Josh was a good one too," I remind her.

"Josh was a dick. You guys were hardly together. He never once looked at you the way Blaise does."

I let the last comment slide. "My heart can't take any more. I'm afraid the next time, I won't be able to bounce back."

"Tatum Marie Thompson. Life is filled with heartbreak. You have lived through more than most, but you survived. You're strong and you have to open yourself up to the possibility of the pain to find the true happiness. They would want you to find love, a love like they shared. I have a good feeling about Blaise. He could be the one your mom was always talking about," she says gently.

"He fixed me breakfast. Yesterday, while I was showering, he made me breakfast."

"See, like I said, a good one. How many times did Josh make you breakfast?"

I don't answer and I don't have to. Leah knows the answer. Never. Josh wasn't a real affectionate guy.

Blaise pulls into his driveway and I pull in behind him. "Leah, I just pulled in. So I've gotta go," I say quickly as I watch Blaise climb out of his truck.

"Okay, be safe and follow your heart. Tell your head to fuck off," she instructs me.

"Love you, Leah." I hit end on my phone just as Blaise opens my door. He holds his hand out of for me. I place mine in his and he helps me out of the car. He leads me to the front door.

"Asher and I live here together, but lately he's been at Grace's more than he's here. It's been weeks since he's actually stayed here," he explains.

The house is a brick ranch with a two car attached garage. He leads me inside and it's not what I was expecting. The house is clean and inviting. You can tell two bachelors live here, but at the same time, it feels like a home.

"I want to show you around, and I will. But right now, I just want you in my arms," he says, leading me down a long hallway. His room is decorated much like what I've seen of the rest of the house. White walls, tan carpet. He has a black and cream bedspread that covers his massive king sized bed.

Blaise kicks off his shoes and pulls his shirt over his head. He pulls his pager, which I assume is because he is on call and his cell phone out of his pants pocket. He empties the other pocket, which consists of his money clip. He unbuttons his jeans and lets them slide to the floor.

Holy freaking hotness! Blaise in boxer briefs is a site to behold. Surely this is to be an experience I will never forget. His colorful tattoos encasing his arms and his eight pack; yes, I said eight. My eyes make their way to the V of his hips and I lick my lips.

"Tate, as much as I want to stand here and let you keep fucking me with those beautiful green eyes of yours, I'm dead on my feet." He comes to stand beside me. "Kick off your shoes," he whispers.

At this point, I would walk around and cluck like a damn chicken just to be able to keep looking at him. He truly is male perfection at its finest. I do as I'm told and kick off my shoes. I'm wearing khaki pants and a short sleeve sweater. I briefly wonder if he's going to ask me to take those off as well.

"Do you need something to lay down in so you don't wrinkle your clothes? You have to go back to work right?" he asks. "Wait," he says.

He quickly walks to the other side of the bed and picks up his phone. I have no idea what he's doing and really I don't care. I'm just taking in the view. I hear him say Harry and I try to focus on the conversation. I hear Blaise tell Harry he ran into me at the firehouse and his dad had a meeting. He proceeds to tell him he has a lot of ideas for fundraising and asked if I could join him." Harry says something I cannot hear. Then Blaise says, "Great, thanks so much, Harry. I'll tell her." He hits end on his phone and places it back on the nightstand. Walking to his dresser, he pulls out a t-shirt and tosses it to me. I hold it up. It's a Murfreesboro Fire t-shirt; on the back is says RICHARDS.

"Harry was thrilled we're working together on fundraising ideas. He said after we're done, to take the rest of the day off. He's says things are slow," Blaise informs me.

"But…I can't just miss work," I reason.

"You can. Boss's orders. Harry is a great guy to work for. Besides, Mom says you are so efficient that you have everything organized and running like a well-oiled machine. It's just one day," he says.

I hold the t-shirt up. "And this?" I ask.

Blaise is at my side in two long steps. "This is my shirt. I want you to be comfortable. I want you to stay with me today. I really do have some fundraising ideas, but more importantly, I just want to spend the day with you." He runs his hands up and down my arms. "I'm going to go get a bottle of water while you change. Can I get you anything?" he asks.

"Water, please." And just like that, my decision is made. I want to spend the day with him, too. I want to feel that peacefulness I feel every time I'm in his arms, and it looks like I'm going to be doing it in his shirt.

CHAPTER 32

BLAISE

I leave the room so she can change. I thought for sure she would fight me. I really do just want her to be comfortable and well, I want to see her in my clothes. The thought of her in my shirt causes my dick to twitch. Shit, this is not what I need. She's not ready and I'm exhausted. I meant what I said; I need for her to be able to give me everything. I want all of her. I'm not sleeping with her until I get it. Yes, it sounds crazy. I know this, but Tatum is different. I already know from just the taste of her lips that one night would never be enough.

I take my time in the kitchen, giving Tatum plenty of time to change. The bowl and spoon from my morning cereal is in the sink so I wash them quickly. The laundry room is just off the kitchen so I fold the load of towels I washed last night.

Not willing to wait any longer, I retrace my steps back to the bedroom. As I walk through the door, I see Tatum standing beside the bed wearing my shirt. She's holding a picture of my family, the five of us. It was taken at last year's Fourth of July party. The sight of her takes my breath away. I take her in. The shirt, my shirt, the one that has my last name sprawled across the back is now the only thing covering Tatum. My eyes continue onward. I'm trying to memorize everything, how the shirt ends and the creamy soft skin of her legs begins.

My fingers are tingling and my arms are aching to hold her. My heart flutters in my chest. I know it's soon and I know it sounds fucking crazy as hell, but I'm in love with this girl. As if she knows what I'm thinking, Tatum places the picture back on the nightstand and turns to face me, a slight blush covering her cheeks.

She smiles softly. "It's a little big," she says, pulling at the hem of my shirt.

I go to her because, really, not touching her when she's here with me like this is just not possible. "You make it look good," I tell her, placing a kiss on her temple. "You know what else you do?" I whisper in her ear.

She shakes her head telling me she doesn't. "What?" she asks so softly I almost don't hear her.

I reach for her hand and lay it flat on my chest, over my heart. "You make my heart beat a little faster," I tell her.

Her beautiful green eyes light up at my admission. Not only are my words affecting her, but she can feel the steady rhythm against the palm of her hand. She does that to me, only Tatum.

I run my finger down her cheek. "Lay with me?" I don't wait for an answer; I pull back the covers and motion for her to climb in. I climb in after her and pull the comforter up over us. I have blackout blinds in my room for nights I'm up all night on a run with the department. The room is in complete darkness since I shut the door when I came back from the kitchen.

Tatum rolls over, facing the window, her back to me. I place my arm around her and bring her back against my chest. Immediately, all tension leaves my body. This feels right. It hits me that Tatum is the first girl to ever be in my bed, in my home. I bought this place after Beth and I broke up. I've never brought anyone here, just family and Grace, of course, but she falls into the family category. This is my home; it's sacred. The thought of using it as a place to "hook up" taints the idea of home for me. Heather and I were usually at hotels since she was traveling; if not, we were always at her place. She never wanted to come here, and I never invited her.

No one meant enough to me to share my home with them. Tatum is stiff beside me. I want to reassure her she's different. That I'm different with her.

"You're the first," I say into the darkness.

"The first for what?"

"The first in this bed, in my home. I've never brought anyone here." I let that sink in before I say, "You're different, Tatum. I will fight every day until you understand what you mean to me. I know this is fast, but my heart tells me this is right."

She doesn't respond for a long time. I feel her relax in my arms and her breathing evens out. We lay in silence for so long I'm beginning to wonder if she's fallen asleep, but then I hear her sweet voice.

"The last few months have been hard for me. There were days when I would have to force myself to get out of bed and keep moving." She pauses. "Then I met you and your family. Your mom reminds me so much of my own, and your dad, he's great. Ember and I have so much in common, and Asher and Grace always make me feel welcome."

I wait for her to mention me; she doesn't. She named off each member of my immediate family and how amazing they are, but nothing about me. Not one to avoid the elephant in the room, I ask, "And me?"

"You…" She stops and I feel her take a deep breath, her chest rising and falling. I try to pull her closer to me, I can never get her close enough, and my hand slips under her shirt. I know I should move it, but I can't; well, I don't want to. Instead, I trace my fingers across her flat belly. Releasing her breath she says, "You're changing me. We seem to have this connection I can't explain. I wake up excited to see if I'll run into you. The future doesn't look as lonely and scary as it did before. You make me feel better about life. You make life better," she tells me.

I don't say anything. Not because I don't want to, but because I can't. The raw emotion in her voice. The conviction that she really feels her life is better because of me. I swallow hard against the lump in my throat. I tighten my hold on her and kiss her cheek. This is what I've been missing. Never again will I give Asher a hard time about his protectiveness with Grace. I get it. When you meet "the one," shit gets real.

This is crazy. This intense feeling of peace and satisfaction I get just from being with her. I've only know her a few months, and I'm sure many might think I've lost my fucking mind, and in a way I have. It belongs to her. All of me belongs to her. I want to shout it from the rooftops, but I won't. I need her to catch up before I go pouring my heart out.

I feel her breathing even out and her body relax. She's asleep, here in my arms. That's the last thing I remember as I drift off to sleep.

CHAPTER 33

I waken by the sound of a muffled curse. "Shit." I sit up in bed and my eyes adjust to my surroundings. There is faint light seeping in from the hallway. I blink a couple times and focus my gaze on Blaise. He's tiptoeing around his room, obviously trying not to wake me. He stubs his toe, I can only assume, for at least the second time and a whispered, "Fuck," falls from his lips. I can't help but chuckle.

Blaise whips his head in my direction. I'm able to make out the smile on his face even through the dim lighting. "Hey you," he says softly, making his way to the bed. He sits down next to me and places his hand on my hip. "I'm sorry I woke you. I was really trying not to," he says.

I cover my mouth as I yawn. "Where are you going?" I ask. He's fully clothed. I guess that means it's my time to leave.

I throw the covers off and start to scoot to the end of the bed. Blaise places a hand on my leg to stop me. His touch against my bare skin sends shockwaves through me. "What are you doing?" he questions me. He sounds pissed off. Really? He's the one leaving.

I gesture to his now fully clothed body. "I assume it's time for me to go," I tell him while scowling at his shirt and jeans.

Blaise is shaking his head in protest. "Tate, I have a run." He holds up his pager. "There is a field fire just out of town. I'm on call, remember?" He gently runs a finger down the curve of my jaw, then his big hands are cupping my cheeks. He runs his thumb over my bottom lip. "Today is the first time I've ever had ill thoughts toward my status with the department. It took everything in me to leave you in bed alone." He places one hand behind my neck and brings my lips close to his. "I was hoping I could be back before you missed me and slip back into bed with you." His lips claim mine. The kiss is gentle; he doesn't push and I'm happy to just feel his lips against mine.

Pulling away, he rests his forehead against mine. "Stay," he whispers.

"I shouldn't. It wouldn't feel right without you here," I tell him. I can see the disappointment in his silver pools. I hate that I've disappointed him. "Call me if it's not too late, and maybe we can grab dinner." The words slip from my tongue effortlessly.

He releases a heavy sigh. "I'll take what I can get." He hands me his phone. I quickly program my number.

"I really need to go. I'm going to have to meet them at the scene as it is." He gives me a quick chaste kiss. "Thank you for today. I like you in my bed." He winks. "Stay as long as you want; help yourself to whatever you need. I'll call you as soon as I can." Dropping another kiss on my temple, he turns and walks out the door.

I throw myself back on the bed and stare up at the ceiling. What am I doing here, in Blaise's bed in nothing but his t-shirt? One look from those silver eyes and I'm weak in the knees. He's says I'm the first one to be here. I can't help but smile at that.

Climbing out of bed, I slowly remove his t-shirt and put my clothes back on. I look at the bed, and I swear I can still feel his arms around me. I decide to make the bed. Blaise was exhausted before this; I can only imagine how tired he will be when he gets back. I make my way into the kitchen and grab a bottle of water. There is a small dry erase board hanging on the fridge. I decide to leave him a note.

Blaise
Call me when you get
in if you're not too
tired.
xoxo
Tatum

Back at the apartment, I find Ember curled up on the couch with her Kindle. "Hey, how was your day?" she asks me.

"Good. I actually went to the firehouse this morning to meet with your dad about marketing ideas, but he had another meeting. Harry told me to just drop in, so he wasn't expecting me," I tell her.

Ember beams. "I love going there; as kids, Dad would take us all the time. Asher and Blaise loved it just as much; they both always said they would volunteer one day."

"Yeah, so I saw Blaise while I was there." I decide to just get it out there.

"Really? And how is my big brother?" she asks.

I shrug. "He seemed exhausted." I dig my phone out of my pocket when I feel it vibrate. Maybe it's Blaise. Swiping the screen, no such luck, just an e-mail.

"Did you talk to him?" Ember asks me.

"What are you reading?" I ask changing the subject.

"Vision of Love. Did you talk to him?" she asks again.

I can't lie to her. "Yeah, he um...well, he actually called Harry and told him he had some marketing ideas he wanted to discuss with me as well. Harry said to meet with Blaise and then take the rest of the day off."

Ember looks at her watch. "I guess that's why you're home early. Blaise must have talked your head off. You said you went to see Dad first thing, right?"

I nod my head. I can't keep skirting around the details when I know she will find out sooner rather than later, especially if Blaise calls when he gets home. I decide to say it. "Blaise actually asked me back to his place." I try to sound casual.

Ember quirks an eyebrow. "Really?" I shake my head yes.

"He's really into you, Tatum. Blaise doesn't invite anyone to his place, ever." Her voice is serious.

Again, I nod my head. "Yeah, he told me that as well."

"So, what happened? Don't worry about it being my brother; I can see you're dying to talk about it. I like the idea of the two of you together. Spill it," she says, shaking her finger at me.

I release the breath I didn't even realize I was holding. "So, Blaise basically said that after holding me in his arms Saturday, he couldn't sleep last night. He said he was exhausted and asked if I would come home with him and lay with him until he fell asleep," I say in a rush, staring down at my hands. Relieved it's out there, but still nervous of Ember's reaction.

Ember doesn't say anything. I look up to see her sitting there with a dumfounded look on her face. She opens and closes her mouth a couple of times to reply, but nothing comes out.

"Ember?"

"Tatum, my brother's in love with you," she says pointedly.

"What? That's crazy talk. He just had a hard time sleeping, that's all," I try to reason.

She's shaking her head no before I even finish. "Blaise doesn't do stuff like that. This is a side of my brother I have never seen before. Well, I have, but only from Asher." She sits up and pats the couch beside her.

I take the invitation and join her on the couch. "Tatum, Blaise is different with you. He touches you every chance he gets. He follows you with his eyes, like you're his last meal. I've never see him this way. Asher used to be the same way; no outward displays of affection, until he met Grace."

"Okay, I can see that, but saying he's in love with me, that's a little farfetched, don't ya think?" I ask her.

She chuckles, "When the Richards men know, they just know. Our dad swears he fell in love with my mom the moment he met her. Asher has a similar story with Grace."

"He can't…I'm not…"

Ember places her hand on my shoulder. "Take your time; you'll get there," she says with a knowing smile.

My phone vibrates and I quickly swipe the screen. It's Leah letting me know she's going to e-mail me a few websites for destination weddings to look at.

"Is there something else going on?" Ember asks. "You jumped when your phone went off, and you seem disappointed at whatever it is."

I can feel my face heat with embarrassment. "Blaise was called out on a run. He said he would call if it wasn't too late. I also left him a note telling him to call if he wasn't too tired. I just…How do you and your mom handle it? How do you not drive yourselves crazy over worrying about their safety?" I ask her. I know I pretty much just laid my cards out on the table, too late to take them back.

She pulls her leg up on the couch and rests her head on her knees. "It's hard, but at the same time, I'm so fucking proud of all three of them. They save lives. What they do is dangerous and heroic, but I thank God every day there are men and women just like them. You just have to remember they are trained professionals."

She raises her eyes to meet mine. "Life inevitably throws us curve balls blazing with unexpected circumstances. Living life, taking risks." She shrugs. "It's something we all have to do in order to understand the miracle of it all; only then do true miracles happen. The best things in life are truly unexpected."

"Not always," I whisper. "Losing my parents was unexpected," I reply.

Ember's eyes mist with emotion. "I'm so sorry you lost them. I'm here if you ever want to talk. We don't know what the greater plan is, and yes, some things, tragedy and death, are unexpected and cause pain. However, that pain brought you here, to my family. You are quickly becoming my closest friend and my brother's in love with you."

I scoff at that. She laughs.

"Okay, my brother is falling in love with you. That pain brought you to us, and you bring so much happiness into our lives." She reaches over and wraps her arms around me. "I'm glad you're here," she tells me.

As she releases me, my phone vibrates.

Blaise: On my way back to you.

A grin spreads across my face at his words. I hear Ember sigh. I look up to see she's looking at my phone. "I told you so," she says with a cocky smile that reminds me so much of Blaise.

Me: I'm back at the apartment.

Blaise: *Dinner?*

Me: When and where?

Blaise: My place. I'll pick you up in ten.

I scramble off the couch, running to my room to change. I drop my phone in the process. Ember must have read the messages from Blaise because she starts singing, "Blaise and Tatum sitting in a tree, k-i-s-s-i-n-g." That's as far as she gets before she stops to yell, "I told you so," at the top of her lungs.

CHAPTER 34

BLAISE

I told Tatum ten minutes when really I was only a couple minutes from pulling into her building. She said it wouldn't feel right staying at my place without me there, so I headed here instead.

I reach the apartment door and hear Ember bust out in song. I smile at my little sister. She has a great personality. The song she's singing is one we used to taunt our friends with on the playground; it's obvious Ember is a kindergarten teacher.

I knock on the door, but they evidently don't hear. I reach into my pocket and pull out my keys. Asher and I both have a spare, as Ember does for our place. I slide the key in the lock and walk in just in time to hear Ember yell, "I told you so."

"Who did you tell what?" I ask, startling her.

She flips her head around and a huge grin lights up her face. "Well hello there, big brother. I thought your ETA was ten minutes," she chides me.

I chuckle. "I might have already been enroute and didn't want to sound too eager," I tell her. It's not like she hasn't already figured out I want Tatum to be mine.

"Did you not think showing up two minutes later would be a dead giveaway?" she asks.

"Honestly, I didn't think about it, and I don't care. I just didn't want to scare her into changing her mind about having dinner at my place," I tell her. "Who did you tell what?" I repeat my earlier question.

"I told Tatum you were falling hard for her. The last ten minutes proves I'm right," she says smirking.

I give her my "duh" look. "It's not like I'm trying to hide it," I say.

Before Ember can respond, Tatum walks in the room pulling her hair up into a mop of messy sexiness on top of her head. "Em, I need my…" she trails off once she looks up and her eyes find mine.

I'm at her side in two long steps. I place my hand on her hip and pull her against me, kissing her temple. "Hey you," I say softly.

"Hey, you got here fast," she says, green eyes sparkling.

"I may have already been just around the corner," I tell her. "You ready to head out?"

"Yes, I just need my phone," she says, holding her hand out to my sister.

Ember throws her head back and laughs as she places Tatum's phone in her hand.

Tatum slides the phone in her back pocket. "Wait, we're just hanging out at your place, right?" she asks me as she looks down at her outfit. She's wearing short blue jean shorts, a white tank top, and white flip-flops. Her hair is pulled up in bundled mess on top of her head and she looks sexy as hell.

"Yes, I was just going to throw some steaks on the grill, but we can do whatever you want," I say.

"Okay, good. I guess I'm all set. I can drive though, so you don't have to bring me home."

"Who say's you'll be back tonight?" Ember says under her breath, but loud enough we both hear her.

My hand falls from her hip and finds her hand. I lace our fingers together. "I can bring you home or you can stay. It's your choice, but I will be driving you. I want to spend as much time with you as I can," I tell her. I sound like a fucking pansy, and I've given Asher hell over being the same exact way with Grace. Now I get it. I understand what it feels like to not give a fuck what it sounds like or who's riding your ass about it as long as it has my girl's face lighting up like it is at this exact moment.

We say goodbye to Ember and I lead her outside to my truck. I lift her inside and wait until she's safely buckled in before shutting her door.

"How did it go?" she asks as soon as we are on the road.

Keeping my eyes on the road and my hands tightly gripping the wheel. "Good. Old man Sampson was trying to burn some boxes and caught his yard on fire."

"I hope everyone's okay."

Not able to control it any longer, I reach over and grab her hand. "No one was hurt. We were able to easily extinguish the fire."

Tatum's chewing on her lip. "Hey, you okay?" I ask her.

She nods her head. "It's just, what you do, it's scary."

"Yes, at times. I've had extensive training, and I like being able to help people." I glance over and see she's staring out the window. Was she worried about me?

I pull into my drive and turn off the truck. I release her hand and quickly walk to her side to help her down. I lift her and hold her by the hips mid-air so we are eye level. "Hey you," I say. That earns me a smile. I slowly settle her feet on the ground. Placing my finger under her chin, I lift her eyes to meet mine. "I'm okay."

Tatum nods and wraps her arms around my waist. I feel something shift inside me. This girl wrecks me. "Let's get you fed."

I lead her into the house. "Make yourself at home. I'm going to fire up the grill."

"What can I do to help?"

I stop and turn to face her. I wait for her eyes to lock with mine. "You being here is all I need." No words have ever been truer.

Tate smiles and my heart sputters. She's beautiful. "What else are we having?" she asks.

"I thought I would pull together a salad and throw a couple of potatoes on with the steaks," I say as I open the patio door to light the grill that's on the back deck.

As I'm lighting the grill, I hear the patio door open. Tatum steps up beside me holding two platters. One has the steaks seasoned and ready to place on the grill, the other is holding three baked potatoes wrapped in aluminum foil.

I lean down and place a kiss on her forehead. "Thank you, sweets." I take the dishes from her and get busy making dinner.

I stand outside with the grill; I'm nervous. I know I have no reason to be, but I want everything perfect. I don't want her to regret her time here. The door sliding open catches my attention. I turn and watch as Tatum walks toward me. Her feet are now bare. She scrunches her nose a little as they touch the hot deck surface. The sun is starting to set, but it was hot today. When she reaches me she hands me a beer. "Here, thought you could use this." She pulls her hand back. "Wait, are you still on call?" she asks.

Could this girl be any more amazing? "No, my shift ended at five. I was only covering for one of the full timers for a few hours."

Tatum walks to the end of the deck and rests her arms on the railing looking out over the backyard. When I started looking at houses, I had planned on proposing to Beth. Once she dropped her dirty laundry all over the place, I continued to look. I was no longer getting married, but I wanted a home. This place has ten acres and a pond in the backyard. Tatum stares off in the distance, watching the sun slowly set.

I set my beer on the table and walk to her. I slowly step behind her. She glances over her shoulder and smiles. "Great view," she says, turning back toward the sunset.

I close the short distance between us, place my arms around her waist, pulling her back against my chest. I bury my face in her neck and breathe her in. Her sweet smell surrounds me. "You smell so fucking good."

She chuckles lightly. "It's the steak you smell."

"Yeah, the food smells great, but that's not it. Your sweet scent, a mix of vanilla and something uniquely you, is intoxicating."

Reluctantly, I pull away. I walk back to the grill and adjust myself as I do. There is no way she didn't feel what she does to me.

"Are we eating out here or inside?" she asks.

"I'm good either way; it's up to you."

Tatum nods her head and walks back into the house.

I remove the steaks and the potatoes from the grill and take them inside. I assume since Tatum didn't come back out that she wants to eat in here. I make my way in the kitchen and the table is set with everything we need. She's just sitting a bowl of salad in the middle of the table. "I figured since you worked out in the heat today, not to mention the heat from the fire, I thought you might like to just enjoy being in the air," she says as she walks back to the fridge and pulls out a gallon of tea. I raise my eyebrows because I didn't have any tea.

She pours two tall glasses and brings them to the table. "I made tea. I hope that's okay."

I nod my head. "I want you to feel comfortable here. Whatever you want, it's yours."

We both make our plates and dig in. We're quiet for the most part, but it's not uncomfortable. We are both obviously starving. Tate does manage to tell me how good it is between bites. It doesn't take us long to devour our meal. I stand to clean up as does she. "You go sit down and relax; I got this."

"Yeah, not gonna happen. You cooked, it's the least I can do," she fires back.

"You're my guest. It won't take but a few minutes. Really, go sit down."

"Well, just think about how fast we'll get it done if we do it together?" she says as she snaps the lid back on the butter and places it in the fridge.

I don't want to argue with her. I want to take care of her; she deserves nothing less. I decide to choose my battles and let her help, and she's right, we're done in no time.

CHAPTER 35

Dinner was great and so is the company. It takes no time for me and Blaise to get the kitchen squared away. I like being here with him, doing simple daily things together. This is something Josh and I never did. I still lived at home, so there wasn't a lot of privacy. When we did get to see each other, Josh always wanted to go out. I'm finding I really enjoy a quiet night in.

"It's getting late," I say to Blaise. I watch as his face falls. He doesn't want me to leave. I want to stay; I really do. The thought of curling up against him with his arms tight around me is so damn tempting, but I can't. This is too much too fast. I need to reel myself in a little.

Blaise releases a heavy breath. "Let's get you home." He grabs his keys and cell from the counter and leads the way to his truck. The drive back to my apartment is fast, faster than I would have liked. Blaise and I passed the time discussing music. Turns out we both enjoy most all genres. We even discussed maybe going to a concert sometime.

We pull into the lot and Blaise turns off the truck. He unbuckles his seat belt and turns to face me. He reaches out and traces his finger down the length of my jaw. "I had a great time tonight. I like spending time with you, having you in my home."

"Thanks for having me; dinner was great." And before I can stop myself I blurt out "Maybe we can do it again sometime."

A smiles lights up his face. He leans over and kisses me. The kiss is soft and sweet and packed full of everything I'm not willing to say and, my guess is, he's afraid to, afraid to scare me away. Blaise has made no secret of saying he wants us to be together. I just…need more time.

He backs away from the kiss, and even though it was slow and sweet, it was all consuming. My chest is rapidly rising with each breath.

"You take my breath away," he says against my lips before he dives in for more.

How he reads my mind, I have no idea. It's weird the way we have this unseen connection. I can't see it, but I feel it. In every fiber of my being I feel it, and I don't know how to handle it.

I go to turn in my seat and the next thing I know, Blaise has his hands on my hips and he's lifting me into his lap. I straddle his hips. My hands find the back of his head and I plant my fingers in his hair. I want him closer. I begin to rock my hips against him. He's hard as stone, and I'm sure this isn't helping, but I can't stop. He places his hands under my shirt and gently strokes my back. His gentle touch makes me want him more.

Lights pulling into the lot blare through the tinted windows of his truck and cause me to break our kiss. It doesn't, however, stop me. I lean down and begin licking and kissing his neck. Nipping his skin and then soothing it with my tongue. I continue to rock my hips and I can feel the pressure building, the release is close.

Blaise grabs my shoulders and pushes me back. "Not here," he says, his voice gruff.

I whimper, because that's not at all what I want to hear. I want him to unzip his pants and fill me. I want this and I want it now.

"Tate, I refuse to take this any further out here in my truck for everyone to see. You have three choices. One, we can turn the truck around and head back to my place; two, we can head up to your room; or three, I can walk you inside and kiss you goodnight. The decision is yours, but I need you to remember something. I won't take you; I won't make love to you until I know you're mine. I couldn't handle being inside you and then never having that chance again. It would kill me," he says, his voice gruff with desire.

I nod my head and slowly climb off his lap. I watch as he adjusts himself in his shorts before he climbs out and comes to my door. He helps me out of the truck and leads me to the building entrance. Never letting go of my hand, he hits the button for the elevator and we stand side by side, hand in hand, all the way to my floor. The doors slide open. Blaise tightens his hold on my hand as we reach my door. We stop and I look up at him, his silver eyes storming with desire. He said I have to choose. I want him, but I'm not ready to say I'm his. From the desire in his eyes, if I get him in my room, I bet I can change his mind. Let's see how easy it is for him to resist temptation.

Decision made. "Tuck me in," I ask softly.

Blaise swallows hard and nods in agreement. I release his hand to unlock the door. He places his hand on the small of my back and follows me in. The apartment is dark. I flip on the light in the kitchen and there's a note from Ember saying she's staying at Jackson's tonight.

I turn the kitchen light back off and head straight toward my room. Once we reach the door, I don't bother with the light. Stopping at my dresser, I discard my keys and phone; then I kick off my flip-flops. My room is not as dark as his. There's a soft glow from the moon shining through the window. The light reflects off his silver eyes, eyes that are drinking me in.

I reach for the hem of my shirt, and suddenly, Blaise is in front of me.

"Let me," he says, replacing my hands with his. I raise my hands above my head. He lifts my tank and throws it behind us.

He has too many clothes on. I reach for his hands and lift his arms in the air. I trace my hands down his chest, tracing his abs until I reach the hem of his shirt. I make quick work of taking it off of him.

We don't speak and, really, words aren't needed. This connection we share takes care of words. Blaise runs his hands up my sides over my ribs. His thumbs gently grazing over my nipple. The sheer bra I'm wearing does nothing to hide his effect on me. His hands make their way to my face and he holds my cheeks so tenderly as his eyes bore into mine.

"I've never seen anything more beautiful." He traces his thumb across my bottom lip, while his other hand finds mine and places it flat against his chest. "My heart feels like it's going to explode," he whispers against my lips.

I open for him and he slides his tongue against mine, smooth and sensual. I stand up on my tiptoes to gain better access, my hands fisted in his hair, holding him close. His hands find their way to my hips and he unbuttons my shorts. I wiggle my hips to help him and they slide to the floor. Blaise unbuttons his and kicks them to the side. The next thing I know, I'm cradled in his arms bridal style. He carries me to the side of the bed and places me on the soft sheets. He climbs over and stretches out beside me.

I move my body next to his and our eyes lock. "I need to hear you say it, baby. I need you to tell me you're mine," he whispers.

"Blaise." I swallow the lump in my throat. "I want this; I want to be with you. I just can't put a label on it. Not yet anyway. My heart can't take losing someone else," I tell him. Honestly, that's what's holding me back. Blaise says he wants me, but what happens when he changes his mind. That leaves me with a shattered heart. What Josh did hurt me, but I've recovered. The loss of my parents devastated me; I'm coping. Having Blaise and then losing him, I wouldn't survive that.

He leans in and places a soft kiss against my lips. "I'm in this, Tatum. I will wait for you to catch up to what I'm feeling. Nothing is going to change my mind or my heart. The sweaty palms, the giddy excitement, the rapid beat in my chest, all caused by you. You're it for me."

He kisses down my cheek and makes his way to my neck. "So sweet," he says, as he tastes my skin. He reaches behind me and unsnaps my bra. I lift up to help him. He slings it behind him and runs his tongue over my nipples, alternating his attention. His hands are everywhere, and yet, it's still not enough. I am worked up beyond belief and I need...I just need him!

"Blaise," I say, breathless. I need more. He said he wouldn't make love to me, so I'm not sure where this is going, but I'm not going to stop him to ask.

His silver eyes come into view. "Patience, sweetheart. I'm going to make sure you get your release," he says against my lips. The kiss is brief. I moan in protest and he softly chuckles. His lips find their way back to my breast as his hand slides underneath the sheer material of my thong. As soon as his finger slides through my folds, I'm begging him to take me. Blaise buries his face in my neck, softly kissing every

170

inch. His fingers tease my entrance and I can't take it anymore. I slide my hand over his and push until his fingers are where I need them to be. I moan his name at the sensation. Blaise growls as he crashes his lips to mine. The kiss is frantic and messy; our tongues seem to keep time with the rhythm of his fingers sliding in and out of me.

I dig my fingers into his shoulders as my release tears through me. Blaise removes his hand and pulls the covers up over me. I immediately miss his body heat. Leaning down, he kisses my forehead. "Sweet dreams," he says tenderly.

"Wait!" I reach for his arm. "Stay," I say. I have too many emotions running through me, but I know I want him next to me. "Please, B," I say, my voice quiet, yet pleading.

Blaise climbs back into bed and lifts the covers. He slides his hard body next to me and wraps me in his arms. I settle back against his chest. This feels right. I hear him sigh as my body relaxes into his. I drift off into a peaceful sleep, wrapped in his arms.

CHAPTER 36

BLAISE

The sound of crying startles me awake. Opening my eyes, I adjust to the scenery. I hear the soft whimper again. That's when it hits me that I'm at Tatum's in her bed. At first, I thought it was just a dream; when in reality, it's a dream come true. I'm not sure how she got all the way on the other side of the bed, but she's too far away. I scoot in next to her and wrap my arms around her. I bury my face in her neck and breathe her in. She releases another whimper. "Shh, baby, I got you," I whisper in her ear.

"Blaise," she says my name and my heart cracks at the pain I hear in her voice.

"I'm right here," I whisper, trying to soothe her with my words. I know she's asleep, but the last time this happened, she admitted it felt like I was there. I need her to feel me. I need her to know I'm here for her. The loss of her parents still weighs heavy on her. The hurt Josh caused keeps her from moving on. If I ever come face to face with her ex…let's just say I hope it never happens. His loss is my gain, and I will fight for her, for us, with everything I am.

I feel her body relax and I know she's now sleeping peacefully. My mind wonders to the nights I'm not here. The nights she has to work through these dreams on her own. I hate it. I hate she's so close, yet so far away. I need to step up my game. I need to prove to her she's what I want. This is my last thought as I drift off to sleep with her tight in my arms.

The morning sun shines through the window as Tatum tries to sneak out of the hold I have on her. "I'm not done holding you," I mumble against her neck.

Her body jolts slightly at the sound of my voice. She obviously thought I was still sleeping. "I have to pee," she whines.

I kiss her cheek. "What time is it?" I ask.

"Six," she whispers.

"Fine, but it's too early to be awake. I'm taking full advantage of this sleep over; you've got three minutes," I tell her as I release my arms, freeing her. Tatum jumps from the bed, grabs my t-shirt from the floor and rushes to the bathroom.

Just as I'm about to go find her to throw her over my shoulder and bring her back to bed, she enters carrying a bottle of water. She takes a small sip and then passes it to me. I'm not really thirsty, but I want my lips where hers have been. If Asher could hear my thoughts, well let's say he has a lot of payback to dish out.

I hand the bottle back to her and she sits it on the nightstand. I pull back the covers, letting her know I want her next to me. Tatum gets the hint and climbs back into bed. She lays her head against my chest and I engulf her in my arms, holding her tight.

I sigh as she relaxes against me. "Thank you," she says softly.

"For what?"

"For being you. For last night." Her hand, which has been resting over my heart, slips around my waist. She embraces me. "I had another dream; you were there."

"I don't think you should be thanking me for something I enjoyed as much as I did. Last night was amazing; you're amazing." I kiss the top of her head. "As for the dream, all I did was hold you. That is something I also take great pleasure in," I tell her. "You want to talk about it?"

She's quiet for several minutes. I can only imagine what she's thinking. The dreams are visibly upsetting to her. "The dream is my mind's own twist to what I imagine happened. I have the details from the officers at the scene. Those details swirl in my mind." She pauses to collect her thoughts. "I've had the same dream for months; up until recently, it's changed. The outcome is still the same, but the scene is different."

I continue to hold her. I'm gently tracing her spine, letting her know I'm here. I'm glad she's talking. She can't keep this bottled inside. My heart swells that she's opening up to me. My girl's coming around; at least, I hope she is.

"In my dream, I drive up on an accident. I recognize the car as one that looks like my parents'. I jump out of mine and run for them; I need to know who it is. I get close enough to see them cut my dad out of the car. His body is…" she trails off. "I can't talk about what I read in the police reports. There are emergency personnel everywhere. Two policemen hold me back. I'm screaming at them to let me through. They won't. Instead, they hold me back. They ask if there is anyone they can call, and I tell them Josh. Instead of giving them his number, I call him. A girl answers, and I hear him calling her "babe." She takes a deep breath. "I'm sure you know how the rest plays out."

"You said it's changed, that the dream is different? How so?" I ask her.

"It is different. It's not as painful as it used to be. It's the same in many ways. I still drive up on the accident. I still run to get to them. I still see them cut my dad from the wreckage." She lifts her head and rests her chin against my chest so she can see my face. "It's different because you're there. Instead of random policemen holding me back, it's you holding me. You and your team are on the scene of the accident. You are the one who holds me on the side of the road. I don't fight you like I do them. Instead, I take comfort in your arms." She lays her head back on my chest. I feels her tears seeping into my skin. "You're there for me," she says softly.

Her tears are breaking my fucking heart and the anger I feel toward her ex is boiling over. I take a minute to compose myself. I need to be strong for her when really I just want to beat the shit out of the asshole who hurt her. When I think I can speak without sounding like a possessive ass, I say, "I will always be there. There is nothing I want more than to be by your side." I want to say for the rest of my life, but I know that would freak her out.

"You're a good man, Blaise Richards." She places a kiss against my heart.

Her alarm goes off, causing us both to jump. Tatum giggles as I reach over and turn it off. I smack her lightly on the ass. "Get in the shower, woman. I'll make you some breakfast."

She squeals and scurries off the bed. I follow her, slipping on my jeans. I watch as she heads to the bathroom; I want to go with her. Instead, I head to the kitchen to make my girl some breakfast.

In the kitchen, I survey the fridge. I gather what I need to make omelets. I'm just placing Tatum's on her plate and buttering her toast when I hear keys in the door. Ember's here. Our alone time is officially over.

Ember looks surprised to see me. "Hey. Something smells good," she says.

"Want one?" I ask, gesturing toward the plate I just made for Tatum.

"No, thanks. Jackson made me a bacon, egg, and cheese biscuit."

"Things seem to be going well with the two of you," I say.

She quirks her brow. "I could say the same for you," she retorts.

I shrug my shoulders. "She needs time."

I smell her before I see her, that sweet vanilla scent. She stops beside me, a faint blush on her cheeks. I bend down and kiss her temple. "Breakfast is ready." I motion toward her plate on the counter as I sit another next to it. Tatum butters the toast that just popped out of the toaster while I pour us both a glass of milk. She carries our plates to the table; I follow her with our drinks.

Ember laughs. Tatum and I both stop and look at her. "You two are so in sync with each other it's scary. You know the next one's move before it happens."

I smile at Tatum and shrug my shoulders. We've discussed the connection we both feel. I'm not surprised someone has picked up on it, especially my sister.

"Oh, I almost forgot. Guess what happened to me last night?"

"What?" Tatum asks her. She spent the night with Jackson, and if it has to do with that, I'm good. I don't need to hear the details.

"Jackson and I were just hanging out listening to the radio and they had a contest to win four seats to the sold out Luke Bryan concert in Nashville. I won!" she squeals.

"No way!" Tatum replies, her eyes lighting up with the same excitement as Ember's.

"Yep. It's this Saturday. Jackson, of course, is going, but I have two extra tickets. Are you guys in?"

I love how my sister groups us together like it's a package deal. I look at Tatum. "It's your call, Tate. I want to be wherever you are," I say.

"Awww," Ember says.

I chuckle.

Tatum's eyes meet mine. "You'll go with me?" she confirms.

"Wherever you are," I repeat.

Tatum addresses Ember. "Sounds fun." She looks at her watch. "Shit, I'm going to be late." She jumps up, grabbing her plate. I place my hand on her arm to stop her.

"I got this. I don't have to be at the shop until noon," I tell her, taking the plate from her hands. "I'll walk you out."

She nods her head and rushes to her room to grab her purse. I walk her to her car, opening the door for her. I tell her to have a good day and give her a chaste kiss on the lips. It's not near enough, but I know she's running behind with all the concert talk.

Walking back into the apartment, I see Ember has already started cleaning up the kitchen. "I was coming back in to do that," I tell her.

"It's fine. Hey, I'm going to reserve rooms for Saturday if I can get them. Do I need two or three?" she asks hesitantly.

"Two. I may not be willing to make love to her yet, but I want her next to me," I blurt out.

Ember's mouth drops open. "TMI, big brother, TMI," she laughs.

CHAPTER 37

This week has flown by. Blaise and Jackson have both been at the apartment every night. Blaise hasn't stayed over again, and I miss him. Leah and I met for lunch; we had a lot to catch up on. She thinks I should take the plunge with Blaise. I distracted her with wedding talk.

Today is Saturday, the day of the concert. He and I are sharing a room tonight; I can't wait. I sleep better when he's with me. I've come to accept that. I have no idea what I'm going to do about it, but I'm no longer lying to myself. Blaise means a lot to me.

"I still can't believe I was able to get two rooms right down the block from the venue," Ember says as we eat breakfast.

"Last minute cancellation for the win," I say.

She laughs.

"Blaise called and said he and Jackson will be here around noon," I say.

What time is it now?" she asks around a bite of her bagel.

"Ten."

"Shit! I need to pack." She scurries from the table and down the hall to her room.

I'm packed and ready to go. I clean up the kitchen and take out the trash. Once back inside, I retrieve my bag from my room after a final check that I haven't forgot anything. I'm wearing gym shorts and a tank during the drive, but I'm bringing a sun dress and cowboy boots to wear to the show.

I set my bag by the door and make myself comfortable on the couch. I hear a light knock at the door then keys. Blaise is here.

He walks into the living room; his eyes light up when he sees me. "Hey you," he says, bending to place a kiss on my cheek. Those two words have become his trademark line each time he sees me. I love it.

"Hey, yourself. You're early," I say, lifting my legs so he can sit down on the couch beside me.

He shrugs. "I missed you."

This man, he has no idea how his words affect me. He wears his heart on his sleeve, and I never have to wonder what he's thinking or how he's feeling. Blaise is a "what you see is what you get" kind of guy and he lays it all out on the table.

He reaches for my hand and laces our fingers together. We sit in silence and watch the rest of "Sweet Home Alabama." I love Reese Witherspoon.

About an hour later, there's a knock at the door. Blaise brings our joined hands to his lips, and places a tender kiss against my knuckles before releasing me as he stands to go answer the door. I hear Jackson's voice and smile. He's almost an hour early himself. I can only assume it's because he wants to see Ember. *We are lucky girls!*

It doesn't take us long to get to Nashville. Jackson drives straight to our hotel and we check-in. I try to split the cost of our room with Blaise, but he shuts me down, complaining about no way is his woman paying. Ember and I laugh at him. Jackson takes his side, of course. I try to reason with him, telling him I'm not his woman. That statement causes him to complain about "stubborn women;" this I laugh at as well.

After the guys get us checked-in, we pile into the elevator. Our rooms are side by side. As we enter our rooms, we agree to meet at four to grab something to eat before we head to the concert, which starts at seven.

Blaise slides the card into the door and the lock releases. He holds the door open for me. I grab my bag from his hand, and he scoffs, "Must you be so stubborn, woman?" he asks.

I giggle. It's fun to watch him go all caveman "me take care of my woman." We're not even officially together. We have spent every spare minute together lately, but still.

"Oh, you think this is funny, huh?" Blaise asks me.

I try to hold it in, I really do, but I can't. I burst out with laughter. "Me take care of my woman," I say in my most manly voice.

Blaise smiles as he stalks toward me. He snakes his arm around my waist and leans in close to my ear. "Are you laughing at me, sweetheart?" he asks, his voice husky.

I shake my head, biting my lip to prevent further swells of laughter to break free. It's useless; I can no longer hold it in. I throw my head back and laugh at his ridiculousness. Blaise retaliates. He picks me up by my hips and tosses me on the bed. His hands slide up on my shirt and find my ribs; then he tickles me. I squirm under him, trying to roll to either side to break free. When that doesn't work, I flail my arms and legs like a crazy person; still he doesn't release. I'm laughing so hard, tears are rolling down my cheeks. "P—please st—stop," I sputter through my laughter.

Suddenly, he stops. I take a minute to catch my breath. I look up at him; his silver eyes are lidded with desire. It's then that I notice our position. Blaise is lying between my legs and they are wrapped around him. This position is intimate. He moves a little, pressing his hardness against my core. I can't help the moan that escapes my lips. Blaise rests his weight on his left elbow while he traces the line of my face with his finger tips.

"You are mine, Tatum." He reaches for my hand, which has just brushed the hair off his forehead. He brings it to his chest to rest over his heart. "Right here, you're mine." Then his lips capture mine.

I don't hesitate to open for him. I know where I want this kiss to lead, but I also know there is only one way for that to happen. Blaise controls the kiss; his lips, soft yet firm, are demanding. His tongue plays with mine. His hard body, every glorious inch of it, is wrapped tight between my legs. His lips travel to my neck, and I melt into him. This man and his intoxicating kisses are going to be the death of me.

Blaise rolls off me and turns on his side. I turn to face him; my legs are intertwined with his, our arms around each other. It's hard to tell where he ends and I begin. "You're beautiful," he whispers against my lips.

"You're not so bad yourself," I say, running my hands up and down his bicep, tracing the lines of his tattoo. It's a flame design, which he and Asher both have. They gave them to each other the day they opened Self Expressions.

He leans in and kisses me, and that's how we spend the next few hours. Passionate kisses, lots of touching, and nothing more. Blaise is sticking to his word. He won't have sex with me until I'm his.

At three-thirty, his cell rings. I can hear Ember's voice. "You got thirty minutes; are you guys getting ready?" she asks.

Blaise chuckles, "Excited much?"

"Yes. So get your asses in gear. I refuse to miss a minute of this concert," she says, hanging up.

Blaise hits end on his phone and lays it behind him on the bed. "We better get ready; we don't want to deal with the wrath that is Ember Richards," he says, laughing.

It doesn't take long to change. My hair is already curled. It is a little messy from our afternoon make out session, but luckily for me, with a little coaxing, my curls pop right back into place.

When Blaise comes out of the bathroom, I have just slipped on the final touch of my outfit, which is my cowboy boots. His eyes take me in, before they lock with mine as he stalks toward me. Without a word, he bends down and kisses me. Pulling back, I smile. "Like what you see?" I say, flirting with him. Being around Blaise just makes everything brighter.

He runs his hands down my back and tugs me closer, as if that's really even possible. "You look amazing," he says.

The knock on the door, along with Ember's voice, stops us. Blaise groans and I laugh.

With one last chaste kiss, he says, "Let's go," and pulls me out of our room.

As soon as we close the door, Ember is linking her arm through mine and leading me to the elevator. Her excitement is contagious.

"You don't get it," she says, a serious expression on her face, "I wanted these tickets. I tried to get them the day they went on sale, both pre-sale and general public, but they sold out. She grabs my arms and shakes me. "I am so freaking excited!" she exclaims.

"All right, you," Jackson says as he throws his arm over her shoulder. Blaise does the same with me. "Where are we eating?"

We settle for a pub on Upper Broadway. After eating dinner, we head back to the venue. It's just a block over, so we walk instead of calling a cab. It allows us to take in the atmosphere. There is nothing like Nashville. Leah and I have been here a couple times for girls' weekend in college. Now it's practically in our backyard.

Blaise has found little ways to touch me all night, hand on the small of my back leading me into a room, gently brushing a fallen hair out of my eyes, hand on my leg at the table. The man has my hormones on overload!

CHAPTER 38

BLAISE

I keep waiting for Tatum to tell me to keep my damn hands to myself. I can't help but touch her. Earlier in our room, it took all of my self-control not to make her mine. All that was separating us was a few thin layers of clothing.

I'm not really sure what's going on with us. We have spent every spare minute together over the last week. I haven't spent the night again, but I want to. I don't sleep well without her. I tried telling myself it was just because I was worried about her. That's a small piece of the giant puzzle. The larger piece is, I just sleep better with her in my arms, safe...with me. I'm no longer fighting any of these feelings or thoughts that pop in my head when it comes to the lovely Tatum. I'm rolling with it. I don't care if I'm pussy whipped well, not technically anyway. I don't care if the guys ride my ass. It's just Tatum; everything else pales in comparison.

My sister is pumped about this concert. Jackson and I have been giving her a hard time. I know Tatum's excited, too. Apparently, it has something to do with Luke Bryan and him shaking his ass. Shit. Give me a V-neck, some tight ass jeans and a mic, and I could do what he does.

It's good to see her smile and let loose. Each day, I start to see some of the sadness in her eyes lessen. Looking back to that first day I met her and looking at her now, she's happy. That's all I want. She can watch Cole, Lee, Luke, and whoever else shake their asses all night long, but at the end of the night, she's coming home with me.

Ember pulls on Tatum's arm, causing her to release my hand. I scowl at my sister and she winks at me. Jackson just smiles at her and I want to call him out on it, but really I can't. He looks at Ember like I look at Tatum. I hope they feel this same...magnetism that I feel with

Tate. If my little sister can find that, well, I couldn't ask for more for her.

I watch as the girls talk and laugh ahead of us. That's my girl.

We arrive at the venue an hour before the concert starts. The radio station Ember won the tickets from included VIP treatment. We get to tour backstage. At first, Ember is disappointed she doesn't get to meet any of the artists, but Tatum reminds her she would still get to go behind the scenes. It doesn't take much convincing for Ember to believe this is still a bonus. Once the tour is over, an attendant leads us to our seats. Front row. Jackson and I smile as we watch our girls squeal with excitement.

The lights go down and the band starts to play. This has the girls on their feet; Jackson and I follow suit. "The opening guy's name is Cole Swindell," Ember says. He's fairly new, but she loves his stuff. My sister is a freak about her music. He's pretty good. I'm enjoying myself just watching my sister and Tatum with huge smile on their faces. They're both dancing and swaying their arms in the air.

Cole says he's going to "slow things down." I watch as Jackson pulls my sister into his arms. I reach for Tatum and bring her back against my chest. I lean down and whisper in her ear, "Hey you." Her body shivers. Not sure if it's my words, or the close contact. Maybe both.

The song is called "Swaying" and it's perfect for this moment. I hold Tatum tight against me. My arms around her, we gently sway to the music. Not able to resist, I bury my face in her neck. All I see is her. I can no longer hear the band. I don't see the thousands of people who surround us. Just Tatum. I am completely consumed by her. This is scary shit. I've never felt this way. Nothing compares to this feeling of her in my arms. I can't help but wonder if she's feeling it too. Surely she is. As the song comes to a close, I get my answer.

Tatum turns in my arms. Her small soft hands caress my face as she stands on her tiptoes and presses her lips to mine. I want to devour every fucking inch of her. I want to take her back to the room and make love to her. Funny how I've said those words before in the past with my ex, but never have they held more meaning than in this moment with Tatum. Making love to Tatum would be a game changer. I know this; that's why I need her to be in this with me, all in, before I do.

Tatum pulls back as the song ends. I bend down and hug her tight while whispering in her ear. "You own me, Tate."

I gently turn her, so her back is once again pressed tight against my chest so she can continue to enjoy the show. She places her hand over mine, which is resting on her belly. Her hands are shaking. I move mine over on top of hers and lace our fingers together.

As the first set ends, the lights come up and the roadies prepare for the next artist, Lee Brice. Jackson and I go and grab us all a drink. Standing in line, he and I are shooting the shit, just waiting, when a group of girls walk up beside us. I recognize them from the shop, but I don't remember their names.

"Hey, Blaise. What do you say you guys come out with us after the show?" the redhead asks.

I'm shaking my head before she's even finished. "No can do. Jackson here is dating my little sister, and I'm off the market myself," I tell them.

One of the girls, this one I've never seen before, reaches out to touch my chest. I grab her wrist and place it gently at her side. "I'm taken," I grit out.

"We won't tell," the redhead says.

What the fuck is wrong with these girls? "Not happening. Enjoy your night," I say, stepping up to the counter to order four beers.

Walking back to our sets, Jackson says, "So you and Tatum are official? Congrats, man." He sounds like he's happy for us.

"Not yet, but we will be," I tell him.

Jackson raises his eyebrow in question. "I don't' see anyone but her." Just Tatum.

He nods his head. "Trust me, I get it." We don't say anything else until we are almost to our seats. We stop at the end of the aisle to let a couple pass. The girls spot us and wave. "I love her," Jackson blurts out.

I turn my head to look at him. "I do. I haven't told her yet; I want it to be special for her," he says, looking me in the eye.

I believe him. "She's loves you, too. She didn't tell me, but I know my sister. Don't break her heart," I warn.

We reach our seats and I bend to place a chaste kiss on Tatum's lips before handing her the beer I brought her.

She laughs.

"What? Is that the toll I have to pay to get a drink? A kiss for a beer?" she asks, smiling.

Her smile lights up her face and those green eyes of hers sparkle. "You'd be amazed at what I would do for one of your kisses," I say with a wink.

The lights dim and Lee Brice takes the stage. I place one hand on her hip and bring her body against mine. She settles against me and we enjoy the show.

The concert is great. All three artists put on a great show. All three artists also sing songs that remind me of me and how I feel about Tatum. Although, here lately, everything reminds me of Tatum and how I feel about her. Not a second goes by that she's not on my mind.

As we walk back to the hotel, I watch as Jackson whispers in Ember's ear. They stop and she turns to face us. "I think we're just going to head back to the room," she says.

I look to Jackson and give him a slight nod, letting him know I approve and he should tell her how he feels.

Tatum looks up at me. "What about you?" she asks me.

As if I would be anywhere she's not. "As long as I'm with you, next to you, I don't care what we do or where we go."

A soft smile graces her lips. "I think I'm ready to head back, too," she says.

Decision made; we head to the hotel. I'm ready for a good night's sleep with Tatum wrapped in my arms.

CHAPTER 39

As Blaise unlocks the door to our room, I reflect on the night. I had so much fun. Ember is a blast to be around and Blaise, well, he's...amazing. He was constantly touching me all night. Nothing over the top, but enough to leave me crazy with want. There were several songs throughout the show when he held me tight and whispered sweet words in my ear. The first one will be forever in my memory. Cole Swindell was singing "Swaying" and, well, that's what we were doing. Blaise whispered in my ear that "I owned him."

Every day, he shows me more and more that he wants this, us. Leah tells me I can't let Josh continue to rob me of my happiness. She claims to be a great judge of character, which she is. She says Blaise is good people. She also continues to remind me that she never liked Josh.

"Ugh. I need a shower; I'm sticky," I say, gently tugging my dress away from my skin.

Blaise bends down and kisses the side of my neck. "You're perfect," he says, pulling back, licking his lips. His gaze is heated. Breaking the trance, he smacks my ass. "You grab a shower first," he tells me. He kicks off his shoes and plops down on the bed. Remote in hand, he winks at me.

I grab his t-shirt from my bag. He'd left it at the apartment and Ember asked me to drop it off to him. I didn't. I kept it and I can't wait to see his eyes when he sees me in it. It's just like the one he gave me that day at his house from the department with his name on it. Only this time, it reads B. Richards on the back, instead of just Richards.

After taking off my boots, I head to the bathroom to wash away the effects of the concert. I quickly strip out of my clothes and climb in under the hot spray. I lean my hair back and let the hot water soak through. It's when I reach for my shampoo that I realize I forgot to bring it in with me. I debate on what I should do. I hate the stuff provided by the hotel. The shampoo makes my hair feel like steel wool and the soap leaves my skin feeling sticky. Ugh!

I want my stuff, and it's just outside the door. "Blaise!" I yell, hoping he can hear me over the running water and the television. Good thing I left the door unlocked.

I watch as the door comes open. Blaise walks in with his eyes closed. It's not like he's never seen me. "Tatum, what's wrong?" he asks. I can hear the panic in his voice.

"I forgot my shampoo and body wash in my bag, can you get it for me?" I ask.

I can see his shoulders relax at my question. "Sure thing, babe." He's back in no time, walking into the room with his eyes closed and holding his hand out to hand me my necessities.

I pull back the curtain. "Blaise, open your eyes," I tell him.

He shakes his head no. "I can't. If I see you, your sexy body dripping wet…" He shakes his head. "I can't."

An instant rush of desire hits me. I want him to see me. It seems like Blaise is the only man who ever really has just seen me, Tatum. I want that. I want to watch as those silver eyes roam over every inch of my bare skin.

His arm is still outstretched, so I grab his wrist with one hand, while taking my supplies with the other, and setting them on the ledge in the shower. "Please, Blaise," I ask. I'm hoping my soft plea will get me what I want. He's always telling me whatever I want. I'm hoping my "please" seals the deal and he can no longer say no.

He releases a heavy breath and slowly opens his eyes. I watch as he takes in every inch of me. His eyes eventually find mine. He swallows hard. "You are the most beautiful creature I have ever laid eyes on," he says, his voice gruff.

I want to feel his body next to mine. "Join me?" I ask before I can talk myself out of it.

"Tate," he says in a strangled voice.

"You said wherever as long as you're next to me. I want you next to me," I throw his words from earlier back at him.

I can see the war raging inside him. He's fighting against what he wants and what he thinks he needs to do. "Baby, I want nothing more than to be in that shower with you, but I can't trust myself. If I join you, I'll want to make love to you and I can't. I need you to be in this, Tatum. I need you to be on the same level as me."

I step out of the shower, dripping wet, and wrap my arms around him. "I want to feel your wet skin against mine," I tell him. I reach for the hem of his shirt and pull it up his toned abs. He's not fighting me, but he's not helping either. I release his shirt and lift both his arms in the air over his head. His silver eyes follow my every move. I pull his shirt up and over his head and toss it on the floor with my dress. My hands wander over his chest and abs. He sucks in a breath. I move my hands to his hair and pull him down to me. "Please, B," I whisper against his lips. He shudders and it's then I know I'm going to get my way.

His hands find my hips and he pulls me tight against him. His lips move gently against mine. I can feel the evidence of what this is doing to him against my belly. He breaks the kiss and begins to unbutton his jeans. Not once does his eyes leave mine. Once he has rid himself of his clothes, he grabs my hand and steps into the hot spray; I follow behind him.

Blaise pulls the curtain back, even though the floor is already a sopping wet mess. This places us in our own little cocoon. "I can't say no to you," he says as he trails kisses down my neck. A soft moan escapes my lips.

His hands are everywhere as his lips and tongue follow right behind. His lips travel down my neck to my breasts as he gives each of them equal attention. I'm soaking up his attention when he drops to his knees. He rests his forehead against my stomach. I watch him. His silver eyes lift to meet mine and I can see how much he wants me. How much he cares about me. Blaise wears his emotions on his sleeve and the look he's giving me right this minute tells me everything I need to know.

He swallows hard. "Tate, baby, I need you to be mine. I need to know I'm the only man who gets to lavish this sweet body of yours with kisses. I need to know I have all your kisses, your smiles. I need to be the person you run to, that you lean on. I need all of you," he says with so much passion and emotion in his voice.

I want that, too. Every damn word he just said is what I want. As I stand here and watch him kneel before me, I know this is real. His emotions are real. This isn't just a challenge for him. He wants me. I want him. I want to open my heart up to him and pray he doesn't break it. I'm no longer resisting temptation.

I run my fingers through his hair. His silver eyes shining with so much hope, yet guarded at the same time. We can't have that. "You have me, all of me. I'm yours," I tell him.

He opens his mouth to speak and then shuts it. Instead, he places a gentle kiss on my stomach and then gets to his feet. His lips find mine and I melt into his arms. He kisses me like I'm the air he needs to breathe. His hands roam over my body, gently caressing. His calloused hands feel good against my skin.

His kiss has me dizzy with want, so he has to steady me as he pulls away. He reaches for my shampoo and squeezes it into the palm of his hand. He turns me so I'm facing the opposite direction as he massages the shampoo into my hair. He then switches our positions so I'm under the spray. Next, he lathers my entire body with body washes, making sure not one inch is left untouched by his hands.

His touch is tender and loving; it surprises me a little. I would have thought as soon as I told him I was his, he would have me up against the shower wall in two seconds flat. Instead, he's taking care of me. I feel the final walls around my heart tumbling down. Blaise Richards is a force to be reckoned with.

Once he's satisfied he's cleaned every inch of me, he grabs my shampoo and quickly lathers his hair. He makes quick work of his body with my body wash and turns off the water. He pulls back the curtain and reaches for a towel and wraps it around me, placing a kiss on my forehead. Stepping out, he places a towel around his waist. He turns back to me and grabs me by the hips, lifting me out of the shower. "Let's get you dried off," he says softly.

CHAPTER 40

BLAISE

She's mine. She said I have all of her. I need to make sure this is really what she wants before I forge ahead. It's not that I don't trust her, I do. I just...need to hear her say it again.

Willing my hands not to shake at the emotion coursing through me, I gently dry her off. I offer to brush her hair, but she declines, saying it's a rat's nest. I love her long dark locks. I leave her in the bathroom to go find some clothes. I pull on a pair of boxer briefs and climb into bed.

A few minutes later, Tatum emerges from the bathroom. Her hair is in a knot of damp curls on top of her head and she's wearing a Murfreesboro Fire Dept. shirt. She must see the question in my eyes. She turns so I can read the back.

B. Richards.

My girl is wearing my shirt. How did she get it?

"You left it at the apartment when you moved Ember in. She asked me to return it to you, but I kinda wanted it for myself," she says with a smile.

"It looks good on you." I wink at her. She throws her head back and laughs. I love that sound.

I pat the bed; she climbs in and lays down beside me. Our bodies aligned. I place my hand on her hip and tug her closer. She's never close enough.

I tuck a stray curl behind her ear. She is so fucking beautiful; I can't take my eyes off of her. It's not just physical beauty, don't get me wrong she has that in spades, but it's the person she is. She's loyal, kind, and loving. She's amazing.

"You're mine?" I ask her again. I need to hear it one more time.

"Yes," she says, her voice soft. "Please don't hurt me."

Over my dead body. "Never," I say, my voice thick. "Tate, you have all the power here. I'm at your mercy. You've changed me from the moment I laid eyes on you. I want this, want you with everything in me," I say; then I kiss her.

I kiss her deep and slow. She moans and tugs on my hair. I know she wants me to unleash on her. We've been building up to this moment for so long. I, however, refuse to fuck her the first time we are together. I want to make love to my girl and that's what I'm going to do.

I roll on top of her, holding my weight with my arms; I don't want to crush her. She readily opens her legs for me and it's then I realize she has nothing on under my shirt.

Not. A. Thing.

Bare, she's totally fucking bared to me. My girl.

Tatum tugs on my boxers and starts to pull them down. She grasps onto them with her toes and her sexy legs pull them off me. My body is screaming for hers. She arches her back so I can pull up on her shirt. I rip it off her, and now we're both bare. Her legs lock around my waist and she tries to pull me into her.

"Babe, I need to make sure you're ready. I don't want to hurt you," I tell her.

"I'm good, B. Nice and wet. Let's do this," she says, pleading.

I chuckle at her "let's do this," as my hand finds her core. Hot, slick, and wet, just like she said it would be. She moans as I slide my finger against her folds.

"Please," she begs.

I pull back to get the condom I had stashed in the nightstand after our shower, just in case.

"What are you doing?" she asks, her voice breathy.

"Condom," I say, kissing her nose.

She's shaking her head no. "I'm on the pill; I want you now."

I still. *Holy fuck!* Never. Never have I ever ridden bareback.

Tatum can sense my hesitation. "What? What is it? I'm clean. After Josh, I got a full check-up."

I cringe hearing her talk about him, especially when I'm about to be inside of her.

"I've never," I say, my eyes boring into hers.

"Me either," she says softly. "But with you, I want to. I don't want there to be anything between us."

Just the thought has me ready to blow. I lean down and rest my forehead against hers, still mindful of my weight so I don't crush her. "You own me," I whisper as I slide into her, no barrier, nothing.

Just us.

The feeling of being inside her like this is like nothing I have ever felt. I can't tear my eyes away from hers as I slowly begin to move. She closes her eyes and moans. "Open your eyes, baby. I want to look into those beautiful greens. I want you to watch what being inside of you does to me." Her breath hitches as I start to move a little faster. I'm not going to last. She feels like silk. My hand glides down and I begin to rub against her with my thumb. I hate this is happening so fast, but I can't stop it. I refuse to go without her. I need her with me.

"Blaise," she moans. "I'm…"

I lean down and place my lips next to her ear. "Let go, Tate." And she does, my name falling from her lips and hers from mine.

Rolling to the side so I don't crush her with my weight, I hold her tight against my chest. My entire body is trembling from the experience. I can't speak and it's work to pull air into my lungs. Never felt anything like it.

Tatum turns in my arms and lays her head on my chest. She rests her hands over my racing heart. "It's never been like that," she says.

I don't say anything; I can't. My voice won't work.

Tatum looks up. "B?" she asks, biting her lip. I can tell she thinks my lack of conversation is for all the wrong reasons.

I kiss the top of her head and hold her close.

"You're trembling," she finally says.

I focus on my breathing to get myself under control. Once I feel like I can carry on a conversation, I roll on my side so we are laying face to face, nose to nose. I trace her face with my finger. "You did this to me. You ruined me for anyone else. That was the greatest experience of my life. Nothing will ever top that," I say to her.

I watch as a tear slips down her cheek. I catch it with my thumb, then lean in and place a soft kiss on her cheek. "Why the tears?" I ask hesitantly. I'm scared to death I just ruined this.

"You, this, us. They're happy tears, Blaise. I haven't felt this way for...well, ever. Not like this anyway. I've never felt so connected with someone. I thought we had a freaky connection thing going before, but this, what we just shared, was intense and passionate. Scary." She pauses as she absent-mindedly traces the tattoo on my arm. "My heart's invested now, and I can't take that back. I don't want to."

I bite back the words *I love you*. Yeah, I do and I want to tell her so fucking bad, but it's too soon. I have to take my time with her, or she'll run. I can't let that happen.

I wrap my arms around her and hold her tight. "Mine too, Tate. I'm in this, you have all of me. It's you and me," I tell her.

"You and me," she repeats my words as we both drift off to sleep.

CHAPTER 41

Waking up in Blaise's arms is the greatest feeling in the world. What comes after that is pretty damn amazing as well. Blaise made love to me again, then we showered...together.

I'm packing up our things and I can't find my hairbrush. "Blaise, did I leave my brush in there?" I call out to him.

He walks up behind me. "This one," he says, holding the brush. I jump. I wasn't expecting him to sneak up on me.

"Yes, thank you." I take the brush and shove it in my bag. "I think I'm all set," I say, zipping up my bag. I turn to face Blaise; he looks nervous.

"What's up?" I ask.

Blaise takes my hand and leads me to the bed. He sits down and pulls me into this lap. He has both arms around my waist and his head resting on my shoulder. "Tell me this is us, that once we walk out that door, we are still us."

I sigh with relief. I was thinking he was going to tell me he made a mistake, that we are a mistake.

"We are us. We are whatever you want us to be. You fought for me, and here I am. What are you going to do with me, Blaise Richards?" I flirt to try and lighten the mood.

He kisses me hard, then says, "I'm going to shout from the fucking rooftops that you're my girl." His hand cups my cheek. "You're my girlfriend," he says as his lips find mine again.

We get lost in the kiss, in just being with each other. Then we hear Ember beating on the door, telling us to get a move on. Blaise pulls back and a huge grin lights up his face. "Girlfriend, I have someone I want you to meet," he says. We stand up, Blaise grabs our bags, and we leave our nest. I have no idea who he wants me to meet, but he seems excited about it.

Ember and Jackson are in the hall waiting on us, and both are all smiles. Looks like they had a great night. Blaise stops and pulls me to his side. "Ember, Jackson, I would like to introduce you to my girlfriend, Tatum. Tatum, this is my sister and her boyfriend, Jackson."

I can't help it, I bust out laughing; the rest of them do, too. Blaise is wearing his sexy smirk. I just shake my head at him. Ember pulls on my arm and we skip off down the hall ahead of the guys.

We beat the guys to the elevator and Ember pushes the button for the door to close. "Okay, talk fast we only have five floors. You and my brother?"

I nod my head yes. "Yes, I can't resist him," I tell her.

She smiles. "Good, finally. He has been head over heels for you since day one. Now my turn. Jackson told me he loves me!" she squeals.

"Ember, that's awesome. I know how you feel about him."

"I've known him for years, through the guys, and, well, he's amazing. He looked so relieved when I said it back." The elevator reaches our floor as the door opens she says, "That tidbit will have to get us through until we get home, but I want deets," she says under her breath. The elevator next to ours dings and our guys walk off, both looking sexy as sin.

Checkout time is eleven and it's ten fifty nine when we reach the counter. Blaise and Jackson check us out and we load up. We missed the hotel's breakfast, so we're all starving. The Richards are expecting us for the weekly Sunday dinner. I offer to be dropped off at the apartment, but Blaise is having no part of that. I'm a little nervous as to what his family will say about us. I work with his mom, and she has been amazing to me, they all have. But now things are different; I'm dating her son.

As soon as the car is stopped, Blaise is out and opening my door. He grabs my hand and our fingers intertwine. He leads me inside. He bends down to whisper, "I have more people for you to meet." As we walk into the kitchen, he blurts out, "Hey, guys, I want to introduce you to my girlfriend, Tatum. Tate, this is my family." He's laughing by this point from the smiles on everyone's faces.

"About time; come here, you." Nancy says as she walks toward us, arms wide open. I assume she's going for Blaise and am surprised when she engulfs me in a hug. "Welcome to the family," she says in my ear, before releasing her hold on me.

"You are—" Asher starts to say.

"Ready to take whatever you can dish," Blaise says, wrapping his arm around me and pulling me to his chest. I relax into him.

Asher throws his head back in laughter. "Best fucking time of your life, bro," Asher says.

"Asher!" Nancy scolds him.

Blaise looks down at me and smiles. "She already is, bro," he says, never taking his eyes off me.

"All right, well, let's eat," Steve instructs.

The food is delicious. Spaghetti and meatballs with salad. We spend a few hours just hanging out with their parents and brother. Blaise continues to dote on me, touching me any chance he gets, pulling me into his lap to sit out on the back deck. I watch as his family takes us in, nothing but smiles coming our way. It seems as though I was nervous for no reason.

When we finally make it back to the apartment, the four of us are exhausted. I don't ask Blaise to stay, but I know he will. I walk back to my room and he follows behind with our bags. I strip down and open my dresser to pull out something to sleep in.

"You won't need it," he says, walking up behind me. He trails kisses down my neck. "You can wear me.I can hear the grin in his voice.

Blaise locks the door and climbs into bed. He makes love to me for the second time today, before wrapping me in his arms and I fall asleep.

The next morning, all four of us wake up late. Blaise and I make plans for me to stop by the shop after work. He has clients until nine. Ember and I make plans to have lunch as she pushes us out the door. I should have been a teacher, summers off and all that.

Walking into the office, Nancy smiles and says hello. I say good morning and head back to my office. I bury myself in work so much so that when I hear a knock on my office door, I'm shocked to see Ember standing there.

"Hey," I say looking at my watch. "Wow, this day is flying by."

"You ready for lunch? We have a lot to catch up on. I called Leah and she's meeting us at the diner," she informs me. "I invited Grace too, but she is helping Asher at the shop." She shrugs.

I had texted Leah yesterday on the way home and told her Blaise and I are official, promising details later. This is perfect; now I won't have to repeat myself.

We're meeting Leah at a small diner in town. I hear the food is amazing, but I have yet to try it. We all decide on the fried chicken salad. Yes, fried chicken defeats the purpose, but we aren't eating it because we are dieting. We are eating it because it's good. At least Ember says it is. My two friends gang up on me first. I replay the weekend with Blaise and most of our moments. I refrain from telling them how he made love to me, just that we did sleep together. Some things are not meant to be shared. Ember then fills us in on how Jackson told her he loves her and she followed suit.

The waitress comes to the table and drops off the check. Lunch has been great, and I really enjoyed getting to see Leah and welcoming Ember to our group. I go to stand and Leah stops me.

"Tate, wait a minute will you?" she asks. "I have some news as well."

I glance at Ember and she shrugs her shoulders. "Sure, what's up?" I ask.

"I'm pregnant," she blurts out.

"What?" I ask a little too loud as I stand up and hug her. Ember does the same. "I'm so happy for you guys." I wipe the tears from my eyes. This is what Leah has always wanted, what we've both wanted. I couldn't be happier for the two of them.

"Yeah, so we actually have a change of plans for the wedding. We are going to fly to Hawaii and do it on the beach."

"Do it on the beach, huh?" Ember says, laughing.

Leah's face turns red. "You know what I mean. We're going to get married on the beach, just the two of us." She looks up to gauge my reaction.

If this makes her happy, I'm happy. "That's amazing, when do you leave?" I ask. I know she wants to be married before she starts to show.

"I'm ten weeks, and my doctor says it's better to fly after the first trimester. So in three weeks from now, I will be a married woman," she says.

Unfortunately, I have to get back to work. We all hug goodbye and Ember drops me back off at the office.

As I walk through the door, Nancy is all smiles. "How was your lunch dear?" she asks me.

"Great. Leah is pregnant. I am so happy for both of them," I tell her.

"That's great. Please send her my congratulations." Her smile is genuine, just like Mom's. "You had a visitor over lunch. He left something for you in our office."

"Blaise?" I ask, confused.

She shakes her head yes. "He tried your cell and couldn't get you. He was worried so he stopped by." She grins. "I like seeing my boy like this." With that, she turns back to her computer and I quicken my steps to see what Blaise left for me in my office.

As I open the door, I smell them. Flowers. I push the door open wider and see a huge arrangement of wild flowers on my desk. I pull out the small card and it reads:

B

Nothing else; nothing else is needed. He's telling me he is thinking of me. I settle into my desk with a huge grin plastered on my face.

As the day wears on, I start to not feel well. By the time five o'clock rolls around, all I want to do is go home and go to bed. I call Blaise to tell him I won't be stopping by the shop.

"Hey you," he answers on the first ring.

"Hey, I'm not feeling so hot. I'm gonna just head home instead of coming to the shop."

"What's wrong?" he asks, concerned.

"I'm nauseous. I don't know if it's something I ate, but I just want to go home and lay down," I tell him.

"Okay, let me call my last couple of clients and reschedule; then I'll be there."

"No, you don't have to do that. I'm just going home to sleep. I don't want you to get whatever this is. You need to stay away."

"Tatum, I don't give a fuck what you've got; nothing is going to keep me away from you. My last client is at eight. A regular of mine, his wife just had another baby and he wants me to add the new baby's name to the other three. It will be quick and then I'm coming to you," he says.

I don't bother to argue; besides, I miss him. "Okay, be safe. I'll see you later."

"You be safe, Tate. Text when you make it home, okay?"

I agree and hang up. The drive home takes forever and the nausea is getting worse. By the time I make it into the apartment, I'm running for the bathroom.

"Not you, too." I hear Jackson's voice behind me. "Ember started about an hour ago."

My phone rings and I point to my purse lying in the doorway. Jackson picks it up and answers. "Hey, Brent. Yeah, both of them. Shit. Okay, yes. All right. Got it. Thanks, man." He hits end on my phone. "That was Brent; he said Leah has been throwing up, too. At first, she thought it was pregnancy related, but Brent doesn't think so. Now that you and Ember are in the same boat, he is convinced you three have food poisoning. Leah told him you all ate the same thing at lunch today," he explains.

Before Jackson can set it down, it's ringing again. "Hey, man," he says into the phone. "Yeah, she's here. Brent thinks all three of them have food poisoning. They ate at the diner for lunch and they all three had the same thing." He pauses, listening to Blaise. "I'm here, man; just finish what you need to do. Ember is sleeping and Tatum looks like she could drop any second. I'll call you if something changes." He disconnects the call as I empty the remaining contents of my stomach.

CHAPTER 42

BLAISE

"Fuck!" I slam my phone down on the counter. Tate is sick and I'm here. I'm supposed to be the one to take care of her.

"What's up?" Asher says, sticking his head around the corner into my room. "Ember and Tatum had lunch with Leah today at the diner. All three of them are sick. Brent thinks they have food poisoning."

"Damn, Grace was supposed to go too, but she declined to come here and work at the shop with me. I felt bad at first, now I'm glad she didn't go." Asher walks in and looks at my schedule sitting on the desk. "I know what Dave wants. They just had baby number four, right?" he asks me.

I nod. "Yeah, another boy. He was hoping this one would be a girl."

"What about your six o'clock?" he asks.

I shrug. "No one that I know."

Grace walks in. "I scheduled that one. They didn't request anyone specific," she says.

"Great, I'll stay and do your six. I'm sure Dave is fine with me inking baby number four's name. If not, I'll explain and we'll do the job for free when you reschedule. Go to her," he tells me.

I don't need to be told twice. I thank him, kiss Grace on the cheek, and rush out the door. My girl needs me.

I break several speed laws on the way to their apartment. The fifteen-minute drive is cut in half. I hop on the elevator and will it to move faster. I have my key out and ready as soon as the doors open. I let myself into the apartment; all is dark and quiet. Jackson is coming out of Ember's room as I'm walking down the hall. "Hey, man, how are they?" I ask.

"Neither one of them has gotten sick for over an hour, which Brent says is a good sign. He says to keep them hydrated with small sips and rest."

"Thanks for being here, man," I say, patting his shoulder and heading toward Tatum's room.

"I thought you had to work?" he asks.

"I did, but since it wasn't a client who requested me, Asher said he would do it so I could be here."

I slowly open the door to her room and see her curled up on her side, sound asleep. There is a large trashcan beside the bed and a bottle of water on the nightstand. Jackson has been taking good care of her.

I slip off my shoes, jeans, and shirt, and slide in next to her. Food poisoning isn't contagious, but I wouldn't care if it was. I gently slide up against her and wrap my arms around her waist.

"Blaise?" she asks, her voice hoarse.

"Hey you," I say softly.

"I told you not to—"

"Shh. It's okay, babe. Asher took my clients so I could take care of you." I kiss the back of her head. "Just rest."

"I'm never eating at the diner again," she moans.

I hold her tight and eventually sleep claims me, too.

A few hours later, I wake to sounds of Tatum getting sick again. I jump out of bed and pull her hair back. "Blaise, you don't have to be here. I don't want you to see me like this," she says through her sobs.

"Tate, I'm in this. All or nothing, baby, remember. I got you," I say as I help her lean against the headboard and hand her a bottle of water. "Swish your mouth out and spit it back in the bottle. I'll get you a new one."

She does as I say and slides back down into the bed. I take the bag out of the can and replace it with one of the extras that Jackson had lying on the nightstand. He was prepared. I expect keeping up with two of them he had to be. I walk the trash out to the dumpster and stop back by the kitchen to wash my hands and grab Tate a fresh bottle of water. I climb back into bed with her, and she curls up against my side and falls back to sleep.

The next morning, both girls make it to the couch, but refuse food. Jackson and I both stay with them and make sure they are keeping hydrated as much as possible. At six, there is a soft knock on the door. Jackson opens it to find my mom and dad. Dad is holding a large pot, which smells a lot like Mom's homemade chicken soup.

Surprisingly, the girls are both able to eat a little soup and a few crackers and keep them down. I hug my parents and thank them as I walk them to the door.

"Take care of our girls," my dad says.

I smile at him including Tate. "Jackson and I have it covered," I tell him.

We're all exhausted from the last twenty-four hours, so we go to bed early. I wrap Tate up in my arms and we drift off to sleep.

The next day, Tatum insists on going to work. I'm on call for the department, so I insist I drive her. I walk her in and stop to talk to Mom for a few minutes.

"Keep an eye on her today. She's no longer getting sick and she was able to hold down the soup last night. She had a piece of dry toast this morning. She says she feels better, just weak."

Mom chuckles, "Blaise, I will make sure Tatum is well taken care of. Off you go; some of us have to work." She winks at me and I smile. I know Tatum is in good hands.

Today has been a quiet day. I mowed the grass and got some things done around the house. One more hour and I can pick Tatum up from work. I plan on bringing her back here tonight.

Just as I'm getting out of the shower, my pager goes off. I rush to get dressed, hop in my truck, turn on my sirens, and head to the station. On my way there, I call Tate.

"Hello?"

"Hey, babe. I just got paged for a run. I won't be able to pick you up. Have Mom drop you off at the station and you can drive my truck home," I tell her.

"That's silly. I'll just call Ember and have her pick me up. I'm sure she won't mind. Besides, how am I supposed to get in that monstrosity without your help?" she asks.

I laugh. "All right, babe. I'll call you when we're done. I'm technically on call until tomorrow morning at eight. I hope this will be the only call we have tonight. How are you feeling?"

"Much better. Ember brought me some leftover soup and I ate the entire bowl with some crackers. I am back among the living," she tells me.

"That's great, babe. Don't over do it. Be safe going home. I'll call you when I get off."

"Be safe, B," she says softly.

"Always, baby," I say as I end the call.

When I get to the firehouse, the truck is ready to roll. I hop into my gear and we're off. Mike, one of the full-timers, fills me in on the way. Apparently, the Williamson's training stables caught on fire. Old man Williamson made a name for himself training horses for events such as the Kentucky Derby. When I say stables, that's an understatement. It's a full-blown facility complete with therapy rooms, three indoor riding areas, stalls, tack rooms, offices, you name it. The building alone takes up the better part of five acres. I have no idea how much square footage that is. I do know if the entire building is on fire, my girl will be sleeping alone tonight.

CHAPTER 43

I call Ember and ask her if she will pick me up. She insists it's no problem and she's on her way. I straighten up my desk and shut down my computer. I decide to wait for her in the lobby. Nancy's there with the local news station pulled up on her screen.

"Hey. Ember is on her way here. Blaise had a run," I tell her.

"Oh dear, yes, there's a fire out at the Williamson's training stables. From what the news says here, the entire facility is up in flames."

My heart drops at the news. I worry about Blaise and Steve being there. "Did Asher get called out as well?" I ask her.

She shakes her head no. "No, but he might have to be with the way this looks." She points to the screen. I walk around her desk and watch the live video feed of a massive fire.

Ember walks in. "It sounds bad," she says in greeting.

"I'm going to call the other auxiliaries and see if there is a schedule. This looks like it's going to keep our guys occupied for a while," Nancy says.

"Schedule?" I ask confused.

"Yeah, most of the wives form the auxiliary for the firehouse. When there are bad accidents and big fires or anything that causes them to be out for long periods of time, they make sure the men have drinks and food to keep them hydrated and keep their strength up," Ember explains.

"How can I help?" I ask.

Nancy smiles at me. "You girls run on home. I'll call when I get more information," she says.

As soon as we get home, I change into jeans and a t-shirt. I want to be ready to go if we get called out to help. Ember is on the phone with Jackson in the kitchen and I'm pacing back and forth in the living room, watching the live news coverage of this five alarm fire.

Ember joins me and sits down on the couch. "Sometimes I think all the media coverage makes it worse. Especially for those of us who have loved ones there battling the fire."

"Yeah, I agree, but at the same time I can't turn it off. They will be the first to report any injuries, and I need to be there if he gets hurt."

"Dad is there, Tatum. If anything happens to Blaise, he will let us know," she tells me.

"What about him? Who calls if your dad gets hurt?" I ask her.

"Dad is more of a facilitator. He suffered a back injury from a fire several years ago, and now he can't carry all the equipment. He's there to oversee the trucks and make sure all the men remain accounted for. It's his job to keep track of who is in what sector of the fire and make sure they are checking in. He's going to keep them all safe," she says.

I take comfort in the fact that Steve is there to keep an eye on all of them, on Blaise. Ember pats the couch beside her and I shake my head no. I can't sit.

Ember's phone rings. I stop pacing and watch as she answers. I can tell from the conversation that she's talking to Nancy. I don't take my eyes off her.

"Well?" I ask as soon as she hangs up the phone.

"Mom said our local auxiliary is heading over in about an hour to take a shift," she tells me.

"All right, where do we meet them? How do I help?" I ask, my thoughts racing. I'll be where he is. If something bad happens, I'll be there this time.

"Tatum, maybe we should sit this one out," she says gently.

I shake my head no. "No, no way. I need to be there with him. If something happens and I'm not there…" I fight back the emotions threating to spill. "I have to be there," I croak out.

Ember releases a heavy sigh. "Tatum—"

"No! I wasn't there when my parents died in that fucking car crash. I wasn't there when…" I take a deep breath. "I need to be there, please, Ember."

"Okay," she says gently. "Under one condition."

She waits for me to agree; I nod my head.

"You have to stay back. If something does happen, you have to let them do their jobs."

"I'll try. I just want to be there," I say.

"All right, I'll call Mom on the way to the firehouse."

Ember tries to distract me on the way there. She talks and I try to listen. I just can't shut my mind off. I can't help but worry. This is all new to me, feeling this about someone. Add in the fear of not being there when something happens. I'm a mess.

Ember pulls into the lot and I see several women filling the back of a van. We get out of the car and find Nancy.

"Hey, girls. We have sandwiches and chips, and coolers of water and drinks. Our shift will run until eleven and then we switch off." She focuses her eyes on me. "Tatum, everything will be fine. I know this is the first for you. Our guys will be okay; we have to stay strong for them. This," she points to the van, "helps keep them going. Just knowing you are there will be all he needs," she assures me.

Ember and I follow the van in her car. Driving toward the stables, I can see the flames lighting up the night sky. We park at a safe distance and help set up. The smoke is thick and makes it hard to breathe at times. I say a silent prayer that everyone's okay.

I focus on keeping everything stocked while crew members come over to take quick breaks from the mayhem. Steve stopped by earlier to tell us the fire spread fast. The owner was able to get all the horses to safety. It started in the back of the stables where the new addition to the training facility was built. More than likely, electrical issues caused the fire.

Time is dragging as we watch the once state of the art stables burn to the ground. Crew members continue to stop by for drinks and food, as a quick relief. It's almost eleven o'clock and I have yet to see Blaise. Nancy and Ember assure me he's fine; he just hasn't felt like he needed a break. This actually doesn't really surprise me. Most of the people who have stopped by were ordered to do so by their chiefs. Blaise is stubborn and his dad knows this. I know he's one of the men who insist on letting others get a break while he stays to battle the inferno. I know this, but I still wish I could see him. I need to see with my own eyes that he's okay.

Eleven o'clock rolls around and another auxiliary comes to take our place. I don't want to leave. I want to stay and…I don't know what. I just know I need to be here. My mind is running through how I can convince Ember to stay when I hear him.

"Tate." His voice is gruff, but it's him.

Blaise.

I whip my ahead around and there he stands. He's covered in smoke and his silver eyes are tired. None of that matters. What matters is that he's here and he's okay. I drop the bag filled with paper supplies and run to him.

Blaise opens his arms wide as I jump on him and wrap my legs around his waist. His arms close around me and it's just us. He holds me tight. I never want him to let me go.

"Hey you," he says softly.

That causes my tears to flow, tears of relief, joy, and sadness. Two little words that mean so much to me. Eventually, I release my legs from around his waist and slide my feet to the ground. Blaise places his finger under my chin and lifts my head.

"You okay?" he asks. He brushes my tears away with his thumbs.

I laugh, "I'm more than okay. I was so worried about you."

He leans down and places a kiss on my forehead.

Nancy and Ember come over and give him a hug. He keeps me tucked into his side the entire time. "We'll be here most of the night," he tells us. "We have the fire under control, so it's not spreading, but this is a big facility."

"We just finished our shift, so we'll be heading home soon," Nancy says.

"I want to stay," I say against his chest.

Blaise wraps both arms around me and brings his lips to my ear. "Go home and get some rest. I'll come to you as soon as we're done here."

"But what if—"

Blaise pulls back and captures my face with his hands. "Baby, nothing is going to happen to me. The fire is secured and no one is inside. The immediate danger is done. We just need to be here to fight flames."

I nod my head in agreement. I don't like it, but I know I won't be able to be at every fire and every accident he's called to. I need to learn to cope with this.

"I'll come to you as soon as I can, okay?"

"Okay." I barely get the words out before his lips crash with mine.

Blaise gulps down two bottles of water and heads back to relieve members of his crew. Ember and I hug their mom goodbye and climb in her car.

"I called Asher, and he's home. Why don't we swing by and pick some clothes up for Blaise." She smiles. "I heard him say he would come to you, and he's going to want to shower and change. That is unless you were planning on keeping him in his birthday suit." She winks.

I laugh, "That does sound appealing, but he's going to be exhausted. I think he would really appreciate clean clothes. Good idea."

CHAPTER 44

BLAISE

It's five in the morning and my ass is dragging. Dad called in today's crew that was supposed to start at eight to relieve us. Standing outside their apartment, I try to be as quiet as I can so I don't wake them. I'm going to have to shower. I hope Jackson has left some clothes here at some point; otherwise, my ass will be naked. Right now, at this moment, I couldn't care less. I just want to shower and crawl in bed with my girl.

Her being there tonight, supporting me, my family, my crew members. I fall more in love with her each day. Beth would have whined and complained, not that she and Tatum are anything alike, thank God. Tatum is the best thing that has ever happened to me.

I make my way down the hall and quietly let myself into her room. She's curled up in a ball on the side of the bed I usually sleep on. She's clutching the pillow tight. I see she also has her cell in her hand. My chest constricts just seeing how much she cares.

I walk into her bathroom and shut the door before turning on the light. I strip out of my clothes and lay them in a pile on the floor. I'll have to clean up my mess tomorrow. I turn on the hot spray and let it massage my tired muscles. I reach for the shampoo and see mine sitting on the shelf beside hers. I smile. Tatum knew I would need a shower. She also knew I would keep my promise and come to her. Like there is anywhere else I would rather be.

I quickly wash away the grime and towel off. I make my way to her bed and gently remove the cell phone from her hands. She stirs and opens her eyes.

"Hey," she says groggily. She scoots back to her side of the bed and I slip in beside her, pulling her into my arms.

"Hey you," I say, kissing the top of her head. I drift off to sleep with her in my arms.

I wake up when Tatum tries to remove herself from my arms. "Quit it, I'm trying to sleep," I mumble.

She chuckles. "I have to get ready for work," she says.

"Don't go. Call in sick," I whine.

"I can't." She leans up and kisses my cheek. I grab her by the hips and settle her on my lap. Her long dark locks are in a jumbled mess and she's wearing my shirt. She is so damn sexy; I want to engrain this moment in my memory. I always want to remember what she looks like, what this feels like, being with her like this.

I reach my hand up and cup her face, gently running my thumb across her bottom lip. "I love you, Tatum." The words slip off my tongue like I've said them a thousand times. I have, in my head.

Tatum leans down, her lips close to mine, her green eyes filled with moisture. "I love you, too." Then she kisses me.

Pulling away from her kiss, I grab her hips and flip her onto her back, and I'm pushing inside of her. Home. Tatum is home to me and home feels fucking fantastic.

Tatum claws at my back trying to get me to go faster. I don't want to for multiple reasons. I'm about to blow and increasing my speed would end this, and I'm not ready for that. We just said I love you for the first time; I want to take my time with her.

Leaning down, I capture her lips with mine, our tongues moving in time with our bodies. I'm not going to last long; she feels too good.

"Blaise," she breathes my name and I feel her clench around me. She's close. I deepen my thrust just enough to throw us both over the edge.

I roll to the side and wrap her in my arms. Once our breathing evens out, Tatum rushes to get a shower so she's not late for work. "There's clothes for you on the dresser," she says, walking toward the shower.

I jump out of bed and slip into a pair of my sweats. She's taking care of me. I smile as I head toward the kitchen to make my girl some breakfast.

Ember is in the kitchen pulling waffles out of the toaster. "Hey. What time did you get in?"

"Around five," I say, popping two waffles in for Tate.

"What are you doing up?" she asks.

"Tate has to get up for work. I tried to talk her into calling in, but she wouldn't," I grumble, and my sister laughs.

Just as I'm taking her waffles out of the toaster, Tatum comes barreling into the kitchen, hopping on one foot as she slides her foot into her shoe.

I place them on a plate and add syrup. I motion for her to sit and eat; she does. I grab her a glass of orange juice and place it in front of her. Leaning down, I place a kiss on top of her head.

She scarfs down her food and quickly stands. I grab her wrist. "I got it, babe," I say. She nods her head and grabs her purse. "Let me walk you out."

"No, you need to go back to sleep. Are you at the shop tonight?" she asks.

"Yes, but I don't even know what's on my schedule."

"Okay, I'll call you later," she says, heading toward the door.

I reach for her arm and tug her back against my chest. "Have a good day," I whisper against her lips, and then give her a chaste kiss. She pulls back and smiles. "I love you." I smile at how good it feels to finally be able to say those words out loud.

"Love you, too" she says with one last quick peck on the lips, and then she's out the door.

"That's new," Ember says behind me. I can hear the smile in her voice.

"No, it's not. Saying it out loud is new, but not the sentiment," I tell her as I walk back to Tatum's room to grab a few more hours of sleep.

I roll out of bed around noon and clean up my mess in Tate's bathroom. After I get my clothes in a trash bag, I throw my bag in the back of my truck and head home to change. Rushing through another shower, and a quick sandwich later, I'm pulling into Self Expressions right on time. I unlock the door and get set up for my first client. Jeff, the artist we recently hired to pick up some of the work, walks in behind me.

"Hey, man. Haven't seen you in a while," he says in greeting.

"Yeah, we seem to be on opposite shifts and the other night, Ash took my two clients because my girl was sick."

"Your girl? Holy shit, dude, it hasn't been that long. You been holding out on me?" he laughs.

I smirk, but don't reply. I'm ready for all they can dish out. Tatum is so worth it.

I'm in the middle of a skull chest piece when I hear Jeff talking to Asher. "Holy fuck, she's hot. I got this," he says.

I just roll my eyes. He can have her and all the others. I got mine and nothing else compares.

"Watch yourself, Jeff. If Blaise hears you talking about his girl like that, you'll not only find yourself unemployed, but knocked out on your ass," Asher warns.

What the fuck! I sit my gun down and tell my client I'll be right back. I rip off my gloves and stalk to the front desk. I make it just in time to see Tatum walking through the front door. She spots me immediately and I huge smile graces her face. My girl.

I hold my arms open and she walks straight into them. "Hey you," I say.

"I missed you today," she replies.

"I'm in the middle of a chest piece, want to come watch?" I ask her.

She nods her head, still smiling. I lace our fingers together and lead her back to my room. As I walk by Jeff, I smack the back of his head with my other hand. No words are needed; he knows she's mine and he fucked up. I'll give him a pass because she is beautiful, and he didn't know she was mine; now he does. No more second chances, not that I think he'll need any. Jeff's a good guy, and if he does, well, I'm good with kicking his ass. It's whatever.

I introduce Tate to my client and verify he's all right with her watching. She sits quietly in the corner watching my every move. I see her cringe a few times as my client grits his teeth. We've talked about it before, and she's not a fan of needles. That's fine with me; I like her smooth, creamy skin just the way it is.

The rest of the night flies by. I know it's because Tatum is here with me. I tell her she doesn't have to stay, but she insists she was good with watching me do what I love.

After closing up shop, she follows me back to my place. She surprised me as I was walking her to her car, saying she packed a bag for work tomorrow. Asher is never here, so we have the place all to ourselves. We don't have to worry about my sister overhearing us. Not that I care really, but I know it bothers Tate.

We shower together, which leads to me taking her hard and fast against the shower wall. I apologize for losing control, but she says she loved every minute of it. I swear this girl was made for me.

We're lying in bed with me spooned in behind her when Tatum says, "I've been thinking a lot about my parents, and my life here."

I hold my breath; I have no idea what she's going to say next.

"When I came here with Leah and Brent, I closed up the house and put the neighbor kid on the payroll to keep the lawn mowed. Leah didn't want me to make a rash decision and sell, then regret it. I put most everything in storage, except for what I brought with me," she explains.

I still have no idea where she's going with this. Is she trying to tell me she wants to move back to Ohio? If that's what she really wants, we'll make it work. I'm sure I can join a paid department or maybe even open another branch of Self Expressions. Or is she saying she's changed her mind about us?

CHAPTER 45

I roll over so I'm facing him. He's beautiful. I know you're not supposed to call guys beautiful, but that's what he is. His dark hair is still damp from our shower; his defined jaw is covered with the day's stubble. I reach up and trace his jawline with my finger. His silver eyes are boring into me. I can tell he's confused and scared maybe?

"I know what I want to do with it, with the house." I scoot closer and lay my head against his chest. His arms are immediately holding me tight against him. "I want to sell it."

I feel the release of air from his lungs and his body relax.

"You're where I want to be. Ohio has nothing for me, and Tennessee, well, it has you."

"Thank God," he says with relief. "What can I do to help?"

"I think I'm good. I'm going to call and make an appointment with a realtor and get it listed. Not much else to do really. I'll eventually need to go through the storage unit and decide what I want to keep and what I don't, but the apartment isn't big enough for that," I chuckle.

"Bring it here," he says. "I have tons of space and Asher is moving into Grace's condo. He's moving his stuff out this weekend. I'll pay to have it moved here and you can go through it as you want."

"Thank you, that's sweet, but I'm not sure I'm ready to go through it all just yet."

"Well, when you are, the offer stands," he tells me.

We lay there in silence holding each other, both at peace. I hear him say, "I love you, Tate, so fucking much," just as my eyes fall closed.

The next few weeks fly by. Work, Blaise, and conference calls with the realtor. Leah's mom set me up with a friend of hers and she's been amazing. She emailed me the contract so I didn't have to drive back to Ohio just to list the house. It's been three weeks since it's been on the market, and there have been a lot of interested buyers. I'm sad, but at the same time, I could never live there. Not without them. So this is just the ending to another chapter.

Today is Saturday and Leah and I are going out for a girls' day. I miss her so much. She and Brent got married last week in Hawaii, and we need to catch up. I pull into the lot and see Leah standing by the door; she waves.

I jump out of my car and rush to her, giving her a huge hug. "I missed you, Mrs. Wethington." She holds up her ring finger to show her wedding band nestled against her engagement ring.

Leah laughs. I follow her into the salon where we are getting manicures and pedicures. Before we know it, we're done at the salon and heading to lunch. Leah claims her appetite has doubled in the last week as she rubs her belly. My eyes follow her movement and I can see the start of a small baby bump.

"Leah, I am so happy for you. You're going to be a mom," I say, excited.

"I know. It's scary and exciting all at the same time."

"Just remember that Aunt Tate is always around when you need a break or a night out on the town," I tell her.

She laughs, "I'm going to hold you to that. Wait, let me get my phone. Can you say that again so I can record it? You know, just in case you change your mind."

I laugh at her antics. I've missed my best friend, my sister from another mister.

The entire day is so much fun. It's been longer than I care to remember since just the two of us hung out like this. We part ways at the restaurant so we can each go home and get ready for tonight. The eight of us are meeting at Backwoods tonight to celebrate Leah and Brent's nuptials.

Blaise is waiting for me at the apartment when I get there. This hinders the process of me getting ready. The man is tempting! Ember texts me and lets me know she and Jackson are riding over with Asher and Grace.

When I finally pull myself away from Blaise, I push him out of my room and lock the door. Otherwise, we would not be going anywhere.

I rush through my shower, careful not to get my hair wet. I don't have time to dry it. I throw on a black sundress with a teal design and Ember's teal cowboy boots. I pull my hair up into a ponytail and call it good.

As I open my bedroom door, I run into a wall of muscle. Blaise. He holds me at arms-length as he checks out my outfit.

"Uh um," I clear my throat to get his attention. His silver eyes shining with mischief capture mine. "Stop undressing me with your eyes, Mr. Richards. We don't have time for that," I scold him.

"Baby, I can't take my eyes off of you. You look hot," he says, pinching my ass.

I laugh and swat his arm away; we really need to leave.

Backwoods is packed tonight. Ember says it's because the band just got signed with a big label. Small town boys making it big and all that. Blaise leads us to a table in the back corner large enough for the eight of us. Just as we go to sit, the other six come walking through the door.

Blaise orders a round of drinks, with a bottle of water for Leah, to toast the happy couple. I don't plan on drinking anything other than water after this shot. I don't want Leah to be the only sober one among us. She's all smiles either way. I love seeing her this happy.

We all toss back our shots and hit the dance floor. The song "It Goes Like This" by Thomas Rhett is playing. Blaise pulls me tight against his chest and I melt into him. I'm not really sure I can even call what we are doing dancing, really. He's holding me close as we gently sway back and forth. I'm in my own little Blaise consumed world and I love every freaking minute of it.

As the song ends, his lips find mine. I stand on my tiptoes to gain better access as I open for him. The kiss is gentle, yet demanding. He's taking what he wants, and I am more than willing to let him.

"I think I need to sit down after that," he says. I can feel how the kiss affected him. I turn so my body is directly in front of him. His hands find my hips as I lead us back to the table, hiding the evidence.

A few feet from our table, a blonde girl and her friend step into our path. "Blaise," she says curtly.

His grip on my hips tighten as he pulls me tight against his chest. His arms snake around my waist. He obviously is trying to send a message to this girl.

"Beth," he says, sounding bored.

Beth...*Oh shit!* This is her. This is the girl he was with who cheated on him and got pregnant by someone else.

"New flavor?" she sneers.

"No. New love," he says, placing his lips against my neck. I shiver at the contact.

"Humph. This one must be making you work for it," she says, pointing to where his arms are around my waist.

"Don't you have a husband to go home to? Oh, that's right. You cheated on him too and he divorced your sorry ass. Best of luck," he says, and guides us to move around her.

"That bitch ain't got nothing on me," she says as we pass.

Blaise stops us and jerks his head around. "You don't fucking look or breathe in her direction. This girl," he reaches for me, "is the most important person in my life. She's off limits to you. Don't talk to her, don't even look at her. Take your cheating ass somewhere else. We don't need your shit," he snarls.

Then, he kisses me. His lips capture mine, possessing me. I can't help the moan that escapes my lips.

"ARGH!" I hear Beth growl.

By the time Blaise releases my lips, she's gone. Good riddance.

As we reach the table, all eyes are on us. Asher raises his eyebrows, asking, "You good?" to Blaise.

He nods his head and kisses my temple. "Never better," he says.

We don't see Beth the rest of the night, and we're able to relax and enjoy ourselves. Brent got a little tipsy, well a lot tipsy, and made sure he told everyone within hearing distance that he knocked up his new bride. Leah just laughed and smiled. They are both radiating excitement and love.

As I survey our group, I realize life is moving on and that's okay. That's what they would want for me. I wish more than anything my parents were able to meet Blaise and his family, but more than likely, I wouldn't be here if I hadn't lost them. It's bitter sweet. I'll miss them every day. I look over at Blaise as he talks with his hands to Asher, Brent, and Jackson. I will love him every day. He's so tangled up in my heart that there is no chance of killing the roots.

Blaise is my future.

It's Monday morning. The weekend flew by. I guess what they say is right, time flies when you're having fun.

As I'm walking into the building, my cell rings. Looking at the screen, I see it's my relator. "Hey, Mary," I say in greeting.

"Tatum, we have an offer. They bid five thousand below asking price. They are pre-approved for that amount. They love the house. It's a young couple with two small children, ages two and four. I think we should take the deal," she says in a rush.

I laugh, "Sounds great to me. The house is great for kids with the big yard. What's the next step?" I ask her.

"Well, since they are pre-approved, we just need to schedule the closing. I had the house inspected last week, so it's within the thirty day guidelines. I'll let them know you accept their offer and call you once I get everything set up. Are there any restrictions on times for you to travel back here?" she asks.

"No, my boss is great. I told him what was going on and that I will need a few days to travel back to Ohio to settle everything. I got two weeks vacation when I started, so I have the time," I tell her.

"Wow, sounds like a great gig," she says.

I look up and see Nancy smiling at me. "In more ways than one," I tell her.

"All right, well, let me get to work on this and I'll be in touch."

"Great, thank you so much, Mary." I hit end and shove my phone back in my purse.

"That sounded like good news," Nancy says with a smile.

I nod. "Yeah, I decided to sell my parents' place back in Ohio. That was the real estate agent; she had a bid and I accepted their offer. I'll need to take a few days off for the closing. I'll know more soon," I say.

"Blaise mentioned that. He seemed pleased you're staying in town. He was afraid you were moving back to Ohio," she says.

I shake my head no. I look up to see her watching me intently. "Blaise is my home now," I say. I slap my hand over my mouth. The words just flew out of my mouth before I could stop them. *Shit!* Nancy is his mom and I just blurted that out. *Way to go, Tatum!*

A huge smile lights up her face. "I'm so glad to hear you say that. My boy is completely smitten with you. I've never seen this side of him, and it's nice. You two are good together," she tells me.

What the hell, I might as well go all in. "I love him," I say simply.

She nods in acknowledgment. "He loves you, too. He told me…well, let's just say you're not alone in your feelings."

I smile at her. "I better get busy." I wave as I walk off toward my office.

CHAPTER 46

BLAISE

After making breakfast for my girl, I head home. I need to shower and change and be ready. I'm on call for the next twenty-four hours with the department. Now that I have Tatum, it seems like balancing the shop, my volunteer time, and my time with her is difficult. I refuse to give up any time with her and the shop, well, that's my dream. I need to talk to Dad about cutting back my hours. I love it and I'm proud to serve the community, but the shop is how I live and, well, so is Tatum.

I do a few things around the house that I've been neglecting, like laundry. I text Tate to see if she's free for lunch; she's not. She has a meeting scheduled. I'm disappointed, but I get it. It's her job.

I decide to try my luck and see if Dad has time to talk. I've been thinking about it all day and I really want to get his take on me cutting back.

When I arrive at the firehouse, I shoot the shit with a few of the guys before heading to Dad's office. I knock lightly on the doorframe.

Dad looks up and smiles when he sees me. "Hey, son."

"Hey, you got a minute?" I ask him. I'm suddenly nervous that he's going to be upset with me. I know that's an irrational fear, but it's there all the same.

"Always for you," he says. Both of my parents have always put us kids first, whatever we needed.

I walk in and close the door. He raises his eyebrows in question, but doesn't say anything. I take the chair across from him and stretch out my legs. "I've been thinking a lot lately about life and how busy everything seems." I decide to ease into it.

"Indeed, life can feel like it's passing you by," he says.

I nod. So far so good. "Yeah, the shop is growing. Asher and I just hired another part-time artist to help out. Grace is taking over for Ember full-time; business is great."

"That's great news. I knew you boys would be a success. You've talked about your own shop since you were teenagers. I'm proud of both of you."

That's Dad. Always telling us how proud he is. My gut clenches at the thought of disappointing him. He's watching me, waiting. He probably already knows what's coming. He's a smart man, my dad. He won't say it for me. I'm going to have to just go for it. "So, I was thinking about maybe cutting back on my volunteer hours here," I say.

Dad steeples his fingers under his chin and leans back in his chair. "I see. And what's brought this change on?" he asks. I can see the mischief in his eyes, eyes that are just like mine. He knows, but he's going to make me say it. My mind drifts back to the Fourth of July party and our conversation.

"Tatum. I love her. The shop is my living, how I support myself. She is the air I breathe and I need more time with her. I want it all with her. I can't be married and have a family and never be home. I won't do that to her or our children," I tell him. I gave him way more information than he needed, but I want him to know where I stand. This is a forever deal for me, and I want to be the kind of husband and father that he was, that he is. "I want to be there for my family like you were," I add.

Dad smiles. "I love being right. So how does Tatum feel about all of this?" he asks.

He really wants to know if she's in as far as I am. I can honestly say without hesitation that she is. "She loves me, too. The marriage and kids thing, has yet to be discussed, but I want that. I know she does as well; we just haven't talked about that for us, for our future."

Dad stands up and walks around the desk. I stand as well. "I'm damn proud of you, son," he says, giving me a hug. "As far as your time here, this is my dream, not yours. I appreciate all that you do and I enjoy working with you. You tell me how much time you're available and I'll make it happen. Hell, you don't have to volunteer at all. I'm

228

proud either way. You have to love your life, Blaise, for you and, well, now for Tatum," he says, leaning back against his desk.

I release the breath I was holding. "Thank you. I'm not ready to give it up completely, but I would like to cut back. I'll talk to Tate about it, about us, and get back with you," I tell him.

"Sounds good. In the meantime, I'll go ahead and start scaling you back a little at a time."

"Thanks, Dad," I say, with emotion in my voice.

He nods his head. "Now get out of my office; some of us have work to do," he laughs and winks.

Just as I walk out the door, the alarm sounds. There is an auto accident, time to suit up. I send Tate a quick text letting her know.

Me: Hey. Just got called out on a run. Will stop by when I'm done. I love you.

Tatum: K. Love you. Be safe!!

CHAPTER 47

Just as I'm putting my phone back in my purse from replying to Blaise's text, it rings. It's Mary. Surely she doesn't have the closing scheduled already.

"Hey, long time no talk," I say in greeting. She laughs.

"Hi, Tatum. I got everything scheduled for Thursday of this week at three in the afternoon. I thought a later time might work so you could drive down the day of and miss less work. The family wants to move fast; they have to be out of their place in two weeks. They love that you have given them immediate occupancy."

"Wow. All right then. Let me talk to my boss and get everything squared away and I will see you on Thursday," I tell her.

"Great. See you then," she say, and we end the call. I look up when I hear a knock on my office door. It's Harry.

"Hey, Tatum. Nancy had a dentist appointment that she forgot about. I told her to go ahead and go. Can you cover reception for the next thirty minutes until we close down for the day?" he asks.

"Sure, no problem at all. Actually, I'm glad you're here. That was my real estate agent. I sold my parents' house, so I need to be in Ohio on Thursday for the closing."

"No problem at all. You have the time, just let Nancy or I know how long you will be gone so we can cover for you," he says with a wave of his hand.

I seriously lucked into the best job ever. Working with Nancy and Harry is great!

"Thank you so much. I'll let you know for sure tomorrow," I say. I need to talk to Blaise first and see what his schedule is. I wonder if he'll come with me.

Harry waves his hand in the air dismissing me as he walks back to his office.

The last half hour of the day feels like two minutes. I pack up my stuff and head home. I decide to stop at the store and pick up the stuff to make meatloaf. That way Blaise can easily heat it up when he finishes with his run. Meatloaf is better cold in my opinion anyway.

The store is quiet. Monday nights must be the best time to shop for groceries. I'm bending down to pull a box of macaroni and cheese from the shelf when I hear a snarky voice behind me say, "Well look who it is."

I stand up to my full height and see no one other than Beth. She's pushing a cart with an adorable dark haired little girl sitting in it. Beth follows my gaze to her daughter and smirks. "She looks just like him, huh?" she says sweetly.

Wait! What? I shake my head at her question.

"Blaise claims she's not his, but look at her; you know she is." She speaks in her sugary voice, the voice that is threating to rip my heart to shreds. He lied to me.

"B—Blaise said the baby wasn't…" I trail off as I study the little girl before me. She has straight dark hair and dark brown eyes. She has Beth's eyes. I'm trying to find something, anything, that will convince me that what she's saying isn't true. Sure she has dark hair, but that doesn't make her his. He wouldn't lie to me or run out on his responsibilities. Would he? Who am I kidding? I've only known him a few months. I allowed myself to fall head over heels in love with him in a matter of months. Do I really know him? I thought I did. Look what happened with Josh and we were together for years.

"The real reason my husband left me is because he found out that she's not his." She strokes her daughter's hair. "Blaise was coming around to the idea of being a dad until you came into the picture. Now he wants nothing to do with either of us," she says. Her eyes find mine. "Please for my daughter, walk away." Her voice is not mean, or hateful; she sounds…sincere.

Suddenly, I can't breathe. I need to get out of here. I don't reply. I push my cart to the check out and, luckily, there is no line. I quickly pay for my items and rush to my car. Once inside, the tears escape like a waterfall running over my cheeks. I need to get out of here. I don't want her to see that she got to me. I can't let her see my heart breaking. I buckle my seatbelt and slowly drive away. I drive to the apartment, grateful that I don't see Ember's car in the lot.

I load up the groceries and make my way inside. I sit the bags down on the counter and begin putting them away. My mind is a jumbled mess. I need time to process all of this. I don't know what to believe; I just don't know. My insecurities from my past are taking control and I hate that. I hate that I doubt him even a little, but she was so…sincere. If she was being mean and nasty it would be easier to think she's just trying to split us up. But when she asked me to walk away, her voice was defeated.

Suddenly, it hits me. I need time away from it all to figure it all out. I pick up my phone and dial Harry.

"Hey, Harry. It's Tatum. I have a few things to sort out with the house and storage before the closing. I thought I would head back to Ohio tomorrow and get that all squared away. Would that be all right? I'll just take the rest of the week as vacation and return to the office on Monday?" I ask. I'm trying to keep the sadness and desperation out of my voice, but I know he can tell how emotional I am.

"Sure, Tatum. Take all the time you need; just don't get any ideas about moving back there. We need you to come back home to us," he says in his fatherly voice. This causes my tears to return. He and his wife have been so good to me.

"Thanks, Harry. I'll be back on Monday," I tell him and we say our goodbyes.

I hit end on my phone and place it on the counter. I need to pack and get out of here. I'll call Leah on my way to let her know what's going on. I run to my room and fill a suitcase with enough clothes for the next few days. I pack my essentials into a separate travel case. I slip my cell charger into my laptop case and call it good. I can stay at the house. I turn off the light and head out the door, silently praying that no one sees me and tries to stop me before I make it out of town.

Car loaded, I strap myself in and type out a quick text to Ember.

Me: Sold parents' house. Headed to Ohio to square everything way. Will be back this weekend.

After reading it three times, I hit send. I immediately dial Leah, but she doesn't answer. I leave her a message. "Hey, Leah, it's me." I choke back tears. "Everything is so screwed up. I ran into Beth and she had her little girl with her. She said she really is Blaise's. I'm so confused and torn. Did I jump into this too soon? I've only known him a few months, maybe he's lying to me. Look at what Josh did." I pause as a sob breaks from my chest. "I'm on my way back to Columbus. I sold the house, so I'm going to spend a few days there before the closing on Thursday. I'll be home this weekend. Call me if you get time. I just need my best friend," I say as I can no longer control the sobs. I hit end and place my phone in the cup holder.

I hear a ding and look down to see my car telling me I have a "Low Fuel Level". Great, I'm not even ten miles out of town. I merge lanes and signal to get off at the next exit. I stop at the traffic light at the end of the exit ramp, waiting to turn left. I watch the light. The light turns green and I watch as the car in front of me starts to move. I follow the line of traffic.

I hear screeching tires and the impact of a hit to my car. My car spins and flips until it finally lands. My heart is racing and my entire body is shaking. I feel slicing pain in my head. I place my palm against my forehead and feel wetness. Pulling back, my hand is covered in blood. That's the last thing I remember before darkness claims me.

CHAPTER 48

BLAISE

The accident took longer than usual. There was a lot of glass on the road. Thankfully, no one was seriously injured. Once we're back at the firehouse, I strip down and hit the shower. I rush through the process so I can call Tatum. I'm excited to talk to her about my discussion with Dad earlier today. I want her to know I want everything with her, all of it.

Pulling my shirt over my head, jeans still unbuttoned, I reach for my phone to call her. The other guys in the locker room are watching with fascination. This is another first for me. I always used to let them come to me, even Beth. Not Tate. Never with Tate. Her phone goes straight to voicemail which is odd. I hit end and finish getting dressed just as the alarm sounds. We have another run; it's another accident.

I follow the guys back to the truck where we suit up. I quickly type a text to Tatum.

> **Me:** Hey. I tried to call, got voicemail. Finished with run, off to another. Will call when I can. Love you! B

"Brace yourself, fellas; apparently, this is a bad one. White female early twenties, t-boned by a drunk driver," Jeffers says from the front seat. He's got his phone to his ear talking to dispatch who also happens to be his sister.

No one says anything, because, really, what is there to say? It's a shitty fucking deal. My guess is ten-to-one the drunk driver walks away with barely a scratch. This is part of the job I hate. I hate the tragedy. The part where you watch as family members are told their loved ones either might not make it or didn't make it at all. This is the hard part.

We arrive at scene and park the truck. The internal radio beeps and my dad's voice fills the airways. "Tell Blaise to stay back. I need to talk to him," he says. His voice is hard. My stomach drops. Something's wrong.

Tatum.

I couldn't get ahold of her. I thought it was odd her phone went to voicemail, but…no, it can't be her. My breathing is accelerated. I can feel the panic start to set in. I reach for the handle of the truck and Asher is there.

"Let me out, Ash," I say, venom in my voice.

"Bro, you need to take a breath. Dad just needs to talk to you," he says calmly. His calm demeanor does nothing to calm my nerves. He is my twin brother after all; I can read him better than anyone. He's not a blubbering mess and neither is Dad. That's when I know for sure, it's her. My girl. I have to get to her.

I place my hand on the door handle and use my shoulder to push with all of my might against the door. Asher stumbles back. I jump out of the truck, and before I take two steps, he has me tackled to the ground. I feel a strong grip on my shoulder, looking up I see it's Dad.

"I need to go to her," I plead with him.

His eyes, glassy with tears, bore into mine. "Son, you need to calm down first. I need to prepare you," he tells me.

"Fuck that! Dad, you know! You know I need her; she's my one. I need to go to her. Dammit, let me go!" I yell at them.

Asher tightens his grip on my arm, while Dad holds the other. "Listen to me, Blaise, the accident was bad. I need you to let us do our jobs. Let us get her out of the car and assess her injuries. You have to stay back and let us work on her. You have to stand down until we know what we're dealing with," my father says, his voice cracking.

Fuck this! My future, my heart, is in that car. She's got to be scared. I need her to know I'm here, dammit. I twist my elbow into Asher's gut causing him to loosen his grip. I then tear my arms from Dad's grip and I'm running.

Running to her.

To my Tatum.

Just as I get close enough to see the car, two of my fellow crew members who happen to be the same size as me, step into my path. "Let us work, my man. You need to stand down," one of them tells me. I can see in his eyes that it's bad.

I feel the pain slice through my heart at the thought of her in any pain, at the mere thought of losing her.

"Tatum," I scream her name. "I'm here, baby," I croak out. My vision blurs and the tightness in my chest makes it hard to breathe. I can hear my name being called, but all I can do is stand there, my arms restrained by my crew as I watch the jaws-of-life prepare to remove my heart from the jumbled mess that is Tatum's car.

I drop to my knees as I hear the first sound of grinding metal. I feel a hand on my shoulder, then a voice, it's Asher. "Blaise, you have to stay strong for her. She needs you to fight. She needs you, brother," he says as he drops to his knees beside me. I feel his arm go around my shoulders and he squeezes. I don't even try to hide the tears that are coursing down my cheeks.

I feel a presence beside me, but I don't take my eyes from the car. I need to see her. I need to make sure she's okay. A hand lands on my shoulder, a firm grip. Dad.

I hear him say Mom is calling Brent so he can notify Leah. I should be the one to handle that call, but I can't. I can't move from this spot without seeing if she's okay.

I can't breathe without her.

After what seems like hours, when in reality it's not more than a couple of minutes, the paramedics are ready to extract Tatum from the car. I jump to my feet. I need to see her as soon as she's out. From the angle I'm standing, all I can see is what a totaled mess her car is.

I watch as they carefully lift her limp body from the car and place her on the stretcher. I take a step and feel my arms being pulled back from both sides.

"Please, let me go to her," I beg my father and Asher.

"Son, let them take care of her. They need to asses her injuries," Dad says calmly.

I know he's right, but I don't like it. I stand on the side of the road watching as they work on her. Her face is covered in blood and I feel my knees weaken at the sight. Oh, God, please save her. Please don't take her way from me, I plead.

Finally, they start wheeling the stretcher toward the ambulance. I twist out of the hold they have on me and I'm beside her in no time. I reach for her hand, but stop myself before I touch her. Her body is limp; she looks so small and frail.

"Sir, you need to step back." This from the ambulance driver. He's from the next town over. Our crew is working on the drunk driver.

"She's my fiancée," I tell him.

He nods his head in understanding. "You can ride as long as you stay out of the way. I won't hesitate to stop this rig and kick your ass to the curb," he tells me.

At this point, I would agree to anything just to be with her. I nod my head in agreement and climb in the back of the squad. I sit next to the stretcher and reach for her hand.

"Sorry, sir, but you can't touch her. Not yet. We don't know the extent of her injuries."

I slowly pull my hand away. I can actually feel my heart breaking at the sight of her. My girl, battered and broken. I close my eyes and send another prayer to keep her safe, to help her pull through this.

Once we arrive at the hospital, she is whisked away and I'm told to stop at the registration desk to give them all of her information. As I approach the desk, I hear my name. I look up to see Leah, Brent, Ember, Jackson, Asher, Grace, and my parents. I choke back the sob that threatens to break free.

"How is she?" Leah asks me.

I shake my head no. "She's still unconscious. They said I have to register her first," I say.

"I'll go with you," she says as she links her arm through mine and we walk the remaining short distance to the registration desk.

We go through the process of registration and are told to go back to the waiting room and someone will be out to update us as soon as they know more.

Waiting, I fucking suck at waiting.

We reach the waiting room. Leah takes a seat by Brent while I pace back and forth. I can't sit. I need to know how she is. I continue to pace. They all try to get me to sit, but I can't. I have to keep moving. This goes on for an hour before we hear the door open and a man in dark blue scrubs enters the room.

"Are you the family of Tatum Thompson?" he asks.

"Yes," we all say. I stop pacing and turn to face him.

"I need immediate family," he says, unsure.

"She has no immediate family. She's my best friend and this is her fiancé," Leah says without missing a beat. I'm glad to see she and I are on the same page.

"No immediate family?" the doctor repeats her words.

Brent opens his mouth to intervene, but I beat him to it. "I am her immediate family. That girl you have in there, she fucking owns me, heart and soul. I need for you to take me to her. She needs to know I'm here," I say, my voice hard.

"Dr Jones is it?" Brent asks. He holds his hand out. "Dr. Brent Wethington. I have privileges here as well. I know this is against policy, but as a fellow physician, I can verify what he says is true. In fact, my wife has power of attorney over Tatum should an event like this occur," he tells him.

Leah's face pales; she apparently forgot, not that I blame her with all that has gone on tonight. "That's right, it's on file here at the hospital. I give full permission for her fiancé, Blaise Richards, to have full access to her and her care." She looks around the room. "Everyone in this room is her family now," she says quietly. "We all love her. Can you please just tell us what you know?" she pleads.

Releasing a deep breath, Dr. Jones proceeds to tell us that Tatum has suffered a severe concussion. She has a gash on her head about two inches long and she lost a lot of blood. Her right ankle is broken, but does not require surgery. They are in the process of setting her up for casting now; then she will be moved into a private room.

"Is she awake? When can I see her?" I ask him.

Shaking his head no, he says, "She has not yet regained consciousness. Her scans are all normal; this is just her body's way of dealing with the stress of her injuries. I expect her to make a full recovery. Once we have her cast in place, she will be moved to a private room, no more than two visitors at a time." He looks down at the iPad in his hands. "As soon as we have her settled in her room, I'll request a consult with Dr. Michaels who is the obstetrician on call tonight," he says.

Obstetrician, wait…what? My confusion must have shown as well as the others' because Dr. Jones begins to explain his previous statement.

"Our blood test shows that Ms. Thompson is pregnant. I'm sorry, I assumed as her fiancé that you knew," he says.

I drop to my knees and run my fingers through my hair. Pregnant? A baby? I'm going to be a father. "I need to see her," I say, my voice pleading.

"She doesn't know. She would have told me. She doesn't know," Leah says as she quietly cries against Brent's chest.

Dr. Jones, nods his head. "I'm sorry, Mr. Richards, I assumed that you knew. I will send someone to alert you once we have her moved," he says before turning and leaving us alone.

Pregnant. Everything I want is dangling in front of me by a thread. I bow my head to hide the tears. I see a small hand appear on my leg.

"Blaise, you have to stay strong for her. She needs you now more than ever." Leah sniffs. "The last tragedy that hit her, she was left by—"

"Don't!" I say, my voice angry. "Don't you dare compare me to him," I choke on the words.

"I'm not…I just…I want you to know that she loves you," Leah says quietly.

240

A sob breaks from my chest at her words. Ember sits on the other side of me and wraps her arm around my shoulders. I lean into her. "I don't know how to be me without her," I whisper.

Nothing else is said. We all sit and wait, wait to hear she's in a room so we can go to her. The doctor said he expects a full recovery, but the baby? "Oh, God, our baby. I need them both."

After about an hour, the same doctor greets us. He tells us Tatum has been moved into a private room and we can go in two at a time. I don't wait to see who's coming with me. I'm on my feet making my way toward the elevators. All I know is I am half of that equation, and I will remain that way until my girl gets to come home. I'm not leaving her. The others will just have to take turns one at a time or break the two at a time rule. I. Am. Not. Leaving. Her.

I stand outside her door and take a deep breath. Exhaling, I slowly push open the door. As soon as my eyes land on her, wet hot tears fall from my eyes. She's pale and connected to a bunch of wires. I walk to the side of the bed and grab her hand. It's cold. Leaning down, I place a kiss on her temple before pulling a chair up beside the bed. I bring her fingers to my lips and pepper them with kisses.

"Hey, baby. It's me, Blaise. You were in an accident, but the doctor says you're going to be fine. I just need you to wake up for me." I kiss her hand again. Reassuring myself that she's here, she's alive. "He actually gave me some exciting news that I can't wait to share with you." I place my hand gently against her belly. "I need you to wake up, Tate. I love you so much, baby," I say, my voice gruff with tears and emotion.

I hear the door open and look up to see Leah. "Hey," she says softly. I watch as she walks to the other side of the bed and grabs Tate's other hand. "Listen, missy, I need you here with me. I need my best friend." She looks at me. "Blaise is here. He loves you and needs you to wake up. Who else is going to keep him in line?" she jokes. I can't help but smile at the effort.

Leaning down, she kisses Tate's cheek. "I'm going to let the others have a turn. I'm not going anywhere," she tells me. I nod in agreement and watch her walk away.

No sooner than she's gone, the door opens and in walks Asher. I feel tears well up again at the sight of my twin. We've always had this freaky connection. I know he can feel my sorrow, just like I can with him. I can't explain it, it just is. Instead of walking to the same side of the bed that Leah had, he heads straight for me. I'm on my feet ready to accept the hug I know is coming. "She's gonna be okay, bro," he whispers.

Pulling back from the hug, we both wipe our eyes. Asher begins to tell me about the drunk driver, how he did indeed walk away without a scratch and that he and Brent have already contacted an attorney. The sound of voices alert us as the door pushes open. In walk two women, one dressed in dark blue scrubs, the other…Beth.

"What the hell are you doing here?" I hiss at her.

Her face pales as she looks between Asher and me. Her eyes travel to Tatum and her skin becomes ashen. "No," she whispers.

"No, what? What the fuck are you doing here? I don't want you anywhere near her," I spit the words at her.

"Sir, you need to calm down. My name is Dr. Michaels. I am an obstetrician. Dr. Jones requested I consult with Ms. Thompson," she explains.

"You," I say, pointing to the doctor, "can stay. "She," I say, pointing to Beth, "cannot."

"Sir, this is my medical assistant. She will be assisting me with my consult on Ms. Thompson." She turns to look at Beth and notices her ashen face as she stares at Tatum lying in her bed.

"Beth?" Dr. Michaels tries to get her attention.

"I'm sorry," she barely whispers. "I let her drive. I didn't think this would happen," she says as she covers her face to hide the tears.

What. The. Fuck? "What are talking about? You let her drive? You need to explain now!" I say, my voice getting louder by the minute. My blood is boiling at the thought of Beth having something to do with Tatum's accident.

"Beth?" Dr. Michaels asks again.

"I saw her earlier today in the grocery store. I had Emily with me and I told her… I told her you were Em's dad. I told her you lied to her and I asked her to leave. I asked her to go so we would have a chance to be a family," she cries. "I saw her in the lot, she was upset. I let her drive." She wails. "I shouldn't have done it. I should have told her the truth when I saw how upset she was." She wipes her cheeks with the back of her hand. "I'm so sorry." She whispers.

"You did what?" This coming from Asher. I'm in shock at her words. Tatum thought I lied to her. She was driving upset. Not that I can blame her with what that fuckwad of an ex did to her, but I wish she would have come to me.

Finding my voice, I say, "Why would you lie to her like that? We had a paternity test. You know I'm not Emily's father. You upset her and let her drive, and now look at her. She's lying here in this hospital bed carrying my baby. Mine! This baby is mine and I want him or her more than my next breath." I stop and take a deep breath. "Get the fuck out of my face. Don't come near me or my family ever again." Beth stands still, not moving. "Leave!" I roar.

I walk back to my chair and sit down. I clasp her hands with mine and lower my head to the bed as emotions wrack my body. I did this to her. My stupid ex caused her to be upset, to be driving upset. How will she ever forgive me?

It's then I hear her sweet voice. "Blaise," she says. I look up and see Tatum awake and watching me.

CHAPTER 49

I hear voices, angry voices. I can tell one of them is Blaise. I struggle to open my eyes. The room gets quiet and I can feel someone squeezing my hands. I can smell him. I fight to force my eyes open. The pain in my head is excruciating, but I need to see him.

When I'm finally able to force them open, I see Blaise sitting beside me resting his head on the bed. "Blaise," I croak out. My throat is so dry.

He whips his head up and faces me. His silver eyes filled with despair. "Hey you," he whispers as he leans over and kisses my cheek. "I missed those beautiful green eyes," he tells me.

"Ms. Thompson, my name is Dr. Michaels. Do you remember what happened to you?" she asks me.

Blaise brings a glass with a straw to my lips; I suck the water greedily. "Yeah. I was on my way back to Ohio when I needed to stop for gas. I got off on the exit ramp and stopped at the red light. The light turned green and I followed the car in front of me. The next thing I remember is the jolt of impact and blood. There was lots of blood." I take another drink that Blaise offers as his eyes study me. He wants to know why I was going back to Ohio. I remember every word of my conversation with Beth; the question is do I believe her? This man here at my side, would he lie to me? No, I really don't think he would. Funny how tragedy can make you see things in a better light.

Dr. Michaels taps away on her iPad. "The report says you were wearing your seat belt which is good. I need to do an ultrasound to make sure everything is okay with the baby," she tells me.

"Wh—what? Baby?" I look at Blaise for clarification.

"I need to step out and find an MA. My last one was escorted out. I will be right back," Dr. Michaels says as she leaves the room.

I look to Blaise. "Baby? What is she talking about?" I ask, confused. Does he know that I know about his daughter?

Blaise gently runs his finger down my cheek. "I have a lot to tell you. Just listen, okay?" he says, his voice gentle.

"First and foremost, I love you so fucking much. To think that I could have lost you." He stops to get his emotions under control. "Second, the MA that Dr. Michaels was talking about is Beth, my ex Beth. When she saw you lying here, she came clean about the lie she told you about her daughter being mine. She's not, Tate. I insisted on a paternity test the day she was born. I would never not be a part of my child's life. I still have copies of the test at home in the safe. I will send Asher to get them," he says calmly.

I try to shake my head no, but the pain prevents the sudden movement. "I don't need to see it. I trust you."

"Then why were you leaving town? You didn't bother to tell me," he questions.

"Honestly, I just wanted some time to wrap my head around this, us. We haven't been together that long, yet it feels like a lifetime. I'm emotional from selling the house, and well, I just needed time," I tell him.

He smiles at me. "Baby, it wasn't just selling the house that has you emotional." He stands up and leans over the bed so we are eye-to-eye, nose-to-nose. He rests his palm against my belly. "We're having a baby," he says, his eyes sparkling. "That's why the obstetrician is here. She needs to make sure the baby is okay. Your doctor says you will make a full recovery; now we just have to worry about our little peanut here. Make sure all is fine," he says, gently stroking my belly.

His words cause a waterworks of emotions to break loose. "I'm pregnant?" I ask again through my tears. I need to hear it again.

Blaise shakes his head no. "No, baby, we're pregnant. You and me. We are in this together, and just so you know, I plan on marrying you and having at least two more," he says with a wink. Then his lips find mine. He's careful of my injuries. The kiss is packed full of tenderness and love.

"I love you," I say once he releases my lips.

"I love you, too," he says just as the doctor enters the room.

"All right, let's take a look at your baby," she says as she and her new assistant wheel in the ultrasound machine.

The doctor explains something about the hormone levels of my blood show that I'm not too far along. By her calculations, a few weeks. She says she will be doing a trans-vaginal ultrasound. When she pulls out a wand, I watch as Blaise's eyes go wide. He doesn't say a word, just holds my hand and stands beside me. Every few minutes he kisses my temple, my cheek, or my fingers. It's almost as though he has to touch me to reassure himself I'm okay.

Dr. Michael's assistant dims the lights and she directs our attention to the screen. I'm grateful for the distraction considering the position I'm currently in.

After a few uncomfortable minutes, Dr. Michaels points to the screen. "There," she says. "There is your baby."

I watch the tiny blip on the screen flutter. So tiny. My hand instinctively moves to my belly. Blaise covers mine with his and laces our fingers together. Tears fall from my eyes. I'm having a baby.

Blaise leans down and whispers in my ear. "We made that," he says, kissing my temple.

"Oh," Dr. Michaels says, and my heart skips a beat.

"'Oh' what? You can't just say 'Oh' and nothing else," I scold her.

"What's wrong?" Blaise asks. I can hear the fear in his voice.

"Nothing, nothing. I'm sorry I frightened you, it's just that...well, you see this dark spot here?" she asks.

Blaise and I both nod our heads. "You see this one here?" she asks.

Again we nod.

Dr. Michaels removes her eyes from the screen to look at us. "You're having twins," she says with a grin.

"Hell yeah!" Blaise says as he places a sloppy wet kiss against my lips. "Twins!" he cheers.

I can't help but laugh. We're having twins.

"Have you been feeling any sickness, Tatum?" she asks me.

I shake my head no. "No, nothing. I had no idea. I'm on the pill," I tell her.

"The pill is not one hundred percent effective. Have you been taking it regularly?" she asks.

I start to nod my head, but then stop. "I had a stomach bug a few weeks ago. I took it, but I wasn't able to keep much down." I look up to find Blaise smiling down at me. "I didn't even think about it; I'm sorry," I tell him.

"Sorry? For making me the happiest man on the damn planet? We're having twins," he says happily.

We all laugh at his outburst.

"It looks as though you are only about three weeks. I was worried due to your numbers being so low, but you are so early in the pregnancy that it makes sense. I see no issues with either baby. I will want to see you in a week for follow-up and we'll keep a close eye on the three of you. Congratulations," she says before she leaves us alone.

Blaise leans down and kisses my nose. "I love you so much, future Mrs. Richards," he says.

"Just because I'm—" He interrupts me.

"Stop. I love you, all of you. I talked to my dad today about doing less time at the department to spend more time with you. I told him I wanted to build a life with you. All of this before we found out about the babies. You're it for me," he tells me.

"I love you, too," I tell him.

Blaise falls to his knees beside the bed and holds my hand to his lips. "Marry me. I want you." He moves one hand to my belly. "I want them, and a few more." He winks. "I want to build a life with you. I can't breathe without you. Marry me?" he says.

Without reservation, I answer, "Yes."

He crashes his lips to mine. "I know it wasn't the most romantic, and I don't have a ring, but as soon as I can break you out of here, I'll do it right and we'll pick out your ring together. I love you, Tatum," he says.

"I don't want you to ask me again. That was prefect," I say, wiping the tears from my eyes.

Blaise stands to his full height and claps his hands together. "Okay, so no more than two people are allowed back here at a time, but I say fuck that. Everyone we love is in that waiting room. They all want to see you and we have news to share. I'm going to round up the troops so we can tell them all at once," he says, beaming. Leaning down, he kisses my cheek and practically skips out the door.

Not two minutes later, the two-visitor rule is shot to hell as all nine of them fill the room. Blaise makes his way to me and stands beside the bed. He reaches down for my hand and brings it to his lips.

"Blaise, you know they're gonna kick us out," his mother scolds him.

He smiles at her. "This won't take long. I just wanted everyone here at once." He looks down at me. "First of all, I wanted you all to be the first to know that Tate and I are getting married," he says.

The room erupts with congratulations and hugs and kisses on the cheek.

"We have one more piece of information." His free hand finds my belly. "We're having twins," he says. His eyes never leaving mine.

More hugs and congratulations erupt. We are a noisy group. I guess that's why we didn't hear the nurse the first time she yelled at us.

"Excuse me. Two at a time. You need to go back to the waiting room," she scolds.

Blaise just shrugs his shoulders and takes a seat beside my bed, never letting go of my hand.

I watch as they leave my room. I turn to look at Blaise. He's texting with one hand, no doubt spreading the word. I will miss my parents every day of my life. I will always feel the sadness deep inside because they will never get to meet my children. I know they are proud of me and watching over us. I also know I have never known a love for another person like I do with Blaise. I found what I've always been looking for. I found what my parents had. I found the man that will always cherish my heart. I found Blaise.

EPILOGUE

BLAISE

Today is my birthday. Tatum insisted that she throw me and Asher a party. I whined, complained, protested, whatever you want to call it, but my lovely wife won the battle. She always does. I never have been able to say no to her.

I watch as she waddles into the kitchen to try to help prepare the food. I know for a fact that my mom will scold her, so will Ember for that matter. It only takes five minutes for her to retreat back to the living room and ease herself back down on the couch. She takes the spot beside Grace who absentmindedly rubs her small baby bump. She and Asher are about four months along. I continue to brag that I'm, of course, the superior twin because my wife is having twins; his, however, is not. The women just laugh at us.

Leah and Ember are sitting on the loveseat opposite the couch. Ember is holding baby Sophie in her arms. She's a month old today. All four of them are glowing with happiness. Ember and Jackson just recently got engaged. Life is good.

I hear my name and I focus my attention back to the guys. They all have the same dopey look on their faces, the same one that I'm sure is plastered on mine. Just as I'm about to re-join the conversation, I hear a loud gasp. I whip my head around to see Tatum with wide eyes. She lifts her head and our eyes lock. She nods once and I'm rushing to her side. It's time. The house becomes a flurry of activity while Asher pulls the Tahoe around.

Brent takes one of Tatum's arms and I take the other, carefully leading her out the door. I help her inside and make sure she's strapped in. I already have both car seats, both our bags, and a bag for the babies loaded in the back. Call me super dad.

Asher stays in the driver's seat as Grace climbs in beside him. I turn to face our family. "We'll be right behind you," Brent says.

I nod in agreement.

I round the back of the car and hear my mom say, "What a special gift to have the babies be born on their birthday." She laughs.

I smile. That thought had never occurred to me. It would be really cool to have my kids born on mine and Asher's birthday; however, I know that's unlikely, yet still possible. Either way, soon, very soon I'm going to be a father.

Asher gets us to the hospital in record time. It helps that Blaise has the emergency lights, which we placed on top of the truck. Even though he gave up working at the department all together, he insisted on keeping the lights for this exact occasion. At first, I said he was being silly; now, not so much. I'm grateful. My contractions are maybe two minutes apart. I'm doing all I can to keep from letting on to Blaise how much pain I'm in. He worries.

I'm whisked into the ER and immediately settled into a wheelchair. A nurse, who looks about Nancy's age, leads us to an elevator. Labor and Delivery is on the fifth floor. Blaise made sure we were pre-registered three weeks ago. Again, I'm glad my husband is always thinking ahead.

By the time I'm in a gown and in a room, the contractions are almost constant. The machine is going crazy about every minute and a half or so. Blaise watches as the lines rise and fall. The doctor comes in and says hello to Blaise, while instructing me to "scoot down." I hate this part, but it's worth it for my babies.

"Well, I have good news and not so good news," he says. "The good news is you are going to be parents today." He looks over at

Blaise. "Happy Birthday, Dad." He chuckles. "The not so good news is that you are dilated to ten and baby A is crowning. There is no time for an epidural." He focuses his eyes on me. "How long have you been in labor?" he asks me.

Shit! I'm busted. I avoid Blaise's stare as I answer him. "The pains started about three am. They have become more constant throughout the day," I tell him honestly.

"What?" Blaise asks. "Why didn't you tell me?" He studies my expression. "The party, really, Tate? You should have told me, baby," he says as he strokes my cheek.

"I thought they were just Braxton Hicks." I pant as another contraction hits. At least I did until about eleven o'clock when they increased in frequency. I just wanted to get through the party.

"AHHH!" I scream.

"All right, Tatum. It's time to meet your babies. When I say three, I want you to push. One. Two. Three."

BLAISE

I'm sitting in Tate's private room holding my son and my daughter as I watch my beautiful wife sleep. I haven't been able to keep my eyes off the three of them. My family, my heart.

I hear a soft knock on the door. I look up and see Asher. "Hey, bro. Congratulations," he says softly. "Everyone is here, and they're chomping at the bit to meet the newest members of the Richards clan," he tells me.

I look down at my children sleeping peacefully, and then up at Tatum. Her eyes are watching me. "Hey you," I say to her.

A smile graces her lips. "Hey, Daddy." She pulls herself into the sitting position. I watch as she winces in pain. My girl is amazing. Twins, six pounds one ounce and six pounds three ounces, my son and daughter, and my wife delivered them both naturally. Lucky for Tate the delivery was quick. Within an hour of checking in, they were in our arms and welcomed to the world.

"Hey, sis," Asher says, kissing her cheek. "The mob is getting restless. I say we keep with tradition and sneak them all in." He winks at her.

"Sure," she says with a bright smile. I carefully stand and walk to the bed. She reaches for our baby boy. I sit beside her, holding our baby girl, while Asher ushers in the troops.

"I love you, Tate, so damn much. Thank you for being you, for being my wife, the mother of my children," I say, kissing her softly.

"Hey, now, isn't that what got you in here today?" I hear Brent say as he walks in.

I chuckle.

Once everyone is in the room, I introduce them to the newest members of our family.

"Everyone, I would like for you to meet Gavin Michael and his sister Addyson Renee." I look down and see Tate's eyes fill with tears.

She looks up to our family. "Michael and Renee were my parents' names," she says softly, barely holding her emotions in check.

My mom comes to the bed and hold hers arms out for Gavin. "Let me give this little guy some loving on behalf of me and his Grandma Renee," she says.

My dad follows suit. "And this little angel needs a kiss or two from me and Grandpa Michael," he says as he takes Gavin from my arms.

Emotion clogs my throat and I fight back tears. I look down and find Tatum watching me. I lean my forehead against hers. "Hey you," I whisper softly.

"I love you, Blaise," she says through her tears.

"I love you," I reply as we settle back, watch our family fuss over our children and pass on the love from those who couldn't be with us, but who I know are watching over us each and every day.

ACKNOWLEDGEMENTS

Where to begin?

My family. You make it possible to follow this dream. I have received nothing but love and support from day one on this journey and for that I am eternally grateful. I love you!!

I have met some amazing friends throughout this process. The indie community is amazing and I am proud to say that I am a part of it. Every time I see a fellow author share my work or that of our peers I can't help but be honored to be a part of this Indie Family.

To my AS101 peeps. I love you all. I have learned so much from all of you. It's a huge relief to be able to bounce ideas and gain suggestions from those of you who are in my shoes or have been there recently.

Toski Covey and Sommer Stein you ladies took my vision and exceeded my expectations. Thank you so much for the stunning cover! The custom photography was exactly what I had in mind and summer...your design blew me away. I can't wait to work with both of you again.

Tami of Integrity Formatting you make my words come together in a pretty little package. Thank you so much for making Tempting Tatum look fabulous on the inside!

Saoching Moose I don't even know where to begin. You have become such a great friend to me. From our daily chats, to our marathon sprints, you are there supporting me every step of the way. You played a huge role in helping me mold Blaise and Tatum's story into one that I am proud of. From the bottom of my heart Thank you for always being there. I love ya, girl!

Mary Tatar, I am blessed to call you a friend. You have been with me since my first release and I am so grateful to have met you. Your trailers make my stories come alive. Thank you for your continued support and trailer making skills!

Love Between The Sheets, thank you for hosting the cover reveal and blog tour. You ladies are amazing and I don't know what I would do without you!

To all of the bloggers out there...Thank you so much. Continued never ending support of myself and the entire indie community is greatly appreciated. I know that you don't hear it enough so hear me now. ***I appreciate each and every one of you and the support that you have given me.*** Thank you to all of you! There are way too many of you to list...

To my Kick Ass Crew, you ladies know who you are. I will never be able to tell you how much your support means. I will never forget all that you have done for me. Thank you!

Last but not least, to the readers. Without you none of this would even be worth the effort. I truly love writing and I am honored that I am able to share that with you. Thank you to each and every one of you who support me and my dream.

With Love,

Kaylee Ryan

CONTACT KAYLEE RYAN

Facebook:

https://www.facebook.com/pages/Kaylee-Ryan-Author/589642871063467

Goodreads:

http://www.goodreads.com/author/show/7060310.Kaylee_Ryan

Twitter: @author_k_ryan

Website: www.kayleeryan.com

OTHER WORKS BY KAYLEE RYAN

Anywhere With You – August 2013

More With You – January 2014

Made in United States
Orlando, FL
13 September 2022

22358082R00143